MW00878791

Blood & BONE

by

C.C. Wood

This book is a work of fiction. Names, characters, places, and incidents are the product of the author's imagination or are used fictitiously. Any resemblance to actual persons, living or dead, business establishments, events or locales is entirely coincidental.

No part of this book may be reproduced, scanned, or distributed in any printed or electronic form without permission. Please do not participate in or encourage piracy of copyrighted materials in violation of author's rights. Purchase only authorized editions.

Copyright © Crystal W. Wilson 2017
Print Edition

Cover by
Jena Brignola, Bibliophile Productions

Editing by
Tania Marinaro, Libros Evolution

Table of Contents

This book is dedicated to all the readers that loved the Bitten series.
You are the reason this book exists.
I hope you love these characters as much as I do.

CHAPTER ONE

Chloe

M Y HEART WAS heavy as my eyes drifted over the pack compound. Homes of varying sizes were nestled in the open field. At the center of the group were several metal buildings used for pack meetings, picnics, and parties.

Over the last eighteen months, I'd come to think of this place as home. The first real home I'd had since I lost my parents and left my pack.

Yet it was time for me to go.

Movement in my peripheral vision caught my attention. I turned and watched as a dark brown wolf loped out of the copse of trees to my left. I recognized him instantly, my heavy heart giving my sternum a hard thump. He was still too lean, his ribs pronounced in his large frame. Idly I thought that I should go over and force him to eat a few sandwiches and a couple of pieces of fruit. It wouldn't be enough and I'd probably have to put him in a headlock before I gained his cooperation, but it was better than nothing. I could tell he still wasn't eating as much as he should. A full-grown male wolf needed to consume thousands of calories per day to maintain their body weight. Every time I saw him, he looked as though he'd lost a few more pounds. It hurt to watch him vanish right in front of me.

As the chestnut wolf paused at the back door of a beautiful two-story house, I stepped back into the shadows on my porch. I watched as his body twisted and shivered until a naked man stood in place of the wolf. Like his animal counterpart, his muscles were leaner than they used to be, his ribs noticeably standing out in his torso. His skin was lightly tanned and his chest was covered with a dusting of brown hair.

Even in his nearly gaunt state, he was arresting. From this distance, I could make out the rugged features of his face. His brow was too heavy and his jaw too strong for him to be considered classically handsome, but they suggested a raw, animal power that some women, including myself, would find irresistible. Though his eyes were cast down, I knew from memory that they were blue. Deep, crystal clear blue, like the waters of an untouched lake, with spikes of pale azure and gray radiating from the center. Beautiful eyes that could snare you and pull you in, no matter how hard you resisted.

He climbed the steps of the porch with innate power and grace as only an animal in their prime would move. As I watched him disappear inside, I knew I wouldn't go over and bully him into eating as I had done hundreds of times over the last year and a half. I would never again look into those dangerous blue eyes or study the way his prominent brow and cheekbones cast shadows across his face.

It was time for me to move on, time for me to finish what I had started two years ago when my parents died.

Even if it meant leaving my mate behind.

CALDER'S REACTION TO my announcement was exactly what I expected. As the alpha of the MacIntire pack in Dallas, he took his responsibilities seriously. The fact that we'd known each other for years meant that he was even more determined to look out for me. That also might have had something to do with his mate, Ricki. She was one of my closest friends and a fierce fighter. I would know since I trained her myself.

"You're not leaving," he stated firmly. "I won't allow it." He stopped walking mid-stride, turning his body toward me. "And you know Ricki won't stand for it either."

I glanced around the compound, making sure there was no one within earshot. Shifter hearing could pick conversations hundreds of yards away if the people weren't whispering. And Calder's voice had definitely been loud.

"Let's walk in the woods," I invited, ensuring that our discussion would be kept private from any prying ears. "And I'll explain."

"You better have a damn good explanation," he grumbled, falling back into step with me as I strode off the road, weaving between houses and heading toward the trees that surrounded the compound.

"I do. And when I'm done giving it to you, you'll let me go."

He grunted. "I wouldn't be so sure. Ricki loves having you around and the pups love you too. If I don't stop you, I'll never hear the end of it."

"Ricki will understand," I stated firmly. "Of that I'm certain."

He cast a sidelong look in my direction that clearly expressed his disbelief.

When we reached the tree line, I released the pent up tension I carried in my shoulders as I breathed deeply, relishing the scent of earth and late spring. Once again, my heart sank as I thought about how I would never come back here. Never enjoy the smell and the feel of this forest around me.

"Okay, so explain to me why you have to leave," Calder insisted. "Because I still don't understand."

I inhaled once again, not only enjoying the perfume of the forest but also searching for any possible eavesdroppers. All I smelled were leaves and a couple of wild rabbits nearby. We were truly alone.

"When I came here two years ago, I only intended to stay for a short while," I began. I glanced up to find Calder studying me intently so I continued. "I'm sure you remember that my parents died only a few months before that."

He nodded, his eyes softening. "Yes, I remember. I'm sorry."

I shrugged, shoving the pain aside. "Well, I came here because the alpha of the Austin pack didn't want me looking into their deaths. In fact, Jacob forbade it and threatened to have me locked up if I went against his orders."

Calder's brows drew down over his eyes. "Look into their deaths? I thought they were killed by rogue wolves."

"That was the official story from the MacArthur pack in Oklahoma, but my grandmother had very good reason to believe that was only part of the story. Since she was having problems with her own pack in North Carolina at the time, she couldn't afford to go to Oklahoma to poke around. She wanted me to do it. When my alpha forbade it, I requested a transfer to the MacIntire pack."

Calder nodded. "That's understandable. But you have to know I would never stop you from looking into the deaths of your parents," he explained.

"I know you wouldn't," I answered, smiling slightly. "I know it's on the tip of your tongue to offer to help me, even though you're running yourself ragged between your responsibilities as MacIntire alpha and taking care of your three pups."

"What, are you psychic now?" he asked.

Calder looked so disgruntled I had to laugh. "No, I just know you well."

"So I'll send someone from the pack with you to help," he stated.

The smile faded from my face. "No."

"Chloe," Calder warned. "I'm still your alpha."

"I'll leave the pack first," I argued.

"Lone wolves don't last long in this world and you know it."

"I won't be completely alone," I stated. "My grandmother is helping me. She's the one who's setting everything up and she knows where I'll be." I paused. "Right now, she's the only one I can trust with this, Calder. Well, other than you and Ricki. But this isn't pack business. It's family. My family. Rogues may have killed my parents, but there's something more to the story and I intend to find out what it is." I had other reasons for leaving, but there was no way I was going to drag Calder into my crushed dreams of mating and family. I had to handle it on my own. It was best to keep that little secret all to myself.

"Why now? Why not when you came here two years ago?" he asked, his tone exasperated. I knew then that he was going to give in.

"Things were heating up with the Faction at that time and that was more important."

The Faction, which no longer existed, was a group of vampires, shifters, and warlocks intent on purifying the supernatural races and taking control of the humans. Their leader, Cornelius the Slayer, had been a powerful *animavore*. A devourer of souls, and he had been stronger than any being I'd ever met. Maybe even powerful enough to achieve the goal.

We'd lost several pack members and Calder had nearly lost his mate, but we had prevailed in the end. Rebuilding the pack and chasing down the few remaining members of the Faction had been our priority for the last eighteen months.

Then there was the matter of nursing Lachlan back to health.

He had been alpha when we battled with the Faction...until his mate was murdered, a witch named Belinda. When she died, we'd nearly lost him. Calder had taken over as alpha and I had bullied, cajoled, and even once pinned Lachlan to the floor to make sure that he ate, drank, and slept instead of pining himself to death. There were some shifters who would have considered what I'd done cruel, but my wolf and I couldn't allow him to die of grief.

"So now it's time?" Calder asked, pulling me back into the present.

I shoved my hands into my pockets. "It's time."

"Well, you'd better say good-bye to Ricki or she'll hunt your ass down."

"I will," I murmured.

"And Lach."

I looked away from those knowing green eyes. "I doubt he'll care."

"Maybe he'll surprise you," he stated.

"Maybe."

Though Calder might have been right, I didn't intend to find out. Facing Lachlan's indifference was more than I could bear. There was only so much pain I could take and I had already reached my limit.

CHAPTER TWO

Lachlan

THE NEARLY INAUDIBLE sound of a light step on the kitchen floor snagged my attention. I blinked rapidly, wondering why my vision seemed dim. Then I realized that night had fallen.

Moving slowly, I pushed myself to my feet, rolling my shoulders and straightening my spine. I'd been sitting on my couch for the last few hours, unmoving.

I knew who was in my kitchen just from his scent. As I entered the room, I squinted as my eyes adjusted to the brightness of the lights. Calder turned from the counter where he was spooning food onto a plate and studied me.

"You look like shit," he stated before turning back to what he was doing.

"Thanks for pointing that out," I replied.

The scent of the food hit my nostrils and my stomach growled loudly.

"Good, you're hungry. That means you'll eat," Calder drawled. "Sit down and I'll bring the food to the table."

I saw that he had filled two plates, which meant he intended to stay. Probably to make sure I ate as well, I thought darkly. I went to the fridge and grabbed two beers off the top shelf. I popped the tops and carried them to the table.

Calder joined me, setting a steaming plate of chicken, potatoes, and carrots in front of me. Three buttered rolls topped the pile of food. Without speaking again, he began to eat.

Though my stomach rumbled, I had no urge to eat. But I did it anyway. I forced myself to take the first bite, chewing the chicken slowly. Then another. I ate until I cleared most of my plate, barely tasting the hot food.

When my stomach felt full, I laid the fork aside and picked up the beer in front of me, knocking back a huge slug.

"Thanks for dinner," I said to Calder, breaking the silence that had fallen between us as we ate.

He shrugged. "You're welcome."

"I'm kinda surprised you didn't eat with Ricki and the pups though," I drawled, draining the last of my beer. "I'd think she needs you to deal with those three."

He laughed. "Not tonight. Her friends are all over, playing with the pups and drinking wine."

"So you escaped."

His eyes twinkling with contentment, Calder laughed again. "There was no escape about it. They kicked me out."

A smile tugged at the corner of my mouth and Calder stared at me as though he were surprised to see the expression on my face. Then I realized I couldn't remember the last time I'd smiled.

"They came over to cheer her up," he continued.

"Cheer her up? Did she finally realize she's stuck with you for the next few centuries?"

"Ha, ha, you're hilarious." He crossed his arms over his chest and leaned back in his chair. "No, she's upset because Chloe left today."

"What do you mean *left?*" I asked.

"Left. As in she packed her stuff and drove out of the compound this afternoon. Didn't she tell you earlier?"

I shook my head. "I didn't see her today." The food I'd just eaten sat like a lead weight in my stomach. "When will she be back?" I wasn't sure why I cared. I hadn't cared about anything in eighteen months so the feeling was foreign to me.

"She's not coming back," Calder replied flatly.

Another strange sensation seized me, and I felt as though I'd had the wind knocked out of me. "Not coming back?" I repeated.

Calder reached out and grabbed his beer, drinking down the last of the bottle. "Nope."

"Where did she go?"

"I don't know," he sighed.

"Why not?"

"Because she refused to tell me." His eyes were serious when they met mine. "But I'm worried. I'm going to snoop around and see if I can't figure out what's going on."

"Why did she leave? Did she tell you?"

Calder exhaled and I understood that he was frustrated. "She gave me a very good reason, but I don't think it's the whole story." He got up and walked over to the fridge, pulling out two more beers and bringing them to the table. "You know her parents died a couple of years ago, right?"

I nodded. It had happened a short time before Chloe joined the pack. When I was still acting as alpha. I hadn't been able to go to the funeral at the time, but I remembered Nadine and Matthew MacArthur well. He was a great alpha. As a couple, they were respected leaders and good people to boot.

"Chloe and her grandmother think that it wasn't just a random killing by rogues, as the pack claimed. Chloe left her old pack because her alpha forbade her from investigating. Then, when she came here, we were dealing with the Faction and she had to put it on hold. She's says it's time for her to pick up where she left off and find out what really happened to her parents."

"You think she's lying?"

Calder shook his head. "No, she's not lying, but she didn't tell me the entire truth either. She's hiding something and I'm not sure what it is. But I'm going to find out."

We fell silent as we both heard footsteps approaching my back door. A few seconds later there was a light knock before Kerry Gayle stuck her head in the door. I felt a shaft of pain when I saw her. A witch like my mate Belinda had been, Kerry was now the head of her coven, having taken over when Belinda died. She had also been Claimed by a vampire named Finn not long after the Faction had been disbanded. Seeing her reminded me of what I had lost.

She smiled at us as she entered, but it didn't reach her eyes. She seemed almost...sad. "Hey, Calder. Lachlan."

"Things getting too wild for you over at my house?" Calder asked with a smirk.

Kerry shook her head and I noticed the envelope in her hand. "Uh, Calder, would you mind if I spoke to Lachlan alone? I have something for him."

Calder studied her for a moment then picked up his beer and headed toward the door. "No problem. I'll just go check on Ricki and the pups."

When he reached her side, she put out her hand and touched his arm. "Don't go too far," she murmured softly, her blue eyes communicating something to Calder that I couldn't read.

He seemed to understand though because he nodded. "I'll be back in a few minutes."

When the door shut behind him, Kerry didn't move from her spot in the center of my kitchen. She looked at me, the sadness I sensed earlier clear on her face.

"You look better," she stated softly.

I shrugged and sipped my beer. "I'm alive." I realized I was being rude and gestured toward the chair that Calder had just vacated. "Why don't you have a seat and tell me why you're here?"

Kerry sighed and sat down, her fingers tightening on the envelope in her hand. "I'm not sure how to explain this. What I have to say is difficult."

The back of my neck tightened at her words, the tension spreading to my shoulders. "Maybe it's best if you just tell me."

She took a deep breath and held out the envelope. "I have a letter for you from Belinda. It, uh, appeared in my library yesterday with instructions to give it to you today."

My heart stopped beating at her words and I stared at the creamy paper she held out to me, my name scrawled across the front in elegant script. Slowly, I reached out and took the envelope from her, hyperaware of the coolness of the paper and the smooth feel of it beneath my fingers.

"Thank you," I whispered.

"Do you want me to, um, stay or would you prefer if I—"

"I'd like to do this alone, if you don't mind," I told her, not taking my eyes from the envelope in my hand.

She released a shaky breath. "I'll ask Calder to—"

"No," I stated, lifting my eyes to hers. "I'll want some time alone after I read this. Tell him I'll call him if I need him."

The witch looked as though she wanted to argue, but she finally nodded and got to her feet. Before she opened the back door, she glanced over her shoulder at me. "I'm sorry, Lachlan."

Then she was gone.

After the door shut behind her, I laid the envelope flat on the table, staring at my name. I could hear the quiet murmur of Kerry speaking to Calder outside, but I had little interest in trying to decipher what they were saying. My entire focus was on the letter in front of me. I didn't want to open it. Didn't want to see the words that Belinda had written to me before she died.

When I realized she was my mate and began my pursuit, Belinda had tried to keep me at a distance. She told me, over and over, that it was for the best if I waited until the threat of the Faction was gone. I'd managed to convince her otherwise. I'd marked her not long before she died.

Sometimes I wondered if she fought our connection so hard because she knew she was going to die and she didn't want me to perish with her.

I heard Calder and Kerry walk away from my back porch and realized I needed to read the letter now. Calder would return in a little while, that much I knew. Whatever Belinda had written on these pages was private. For my eyes only. I didn't want to share any of that with Calder or anyone else.

I flipped the envelope over and ran my fingers across the wax seal affixed to the flap. There, in the crest, was a wolf. It was Belinda's crest, one she used when sending correspondence to other Covens. A magical seal that could only be opened by the person the letter was intended for. I'd laughed the first time I saw it, saying it was clear that she was meant for me.

I slid my thumb beneath the flap and the seal released easily. I withdrew several small sheets of cream-colored stationary, Belinda's beautiful handwriting covering the pages.

I yearned to read it, to hear her voice speaking to me in my mind, yet I hesitated because I knew the heartache it would cause. It would hurt to remember her. Hurt to hear the words as though she were right here with me again.

I steeled myself for the pain and began to read.

My dearest Lach,

I met you today for the first time and already I am overwhelmed with what I feel for you.

I knew I would meet you, you see. I've had visions of you for months. But they didn't prepare me for what I would feel today.

Our futures are intertwined. Tangled together, not only with each other but also with others. We are destined to be lovers, more than lovers. It feels strange for me, knowing all this when you do not.

Perhaps it is because I know how this will all end. By now, I'm sure you've realized what I already know—that I am not long for this world. I do not know when or how, but I will be forced to leave you behind. I thought I had made peace with it…until today.

But destiny does not change on a whim. What is coming to pass is for a larger purpose, greater than either of us. And, even now, I understand that you aren't wholly mine, even if you do not.

When I am gone, Lachlan, you will be needed more than ever. I know you will want to die with me, that you will do your damnedest to wither away, but you can't. I don't want that for you. I want you to live. I want you to cherish each year. If not for yourself, for me. Your existence is more precious to me than my own and all I want is for you to have a full and happy life.

I can see you now, in my mind's eye, shaking your head, but I'm demanding that you don't ignore my desire. That's right. Your mate is demanding something of you. And I know you, Lachlan. You will do anything in your power to give me what I want.

And what I want is for you to live…and to love again.

Don't deny yourself happiness because I am gone. THAT ISN'T WHAT I WANT FOR YOU. And you shouldn't want that for yourself.

Let me go, my love. Release yourself from the pain and the grief. It is time.

With my heart and soul, I love you.

Belinda

As I finished reading her words, my heart pounding in my chest and my lungs burning, a single drop of liquid hit the page next to her signature. I blinked, trying to focus my gaze on it as it was joined by another droplet. Lifting a hand, I touched my cheek, feeling the wetness on my skin.

I lifted my fingers to stare at them and realized I was crying. With a howl, I shot to my feet, my chair crashing to the floor behind me. As I lurched for the back door, I was already tearing at my clothes, leaving the tatters to fall where they would.

As soon as my feet hit the back porch, I launched my naked body into the air. When I landed in the grass, it was on four paws. Another howl tore from my throat and the sound felt as though it was ripped from my very soul.

Then I ran as if the hounds of Hell were behind me.

CHAPTER THREE

Chloe

M Y CELL PHONE rang, right on schedule.

"Hi, Gram," I greeted as I answered.

"Hi, darlin'. How are you doin' today?"

"I'm good. How are you?"

"Fine as I ever am. How's the fishing going?" she asked.

I looked out into the trees surrounding the cabin as I answered. "Frustrating. I'm having trouble getting a single bite."

"Maybe you're using the wrong bait."

I shook my head and sighed in frustration. "No, I think my bait is fine. I just think I'm going after the wrong fish."

"Hmmm. So what kind of fish should you be going after?"

"The biggest I can find," I replied.

To anyone listening, our conversation would seem a bit odd but not necessarily out of the ordinary. What they wouldn't realize is that we weren't really talking about fish at all.

"Think you can track him down?" she asked.

"I'm closer than anyone realizes."

"Well, let me know how that goes."

"I will. Love you, Gram."

We disconnected and I turned off the burner phone, setting it down on the railing that ran around the front porch. I took a deep breath and looked out over the property that Gram had arranged for me in Oklahoma. Outside of Tulsa, the small cabin and surrounding acreage were secluded. My closest neighbor was several miles away. There were trees all around the cabin and a small pond in a meadow several hundred yards away. It was tranquil and exactly what I needed.

Leaving the pack had thrown me off balance. I hadn't expected it to be this difficult. I missed Calder and Ricki and their wild pups, but most of all, I missed Lachlan. Though he made it clear he'd rather not deal with anyone as he grieved the loss of his mate, he'd slowly begun to open up to me. We would sit together for hours by the lake on the MacIntire compound, sometimes in silence and sometimes reminiscing about our childhoods.

Being here at the cabin reminded me too much of what I was missing.

Realizing that I was sliding into the dark swirl of thoughts that had plagued me since I left the compound, I pushed myself away from the railing, snatched up the burner phone, and went inside the cabin. I wasn't here to nurse a broken heart or wallow in loneliness. I had a job to do.

I missed my parents fiercely. In the past two years, there were so many times I wished I could have talked to them or asked for their advice. They weren't traditional wolves by any means. Though my father was the alpha of the MacArthur pack, my mother had a huge role in his leadership. She tempered his ferocity and helped him understand the perspectives of others.

Though the name of the MacArthur pack hadn't changed, my grandmother had been hearing rumors that nothing else was the same. Darrell Whelby took over the pack after my parents' death, and I'd hoped he would follow their example. He'd been their second in command for nearly twenty years. I grew up around him, played with his children. He was the current chief of police in

Prater and every one of the four officers who worked with him was a pack member.

People said Darrell ruled with fear and cruelty, yet no one had approached the Tribunal to have him removed, so I didn't know how true those claims were. They didn't fit in with the Darrell I knew, but I couldn't be sure. After years as the enforcer for the Austin pack and then the MacIntire pack, I'd done things I never thought I'd do. Things that would have sickened me when I was younger but I knew they had to be done. Sometimes I even relished it. A good enforcer often had a dark side. It was a necessity in doling out punishment to those who broke the rules.

Then there were the whispers that Darrell had something to do with the death of my parents. That was what had truly gotten my grandmother's attention. My father, Matthew, was her only son. His death had broken something within her. She'd wanted to come to Oklahoma when the rogues that killed him were caught, intent upon meting out her own brand of justice. Unfortunately, Darrell and the pack mates with him had slaughtered them during the fight.

Though Sophia MacArthur was frustrated that she didn't get to spill their blood with her own hands, she was satisfied in the belief that justice was served.

Until a few months later. An anonymous voice on the phone had insisted that Darrell Whelby had been involved in the plot to kill my parents all along. It was enough to set my grandmother on the path that led me here. She'd quietly dug into Darrell's past and the months leading up to that horrible night.

What she'd found was enough evidence to make us both question exactly what had happened.

It had taken two long years to get here, but we were finally going to get some answers.

For the past week, I'd been snooping around online, looking

for any information on Darrell and other members of the pack. I was amazed at the kind of shit I found on their social media accounts. I didn't have all the information I wanted before I approached Darrell, but I had a better idea of what their habits were and how to find them.

Unlike the MacIntire pack, the MacArthur pack didn't have a compound. They all lived in Prater, Oklahoma. There were a few humans in the town, but the majority were half-bloods. One of their parents or grandparents had been a shifter but their blood had been so diluted they could no longer transition. They knew us for what we were and didn't care.

The arrangement shouldn't have worked, but it did.

Unfortunately, that was going to make it more difficult for me to be sneaky. With so many shifters in one place, I'd never blend in. Those who knew me would recognize my scent immediately and those who didn't would still know that I wasn't a pack member.

My only option was to approach the pack as the prodigal daughter and hope that they would welcome me back into the fold. There were many who hadn't wanted me to leave the pack, who'd thought I was abandoning my birthright. They hadn't understood why I didn't want to lead.

But my parents did.

Especially my mother. I had the same itchy feet that she had in her youth, always wanting to go, to do, and to *see*. It was a rare trait in a wolf shifter, but one that she understood all too well. She knew I would be ready to settle down eventually and that I would be back, even if no one else believed it.

Now I just had to convince them.

I picked up my burner phone and turned it on. Slowly I typed in Darrell's number. My thumb hovered over the button to connect the call as I took a deep breath. On my exhale, I pressed it and lifted the phone to my ear.

Darrell answered on the third ring.

"Chief Whelby."

"Hi, Darrell, it's Chloe."

There was a long pause before he exclaimed, "Chloe MacArthur! Girl, it's been years since I've heard from you. How are you doing?"

I managed to put a quaver in my voice when I answered, "Not so good, Uncle Darrell. I, uh, had some problems in the MacIntire pack and…" I trailed off, trying to make it sound as though I were holding back tears. "I-I have no where else to go."

There was another long silence, this one rife with tension, which immediately made me suspicious. Finally, Darrell spoke. "Well, you come on back to Prater, darlin'. We'll take good care of you."

"Thank you so much, Uncle Darrell," I said softly. "It means so much to me."

"When can we expect you?" he asked, his own voice growing affectionate.

"Is tomorrow too soon?" I asked.

He laughed a little. "Not at all, darlin'. I'll see you then and we'll find you a place to stay." He paused for a second. "I'm not trying to pry here, Chloe, but why are you coming to us instead of your grandmother, Sophia?"

I had my answer ready. "She's furious that I'm leaving a third pack. She didn't want me to leave Mom and Dad to begin with, but she said that this is the last straw." I sniffled. "She said she's done with me." It was all a lie of course, but Darrell wouldn't know that.

While Gram didn't understand my wanderlust, she loved me enough to let me go my own way. Mostly because she knew I was too much of her granddaughter to be dissuaded. When Sophia

MacArthur wanted something, she found a way to get it. I was just like her in that respect.

"Oh, my poor Chloe. Well, you come up here tomorrow. If you don't mind something a little old and run down, I have a small cabin outside of town that you can use. That way you'll have a little privacy while you get your head together."

"That sounds perfect, Darrell. Thank you so much."

"Call me when you get into town, okay?"

"I will," I promised.

"See you tomorrow, Chloe."

"Tomorrow, Darrell."

I disconnected the call and set the phone on the table in front of me. Then I smiled.

It wouldn't be long before I had the truth.

CHAPTER FOUR

Lachlan

I GROANED AS I pushed the bar away from my chest, trembling from the effort. I settled the weights back on the rack with a clang and lay there panting. Fuck, how had I let myself spiral so far down that I could barely lift such a light amount?

Moving slowly, I rolled up into a sitting position and grabbed the bottle of water by my feet. Nine hundred pounds might be more than a normal human could bench press but it was the weight I used to load on the bar for a light workout.

I looked down at my shirtless torso and noticed that at least my ribs weren't quite so pronounced any longer. Over the last week, my appetite had returned and I'd gained weight. My muscles were still leaner than they used to be, but the bulk was returning.

I heard the door slam overhead and Calder's light step across my kitchen.

"Lach?" he called.

"In the basement," I answered.

He came down the steps, stopping on the bottom to study me. "You still look like shit," he commented, "But I'm glad to see that you're putting on weight."

It seemed like he said that every time he saw me these days. I laughed, the sound rusty and harsh. God, when was the last time

I'd laughed? More than eighteen months ago, that was for sure.

"Fuck, Calder, if I'd known you were coming, I would have put on some make-up for you."

He grinned, his green eyes twinkling with mischief. "I'll be sure to call ahead next time and bring my camera."

I flipped him off as I lifted the water bottle to my mouth to take another huge gulp. "What's up?" I said after I drained the last of the liquid.

The smirk on his face faded as he came further into the make-shift gym I'd set up in my basement, settling his ass on another weight bench. "I just got a call from Brian Kirkpatrick."

My brows lifted. "The alpha down in Houston?"

He nodded. "Yeah and something…feels off. He says he wants to meet. That he has something important to discuss with me but that we have to do it face-to-face."

"Is it about the Faction?"

Calder shook his head. "I don't think so. He said it was personal. But there's just something about that guy that gives me a bad feeling."

I knew exactly what he meant. Brian Kirkpatrick was not an alpha to be trifled with. He was ruthless, cunning, and had a deeply rooted sadistic streak I'd only seen in action once, but once was enough.

"Are you taking the meet?" I asked.

"That's why I'm here," he replied. "I wanted your advice."

I got to my feet and moved over to the chin up bar I had set up in the corner. "What do you mean?"

Calder grunted in frustration. "I mean, do you think I should take the meet or not? I've only met him a couple of times, but you know him well. Is this likely to turn into a clusterfuck, or do you think he just wants to talk?"

I hopped up, grabbing the bar and began to pull myself up,

smooth and slow. "As alpha, you can't afford to offend your closest allies, Calder. I wouldn't want to do it, but I would. If he needs help and we can provide it, we should. Because you never know when the situations will be reversed."

He was silent for a few moments as I continued to do pull-ups. "I want you there," he finally stated. "You have excellent instincts and it's time for you to get involved in the pack again." It wasn't the request of a friend, but the command of an alpha.

My rhythm faltered for a moment before I continued. "Okay. Then I'll be there. When's the meet?"

"Tomorrow."

I stopped and dropped back down to the ground, turning to face him. "Tomorrow?"

He nodded.

"That's pretty damn quick."

"Exactly," Calder replied. "I'm not sure I can trust him. I feel like he's up to something, but I can't figure out what the fuck it might be."

"I agree. He's up to something." I stared down at my shoes for a moment, thinking. "I'll make some calls, see if I can find out if he's in a dispute with another pack or something. What time tomorrow?"

"Ten a.m."

"I'll be there."

CALDER DROVE US into McKinney for the meeting. To anyone else, he would appear relaxed, but I knew better. There was a tension inside him, humming just beneath his skin.

It wasn't unusual for the alphas of nearby packs to request meetings to discuss working together or alliances, but this one was unexpected. There had been no rumors of unrest among the Houston pack or challenges from others.

Though it could be dangerous to discuss pack business in public, he decided that a busy restaurant would be best for today. If the Kirkpatricks had an ambush in mind, they would think twice in a place full of humans. In fact, the restaurant we'd agreed upon was also frequented by cops. Another deterrent.

When Calder pulled into the parking lot at the greasy spoon we'd selected as a meeting place, I turned toward him.

"What's the plan?"

He exhaled, his fingers tapping the steering wheel. "I'll do most of the talking. Watch them. Maybe you'll pick up something I won't."

We walked inside, a half an hour early for the meeting. It was intentional. We wanted to make sure that we were waiting when they arrived.

The waitress came over, her eyes moving first over Calder until they reached his wide platinum wedding band. She looked disappointed until she saw me sitting next to him. Her mouth curved in a flirtatious smile that did nothing for me.

"What can I get you two?" she drawled.

"Just coffee," Calder replied, all business.

She nodded and strutted away, hips swaying.

Calder and I were still drinking our first cup when Brian Kirkpatrick entered the restaurant, his son, Brayden, right behind him. They were early. Twenty minutes early.

Brian smiled and came over, greeting us with firm handshakes and back slaps. Brayden was more reserved, his eyes moving over the crowd inside the restaurant as though he were looking for someone. Brian and Brayden looked more like siblings than father and son, both tall, muscular, and blond. The only difference was their eyes. Brian's were dark brown, almost black, and Brayden's were pale blue. The color of ice. Still, despite the variation in color, their eyes held the same cold detachment. They could hide it well when they wanted, but they were ruthless and brutal. Completely without mercy.

Despite Brian's friendly greeting, I wasn't fooled and my focus sharpened.

With the pleasantries out of the way, Brian and Brayden sat in chairs across from us, which meant the waitress came over once again. When she aimed her winsome smile at Brian, he grinned back, his appreciative gaze moving over her body in a way that had her preening.

"Hi, there," she greeted them. "What can I get you gentlemen?"

I noticed that Brayden barely looked her way, his gaze still searching the other patrons.

"Coffee, darlin'," Brian answered her with a wink.

She grinned and turned, adding an intentional sway as she walked away. Brian took the opportunity to stare at her ass and I bit back a grunt. Clearly he still fucked anything that moved. He never mated, choosing instead to impregnate several she-wolves in his pack over the years. Though he was over one hundred years old, he looked as though he were approaching his mid-thirties, still strong and handsome. He took advantage of that as often as he could, with she-wolves and human women alike.

When the waitress returned, she leaned over, giving Brian a clear view of her assets down the partially unbuttoned top of her uniform. I ignored his leer and turned my eyes toward Brayden. He looked distracted and angry, his fists clenching and unclenching as he continued to scan the people inside the restaurant. Whatever he sought wasn't here and it raised my suspicions.

After finishing her banter with Brian, the waitress left us again and Calder looked at Brian.

"It's good to see you, Brian. How have you been?"

"Good, good," the other alpha replied as he sipped his coffee. "Busy with business. You?"

"Things have finally settled down."

Brian's eyes flicked to me. "Good to see you up and about, Lachlan."

I nodded instead of answering aloud.

"I was sorry to hear about your mate," he continued.

I waited for the usual stab of pain, but it was muted. It made me uncomfortable. I had become so accustomed to the sharp edges of my grief that this dull ache felt like a betrayal to her memory.

"Thanks," I murmured, my voice rough.

Brian tilted his head in acknowledgement before turning back toward Calder. "So, where's your enforcer today, son? I thought she would be with you."

Something, an instinct maybe, made me look at Brayden. He leaned forward slightly in his seat, his eyes glued to Calder. For some unknown reason, he was extremely interested in the answer to his father's question.

Calder must have caught Brayden's reaction though he seemed entirely focused on Brian because he replied, "She's away, handling some pack business for me."

"Oh, really?" Brian said, leaning back in his chair. "Well, that's too bad. She and Brayden used to be very close, if you know what I mean."

My brows lifted at his implication. As long as I had known Chloe, she had never mentioned Brayden Kirkpatrick. Ever.

"Ah, well then she'll be sorry she missed this meeting," Calder stated smoothly. I knew he'd caught on to what Brian was insinuating but he wasn't going to address it. "So what do you need today, Brian?"

The Houston alpha shrugged. "We're in the area for business and I didn't want to come into your territory without speaking to you first."

Calder arched a brow. "That was very courteous of you, Brian, but don't worry. If you ever need to come to Dallas in the future, a phone call is more than sufficient. I hate to take up your time when you have business to handle."

"Thank you, Calder," Brian replied. He drained his coffee mug and looked over at his son. "Bray, we should probably get going."

Brayden, who hadn't spoken since we sat down, shrugged and got to his feet. When Brian reached for his wallet, Calder waved a hand.

"It's taken care of, Brian," he stated.

"Thank you." Brian smiled as we all stood and shook hands once again.

Father and son left as Calder and I paid the bill for our coffee, neither of us speaking. It wasn't until we got into the car and were heading back toward the compound that Calder said a word.

"Did you buy any of that bullshit?" he asked.

"No. They're up to something."

"Any ideas what that might be?"

I stared out the window as we drove out of the city, buildings and neighborhoods thinning out. "I do."

"Chloe," Calder muttered, his voice low. "Dammit, this has something to do with her, doesn't it?"

I nodded, twisting my head back toward him. "Did you see the way Brayden acted when his father brought her up?"

"Yeah," he affirmed. Calder's tone was dark and angry. "I didn't like it."

"Neither did I."

My right hand ached. When I glanced down, I realized I'd balled it into a tight fist. So tight that my knuckles were white and cracking from the tension.

"We need to find her and figure out what the hell is going on," Calder stated.

"I'll handle it," I told him, forcing my hand open and flexing my fingers. "You need to be here to keep an eye on the Kirkpatricks."

I wondered what in the hell the she-wolf had gotten herself into. Whatever it was, I would discover the answer. Then I would help her straighten it out, whether she wanted me to or not.

CHAPTER FIVE

Chloe

I FLOPPED DOWN on my back in the middle of the field, shifting into my human form. My breath was still coming hard from my run, my lungs pumping as I fought to suck in air.

The sun was warm, beating down on my naked flesh. I tilted my head back and drank it in, relishing in the way the gentle heat loosened my muscles. It was early May and the temperatures in Oklahoma were perfect, still cool in the mornings and evenings but warm during midday.

I'd been in Prater a week and was still no closer to finding the answers I was looking for. In fact, I'd barely seen any of the other pack members. As soon as I arrived, Darrell had whisked me out to a rustic little cabin a few miles outside of town. Away from most of the pack.

I wasn't sure if it was because he wanted to keep me away from everyone or if he thought I needed the privacy. Considering the suspicion I sensed from the few pack members I'd seen, I thought it was the first.

Though I didn't see many of the wolves in the MacArthur pack, I could still tell that there was something going on. It was obvious in the way the shifters carried themselves. The hushed tones of their voices when they spoke. The way their eyes darted quickly when I caught them watching me in town. The fact that none of them would utter more than two words to me at a time.

Darrell had been conveniently busy over the last few days and every wolf I came across would scurry away as fast as possible when they saw me coming. At this rate I'd never find out what happened to my parents.

I groaned in disgust at my defeatist attitude. I could hear my grandmother's voice now, telling me that I never would find what I wanted if I didn't get my head out of my ass and quit focusing on the problems rather than the solutions.

As I lay naked in the grass, staring at the sky, the wind shifted. A scent drifted in the air, one I knew well. At first I thought I was dreaming. It had been three long weeks since I saw Lachlan, but I swore I could smell him at night as I drifted off to sleep.

And I dreamed about him. Lush, sexy dreams where he would touch me in all the ways I needed him to. More than that, he would smile at me. *Love* me.

The dreams were as heartbreaking as always because I knew it would never happen. He'd lost his mate nearly two years ago. In the haze of his grief, he would never know that he was supposed to be mine.

I hadn't even realized it until around the time Ricki had gotten pregnant. She and I had been training and it was the first time she managed to knock me on my ass. I'd fallen and cut my arm badly enough that it wasn't healing right away. Lachlan had insisted on inspecting the wound and cleaning it with his saliva, which was common among shifters. Our saliva held healing properties, similar to a vampire's though not as strong.

As his tongue swept along my skin, I'd felt the stirring inside me. Not desire. Something deeper. It was as if my soul recognized him and sang.

It was both the most intense and worst moment of my life.

I now understood what shifters meant when they talked about the call their bodies had for their mate. The yearning.

Yet I could do nothing about it.

Lachlan was damaged. Irreparably so. There would be no mating with him, no future. Everything I wanted was dangled in front of me, forever to be tugged just out of reach.

Still, I stayed. I told myself that Calder needed me to help with the pack as they recovered from their battle with the Faction. That he needed me to track down the remaining members and eradicate them.

Finally, I had to admit to myself that I stayed because I wanted to be close to Lachlan and help him heal. Even if I would never have him, I couldn't live with the idea of his death. I nursed, bullied, pushed, persuaded, and coaxed him into eating, bathing, even sleeping. There were days that I felt like only my will alone kept him breathing. As much as the thought hurt like hell, I would have done everything within my power to bring Belinda back to him just to see his heartbreak eased. He deserved happiness, even if it wasn't with me.

Once again, the wind shifted, bringing with it the scent of Lachlan and interrupting my thoughts. I closed my eyes and inhaled deeply. Then I heard the brush of denim on the tall grass and knew I wasn't alone. Nor was that scent a figment of my imagination.

I rolled to my feet in a flash and gaped as Lachlan walked through the grass toward me. My stomach twisted at the sight of him. In the last three weeks, he had gained weight, his frame no longer frighteningly gaunt. Though he still hadn't achieved the bulk he'd had when I first met him, he looked healthy and strong.

The biggest surprise was his hair. When I left, it had been long, just brushing the collar of his shirt and falling into his eyes. Now it was shorn close to his scalp, no more than a half inch long. The thick beard that had once adorned his jaw was also gone, his skin shaven smooth.

Without the hair to hide his features, the angles of his face stood out in bold relief. The sharp slant of his jaw and the high formation of his cheekbones and brow ridge were naked. And his eyes. They were so bright and brilliantly blue that it made my chest ache to look into them. He looked dangerous and beautiful, every inch the alpha wolf.

I tamped down hard on my body's response. I was downwind of him so he wouldn't be able to smell any changes in me, but I was also naked as a jaybird.

Then it hit me that he shouldn't even know where I was. I hadn't told anyone and I'd taken the battery out of my phone and hidden it in the cabin I'd left behind. Any arousal I'd been feeling moments ago was immediately quashed.

"What are you doing here?" I asked him, striding forward.

"Looking for you," he replied, his eyes locked on my face.

His jaw was hard and his body tight. I understood then that he was angry. No, furious.

"Why?" I questioned, lifting my chin. "I left the MacIntire pack and what I do now isn't any of your concern."

He growled low in his throat and reminded me once again of the fact that he was an alpha wolf, not to be challenged.

Unfortunately, he seemed to have forgotten that I had dominant instincts of my own and my hackles rose. I growled back, prowling toward him.

"Don't threaten me," I stated. I pitched my voice low and it vibrated with tension. "We aren't on your turf any longer, Ian."

He blinked at me in surprise. "What did you just call me?"

"Ian," I repeated, meeting his eyes levelly.

"How did you…" Confusion momentarily replaced his fury before his eyes flashed once again. If anything, my use of his first name only intensified his anger. "Don't call me that. No one calls me that but—"

He didn't finish his sentence. I knew what had been on the tip of his tongue however. No one but his mate would ever have the guts to call him Ian. In fact, I didn't think I'd ever heard Belinda call him by his given name either.

He hated it and went to great lengths to make that clear. Half the MacIntire pack had probably forgotten that Lachlan wasn't even his first name because it had been so long since anyone dared use it.

I kept walking, brushing by him on my way back to the cramped hunting cabin that I was staying in. "You need to leave."

"Not until you tell me what's going on," he retorted.

Though he moved silently, I knew he was following me.

"I told Calder. Ask him."

His hand hooked around my elbow, spinning me toward him. I reacted without thinking, my body moving on autopilot as I twisted his wrist and swept his legs from beneath him. To my shock, he used his downward momentum against me, dragging my body with him as he hit the ground. Then he rolled us so that he was straddling my waist.

Lachlan leaned forward until those burning blue eyes filled my vision. "That's not what I'm talking about."

I bucked, throwing him off and reversing our positions. This time it was me straddling his hips with my face lowered toward his. "Then I don't know what you mean," I snarled. "I'm here to investigate my parents' death, nothing more."

"Then why did Brian and Brayden Kirkpatrick seem so interested in your whereabouts when they requested a meet with Calder last week."

Surprised, I straightened and stared down at him. "What?"

"The Kirkpatricks paid us a visit in Dallas last week and they asked about you. Brayden seemed especially keen."

A sneer curled my lip as I got to my feet and leaned down to help him up. "I'll bet."

Lachlan took my hand but didn't release it when he rose from the ground. "Is there something between you and Brayden Kirkpatrick?"

I felt my lip curl even further, this time in disgust. "Hell, no. I can't stand that dick."

He studied me. "Did he do something to you?"

I pulled my hand from Lachlan's grasp and gestured for him to follow me to the cabin. "Yeah, he would drive in from Houston and pester the shit out of me the entire time I was in Austin. Kept saying I would make the perfect mate. It was creepy as hell. I was almost relieved when Jacob forbade me from looking into the murder of my parents because it gave me an excuse to get out of there and away from him."

"Did he—"

"God, no. I mean, Brayden tried to kiss me a few times and got a little pushy when I told him no, but nothing more than that. He was never dangerous, just...annoying."

I entered the cabin, Lachlan on my heels, and moved straight toward my clothes. Nudity wasn't usually something that bothered me. As a shifter, I was accustomed to being naked in the presence of others before or after pack runs. However, being around Lachlan made me more aware than ever of my exposed skin and my body's response to his proximity.

Once I was dressed, I faced him once again. Lachlan was looking around the cabin, his eyebrows lifted.

"This is an interesting place," he commented.

I laughed. "Yeah, it's a little on the rustic side."

The cabin was finished inside, but barely. It was basically one large open room with a huge, overstuffed sofa and twenty year old television in one corner, a small dining table in the other, a tiny kitchen just behind that, and the bed in the final corner. Through a door at the back of the living space, there was a miniscule bathroom. It hadn't been very clean when Darrell brought me out here, but I took care of that easily enough.

When I looked back at Lachlan, he was grinning at me. My heart turned over at the expression on his face because I hadn't seen him smile like that in years. Not a genuine, amused smile or a real laugh.

I ignored that smile, and the effect it had on me, and put my hands on my hips. "Now, tell me why you're really here, Lachlan."

CHAPTER SIX

Lachlan

I COULDN'T TAKE my eyes off of Chloe as she stood before me, her hands on her hips. It had only been three weeks since I last saw her, but she looked different.

Her hair was lighter, the dark gold streaked with brighter honey and caramel highlights, and her skin had a light tan all over. Probably from lying naked in the sun as she had been when I found her this afternoon.

It was as if I were seeing her with new eyes.

She moved, crossing her arms over her chest. "Answer me, Lachlan."

"I told you. The Kirkpatricks came to see us last week and they asked about you. Calder and I are concerned."

"What exactly did they say?"

"Brian asked about you. Where you were."

She waited a beat. "And that's it? Wow, you should have had him incarcerated."

Frustration began to simmer within me. "It wasn't what he said, Chloe," I began. "It's how they reacted. Especially Brayden. It wasn't just mild curiosity. His body language wasn't right and neither were his eyes."

Chloe stared me down in silence for a moment, something I

wasn't accustomed to. In all my years as alpha of the MacIntire pack, very few of my subordinates would meet my gaze for such a long period. The wolf within me saw it as a challenge. Strangely, when Chloe did it, my wolf liked it. He wanted her to watch us.

"Okay, so Brayden's behavior was strange. It's not as if he knows where I am." Her head tilted to the side. "Speaking of finding me, how did you?"

"We called your grandmother," I admitted.

She grinned, her hazel eyes sparkling with mischief. "Oh, I bet that was fun. I'm kinda sorry I missed it."

Fun wouldn't be the word I would use. More like painful. It had taken Calder and I an hour to convince Sophia MacArthur that Chloe might be in danger. Even when we had, she still hesitated to share her granddaughter's location. When our conversation was over, Calder had looked at me and said, "I'm so glad that she-wolf lives on the East Coast because I have to tell you, if she ever moved here and wanted the pack, I'd just let her have it."

I couldn't blame him for saying that. Chloe was tough, nearly unbeatable in a fight, but only because her grandmother taught her everything she knew. At two hundred and twenty years old, Sophia MacArthur was still strong and vibrant. And dangerous as hell. I'd heard stories about the way she took apart any opponent who was stupid enough to challenge her for the position of alpha for her pack. It rarely happened any more, but when she first took control, there had been quite a few wolves that thought that a female alpha would be easy to defeat. They'd learned their lesson swiftly and without mercy, recognizing their error in judgment just moments before they died.

Sophia MacArthur didn't take prisoners. She kicked ass and took names.

Chloe spoke, jerking me out of my thoughts. "Well, as you can see, I'm perfectly fine," she stated, unclasping her arms and spreading them wide. "No Kirkpatricks here. I'm safe and sound."

"And how's your investigation into your parents' murder going?" I asked.

She growled beneath her breath. "I'm at a dead end. Everyone in the pack is avoiding me, including Darrell."

"Maybe I can help," I offered.

She scoffed. "Considering my cover story is that I had to leave the MacIntire pack because Calder and I had a falling out, I don't think that will work. The last thing I need is to make them suspicious. Then I really would be in danger."

"So, let's adapt the cover story to accommodate my presence."

"How?" she asked. Her expression was skeptical.

My palms grew hot and clammy. Calder and I had discussed the best way for me to stay close to her during her time with the MacArthur pack, and we had agreed upon a course of action. But now that I was facing her, about to utter the words, my head felt light and my stomach hollow.

"We'll tell them I'm your mate and you left because I rejected you. But I've changed my mind and I came after you."

I expected Chloe to laugh at me. Maybe even tell me to fuck off.

She did neither of those things. Instead her arms wrapped around her waist as if she needed to hold herself up and her face paled. "What?"

I shrugged. "It's a cover story that allows me to remain close to you without drawing too much attention. Everyone here knows what happened to my…last mate, so no one would be surprised if I'm reluctant to take another. It also explains why you would leave a second pack in two years."

Chloe merely stared at me, shaking her head slowly. She looked horrified. "No, Lachlan. I can't do that."

"You can and you will," I commanded. "Your grandmother

agreed it's a sound plan. She didn't like the idea of you being here alone to begin with and she said she would feel much better knowing I'm here to guard your back."

She didn't respond aloud, just kept shaking her head as though she couldn't believe this was happening. I thought she would be annoyed by my proposal, but her reaction was completely unexpected.

"Chloe, what's wrong?"

Before she could speak, I heard a truck pull up the driveway and I twisted toward the front door, a snarl reverberating from my chest into my throat as a door slammed and swift steps came up the front porch. When I yanked it open and stepped outside, I nearly ran into another male.

The wolf stood before me, his light brown hair neatly combed and his brown eyes narrowed. After a moment, I realized I was looking at Darrell, the current alpha of the MacArthur pack. Only he wasn't truly an alpha. He might have been the oldest and strongest male of his pack, but he didn't have the presence of a born alpha. I felt no urge to lower my gaze or a push of dominance from him.

He took a step back, hesitating for an instant before he stood his ground. "Darlin', everything okay?"

I nearly sneered. As if he could protect her. She was more dominant than he was and we all knew it.

"Everything's fine, Uncle Darrell," she said from behind me.

I straightened. It had been decades since I'd seen Darrell Whelby and I hadn't recognized him.

"Darrell," I greeted, nodding my head at him.

The fear in his eyes gradually vanished as he took in my appearance. His brows lifted when he finally recognized me. "Damn, Lachlan. I didn't realize that was you. You look different."

He stepped forward and held out his hand. I took it, shaking it firmly, and bit back a growl when his eyes met mine before skittering away.

"What brings you here?" he asked, releasing my hand.

"I came to see Chloe."

This time, when his gaze rested on me, it didn't move away. "The way I hear it, your pack was done with her."

I shook my head. "It was a misunderstanding, Darrell. I'm afraid that it's my fault Chloe left and I'm here to get her back."

"Oh, really?" He sounded skeptical.

Chloe's hand clamped on my bicep in a warning and I knew I only had seconds to act before she opened her mouth and screwed up the plan that Sophia, Calder, and I had developed.

Moving swiftly, I reached back and wrapped an arm around Chloe, tugging her into my side. "You see, when I realized that she was my mate, well, I didn't have the best reaction."

As I suspected, Darrell knew about what happened to Belinda and his face softened. "That seems understandable."

Beside me, Chloe's body was as tight as a bowstring and vibrated with her desire to deny everything I was saying. I squeezed her shoulders tightly and quickly continued.

"It took me a while to realize my mistake and I'm here to apologize."

"Lachlan…" Her voice was low and carried a warning note.

Ignoring her and preparing to protect my balls in case Chloe decided to retaliate, I said, "As you can see, I have a lot of convincing to do before we return to my pack."

Darrell's eyes moved over both of us and just when I thought he was going to challenge my words, he smiled a little. "Well, son, you're going to need all the help you can get. My niece is a handful."

"One of the reasons I admire her so much," I replied.

Chloe's elbow jabbed me sharply in the gut, making me grunt

in pain. "Now that the two of you are finished talking about me as though I'm not here, what brings you by, Darrell?"

His smile widened into a huge grin and he shoved his hands into the pockets of his pants. "I came to invite you to a barbeque. The pack is having a big dinner tonight in town and I thought you might like to get out of this cabin for a while."

"That sounds great," Chloe agreed, nudging me again as she tried to step out of the circle of my arm.

For some reason I couldn't fathom, I didn't want her to. Instead, I jerked her closer to me. She growled softly and Darrell's grin morphed into a laugh.

"Damn, this is gonna be fun," he stated gleefully, rubbing his hands together. "We're eatin' at six, but come by early around five or so. We'll have a beer and I'll give you some tips for handling a MacArthur woman."

Before Chloe could react, he turned on his heel and walked out of the cabin, shutting the door behind him.

As his footsteps faded from the porch, Chloe shoved me away and whirled to face me. The earlier pallor of her face was gone, replaced with a bright flush. Her fists were clenched by her side and anger rolled off her in waves.

She waited until Darrell started his truck and drove away before she spoke.

"What the fuck was that?" she growled, her voice barely a low rumble in her chest. Her eyes were changing and I knew she was holding on to her control by a thread.

Without thinking, I reached out and cupped her cheeks, leaning forward. "Please let me help you, Chloe," I murmured. "Let me repay you for everything you've done for me."

CHAPTER SEVEN

Chloe

LACH'S HANDS WERE warm on my face and oh-so-gentle. His touch was muddling my mind, making it difficult to think. The anger that had filled me moments ago drained away.

Let me repay you for everything you've done for me.

His words rang in my ears, reminding me that he had no desire for me. He was too broken to realize what I truly was to him. Even if he did, I was certain that his real reaction would mirror his fictional one. He would reject me.

Spurning a mate in our culture was rare. Our very nature urged us to claim our mate, our wolf often pushing us even if our human heart resisted. However, if anyone could master his wolf, it would be Lachlan.

I tore myself away from his hands, putting several feet between us. "I appreciate why you want to help me, Lach, but it's not necessary. There is no debt to be paid. I did for you what I would have done for anyone in my pack."

The imploring expression left his face, replaced by determination as he crossed his arms over his chest. "I'm glad you feel that way, but I'm not leaving. I came to help you and I'm staying." Then he pulled out the big guns. "Sophia wanted me to tell you that if you don't accept my help, she'll be on the next flight out."

Shit. I shuddered to think what would happen if my grand-mother came here. She didn't have the patience to ask subtle questions or observe for long periods of time. She would definitely discover what happened to my parents, but it was extremely probably that there would be blood spilled when she did, and not all of the people she spoke with would be guilty.

"Fine," I relented, knowing that I had no other choice. "You can stay, but you're on my turf now. You aren't my alpha any longer and I won't follow your commands without argument."

Lach's reaction surprised me. He laughed. "When did you ever follow orders without arguing?"

I shrugged one shoulder. "You have a point. Now, if you have thoughts or suggestions, I'm willing to listen, but Gram and I have a plan and I don't intend to deviate from it."

"Sophia already made that perfectly clear."

I couldn't help but smile at his tone. "Good. Now, let's figure out how we're going to handle the barbeque tonight."

"Oh, I'm allowed an opinion now?"

I rolled my eyes. "Lach."

"Just kidding."

Once again he was smiling at me, a smile I hadn't seen in years. Ignoring my body's reaction to it, I grinned back. Even if he never realized that he was my mate, I would have to be satisfied in the knowledge that he was happy and alive.

SEVERAL HOURS LATER, we made our way into town. As we climbed out of Lach's truck and walked toward the park, we noticed the crowd of shifters gathered around tables and a huge smoking grill. Children ran around on the grass, swarming a playground filled with brand new equipment.

My heart ached at the memories the picture evoked. While I was growing up, my parents arranged pack gatherings like this all the time. This was a painful reminder of a happier time.

As Lachlan and I approached the group, he reached out and took my hand, squeezing gently. I tugged my hand away, ignoring the way he growled at me beneath his breath.

During our conversation at the cabin earlier, I'd argued with Lachlan that the pretense of us being mates wasn't necessary. Honestly, I feared that my sanity would be destroyed if I had to go along with that harebrained scheme. Mostly because there would be no pretending on my part.

Acting the part of the smitten mate would likely kill me.

Lachlan finally tired of arguing with me and merely pulled out his phone, dialed my grandmother, and handed it to me. She made it very clear that I was to adhere to the plan that she, Calder, and Lachlan had concocted or she would take over.

I compromised and told her that he could put on the show of a mate trying to woo his she-wolf, but that I would behave as though I were resisting.

When I shared that, my grandmother laughed loudly. "That's a good plan, darlin'. And it's a damn sight more accurate. Any mate that rejected you would have to work his ass off to earn your forgiveness, wouldn't he?"

While what she said was true, my motivation wasn't realism. It was self-protection.

As we drew closer to the crowd, people shifted, moving out of our way, clearly avoiding us. Everyone suddenly seemed busy, looking everywhere but directly at us.

Except Darrell. As soon as he spied us walking through the crowd, he grinned and came over.

"I'm glad y'all made it," he greeted. "Let's get you somethin' to drink and give everyone a chance to say hello to you."

I nearly laughed at his words. I seriously doubted anyone would speak to us. I wasn't sure why. We followed him through the crowd and I watched the wolves around us carefully.

Though I had trouble believing it, there were many rumors about how Darrell ran his pack. Rumors that said he was cruel and violent, that he would force unmated she-wolves to submit to his sexual appetites when he wished. The Darrell I'd known when I was a child never would have done those things, but that Darrell also hadn't been the leader of the pack. Power could twist weak men, turning them into unrecognizable degenerates.

So I watched the way his pack mates reacted to him and what I saw made my jaw clench.

The females smiled and glanced his way, but none looked directly at him. Several even cringed ever so slightly when he brushed by. The males hunched subtly in his wake, as though they worried about offending him. The only pack members who didn't seem to fear him were the four males that also served as the town's police force.

Once again, Lachlan's hand found mine, squeezing hard, and I knew he noticed it too. I also left my hand in his. I needed the comfort of his touch. Something was wrong in the MacArthur pack and the knowledge made my gut burn with rage. My parents had always been firm but fair with the wolves they led. Though alphas were not elected, they wanted their pack members to be happy and healthy and to maintain peace.

Even though our walk through the park was short, I saw more than enough to convince me of the veracity behind the rumors.

Somehow I managed to school my expression to hide my fury and disgust. Glancing at Lachlan out of the corner of my eye, I saw that he'd pasted a smile on his face, but I could still see the tightness of his jaw and around his eyes.

Two picnic tables were set up, one holding drinks and the other food. Darrell nodded to a female standing next to them and she fished two beers out of cooler and brought them over.

"Go grab one for me too, will ya darlin'?" Darrell asked her as she handed the bottles to Lachlan and I.

"Yes, sir," she murmured with a bob of her head before scurrying away to do as he asked.

When Darrell faced us, his eyes dropped to our hands, which were still clasped together, and his face darkened. I jerked my fingers away from Lachlan's grasp and growled low in my throat.

Darrell's expression cleared a little and he laughed. "Don't worry, Lach. She's just like her grandmother. You'll work your way around her in the end."

My lip wanted to curl into a sneer at his words but I bit it back. He was right on one account though—I was just like my grandmother. I would wait until I had proof that he was mistreating his pack and that he participated in my parents' murder. Then I would make him pay.

CHAPTER EIGHT

Lachlan

BY THE END of the evening, I was convinced there was definitely something wrong in the MacArthur pack. Though Darrell never said or did anything the least bit aggressive, the pack members were beaten down. There was no other way to describe it. The she-wolves scrambled to make sure that their alpha's every need was attended to, even before he had a chance to ask.

The males weren't much better.

No, it was only Darrell's deputies that seemed normal, but even that was suspicious.

It had taken several hours, but the pack members had finally begun to thaw toward Chloe. Even then, it only began after a she-wolf approached her. The female looked to be in her forties, which meant she was likely over two hundred years old. Maybe more. Our kind aged slowly, decades could pass and it would appear as though we had just aged by a few years.

"Chloe MacArthur, it has been too long," she greeted, pulling Chloe into a hug. "How are you, child?"

"I'm fine, Miss Emma," she replied, hugging the woman in return. "How are you?"

"Feeling every one of my years," the she-wolf answered as she released her from the hug.

For the first time since we arrived at the barbeque, Chloe smiled and genuinely meant it. "Come on, I want you to meet my friend, Lachlan."

She turned toward me, holding Miss Emma's hand. "Lach, this is Emma Copeland. She's a teacher at the elementary school here and one of the best she-wolves I know."

I held out my hand, happy to meet someone who could make Chloe smile like that. "Hi, Mrs. Copeland. It's nice to meet you."

The older wolf took my hand and just held it rather than shaking it. "Call me Emma." She paused. "You look just like your father, Ian," she stated, her eyes misting over. "I know you don't remember me. The last time I saw you, you were just a pup, barely out of diapers."

"You knew my father?" I asked, ignoring the fact that she used my first name. A name I'd hated all my life.

She nodded. "He was a good man, a fierce wolf, and one of the best alpha's I've ever met."

"Thank you."

"From what I hear, you're just like him."

I shrugged, feeling uncomfortable with the comparison. For years, my father was the yardstick I'd measured all my accomplishments against. "Thank you, ma'am."

She smiled at me and smoothly changed the subject. "So I hear you're my little Chloe's mate. I also hear you've already mucked it up."

"Uh, well, you see, Miss Emma—"

Before I could formulate an intelligent response, the she-wolf laughed and turned back to Chloe. "Good for you, girl. Don't let him get away with anything this early on or he'll try to walk all over you for the rest of your lives."

Chloe arched a brow at me. "That's excellent advice, Miss Emma."

The older she-wolf laughed as she took in the two of us. "Y'all make a lovely couple. I'm so glad I got a chance to see it." She laced her arm through Chloe's and looked up at me. "Why don't you go get us something to drink, Ian, and give me a chance to catch up with Chloe?"

I sensed that she wanted to talk to Chloe privately, so I did as she asked. I took my time, giving them a chance to discuss whatever it was Miss Emma had on her mind.

When I returned, they both looked a little upset, but their conversation seemed to be finished.

We talked for a while until Miss Emma's mate, Tom, came over. After introductions and some catching up, Tom told Emma he was ready to leave.

"I'm ready to go myself," I murmured to Chloe. I'd been on edge the entire time we were at the barbeque and it was beginning to take its toll. There was a dull ache behind my eyes and fatigue dragged at my body. I hadn't spent this much time around a group of wolves in months.

"Me, too," she agreed.

We said our good-byes to Darrell and his son, Carter, before walking toward the parking lot. I wasn't sure why, but I wanted to reach for her hand again. I suppressed the impulse and kept pace with her, my eyes sweeping the dark cars and shadows for threats. From the moment we entered the park, I felt unease prickling the back of my neck. It wasn't just from the way the pack reacted to their leader. It was something more sinister, but the reason eluded me.

"I'm driving," Chloe stated firmly as she skirted around the hood of my truck.

"It's my truck," I argued, even though my heart wasn't in it.

She held her hand out for the keys. "But I know the area and it's dark. It's better if I drive."

Since the ache in my head was rapidly becoming a harsh throb, I let it go and dug my keys out of my pocket. When I climbed into the passenger seat, I noticed a slip of paper in Chloe's hand.

"What's that?"

"It was in the driver's seat," she answered in a low voice, unfolding the note.

I leaned over and read over her shoulder.

They know why you're here. Be careful.

Without speaking, Chloe gave me the paper and started the truck. I read the words again, unsure of the motivation behind them. They could be a promise of future violence or a heads up to watch our backs.

I waited until we were on the road, away from the park, before I spoke again.

"Do you think this is a warning or a threat?" I asked her.

She kept her eyes on the road in front of us when she answered. "I think it's a warning from whoever contacted my grandmother."

"I'm not so sure."

My reaction caused her to glance at me. "Why do you say that?"

"My truck was locked. They got the note inside without setting off the alarm. It seems to me as if that's their way of saying, *we know why you're here and we can get to you anytime we want.*"

Chloe nodded. "That's a good point. Either way, we need to be careful."

"Who are *they?* Darrell? His officers?"

"Probably," she replied.

I lifted the paper to my nose, inhaling deeply. All I smelled was Chloe and lavender so strong it made me sneeze. Whoever wrote this note was covering their scent.

"Bless you," Chloe said. "What are you doing anyway?"

"I'm trying to see if whoever wrote this left their scent, but all I can smell is you and lavender." My nose twitched again and I lowered the page, fighting the urge to sneeze. "A lot of damn lavender. Did you recognize the handwriting?"

She frowned and shook her head. "No, I didn't. So the messenger didn't want to be identified. I guess that makes sense. If I was actually working for Darrell, I would probably take the note straight to him."

"What's with him, anyway?" I asked. "He seems nice enough, but his pack is terrified of him."

"I know," Chloe stated, her hands tightening on the steering wheel until the leather creaked. "I don't like it. I've known Darrell since I was a pup and he was always just...Darrell. He would give me piggyback rides and sometimes he even shifted and let me play fetch when I was little. What I saw at the barbeque today doesn't fit in with my memory of him. There is no reason his wolves should be so afraid of him unless he's doing something heinous to them."

"Do you think he had anything to do with the death of your parents?" I asked.

She was silent for so long that I thought she wouldn't answer. Finally, she spoke, her voice low and vibrating with anger. "I didn't before but now I'm not so sure. I intend to find out. If he did, then I'm going to kill him."

Chloe turned down the dirt road that led to the secluded cabin, the truck bumping along the rough terrain. I had to give her credit though, she was as careful with my vehicle as I was.

"Stay in the truck and let me look around before you get out," I stated, unbuckling my seat belt.

The look she gave me should have singed off all my hair. "I don't think so, Lach."

"Chloe, I'm telling—"

Her seatbelt clicked then her face was suddenly just an inch away. "Listen to me good, Ian Lachlan, because this will be the first and last time we have this conversation. You and I both know that I am more than capable of taking care of myself. I was the fucking enforcer of the last two packs I joined, which means I had to kick a lot of ass. We also both know that I am the better fighter of the two of us. Added to that, you aren't back to your full strength and it's unlikely you will be anytime soon because you barely ate a damn thing at the barbeque tonight. You and I will get out of this truck together and check the property *together*. Have I made myself clear?"

Though her aggressive behavior pissed off the wolf within me, I still found myself biting back a smile. Calder would have been laughing by now, not at her anger, but at me for thinking that she needed my protection. More than once he'd said he was glad Chloe didn't want to be the alpha of the MacIntire pack. He knew he couldn't take her in a fight. He might hold his own, even get in a few good licks, but in the end she would rip him to shreds and smile while she did it.

"You're right, we should do this together," I conceded.

Her brows lifted in surprise and she leaned back in the driver's seat. "You're not going to argue?"

"Hell, no. I don't know what I was thinking. In fact, now that you've pointed all that out to me, I think I'll stay in the truck and let you go look around by yourself."

The anger disappeared from her face and her hazel eyes sparkled in the shadowed cab. In the dim moonlight, I saw the corner of her mouth tug up. "Okay then. I'm glad you see reason."

When she reached for the door handle, my hand whipped out quickly, grabbing her right wrist and jerking her back over into my space, though not as close as she'd been before.

"Just one thing," I said. "If I do or say something that you don't like, do not get in my face like that again. You can talk to me with respect or not at all."

I expected her to get mad and tell me to go fuck myself. Instead she studied me for a moment, an enigmatic expression on her face. "You're right. I'm sorry. I let the stress of the situation get the best of me, but it won't happen again."

I blinked at her for a second, confused. At her gentle tug against my grip, I released her hand.

"Are you ready to get out?" she asked, her face unreadable.

I didn't get the sense that she was angry, or even hurt. All I saw was acceptance.

"Yeah. I'm ready."

With that, we both opened our doors and stepped out into the night.

CHAPTER NINE

Chloe

THERE WERE NO wolves around the house, only nocturnal animals and trees. I couldn't hear Lachlan as he moved around the property near me, but I could feel him all the same.

When it became clear that everything was safe, I approached Lachlan. "I'm ready to go inside and take a bath. It's been a long day."

He nodded, falling in step beside me as I walked back toward the cabin. We moved in silence through the cool night air. Once we were inside, he moved toward the kitchen. To my surprise, he began digging in the fridge and pulled out the leftover spaghetti from my meal last night.

I didn't say a word. Grabbing a clean pair of pajama pants and a t-shirt, I went into the tiny bathroom and shut the door. The bathroom was just as rustic as the rest of the cabin, but there was a long, narrow claw foot tub set against one wall. The exterior was chipped and discolored, attesting to its age, but it was deep enough that I could submerge my entire body from shoulders to toes. I assumed that Darrell had gotten the tub for free from someone who was remodeling their bathroom and decided to install it here.

Regardless of where it had come from, I was glad to have it. I'd been tense and on edge all night, my muscles tight with unease from being surrounded by Darrell and his cronies and awareness from being so close to Lach. I needed a break from both.

I ran the tub full of scalding hot water, pouring in some lavender bath salts that I'd picked up from the store in town last week. As I inhaled the scent, my mind wandered back to the note that had been left in the driver's seat of Lachlan's truck. Despite his suspicions, I believed that the writer wanted to help us rather than warn us off. I only wished I could figure out who'd left it. It was clear that not all the members of the MacArthur pack were content with Darrell's leadership.

Until the author of that note realized that they could trust me, all I could do was wait. Here, with Lachlan.

I exhaled, sinking deeper into the water and letting my head rest against the back of the tub. I'd left the MacIntire pack to escape the pain of yearning for him so badly yet knowing I couldn't have him. Though I no longer believed the wound left by grief was mortal, Lachlan was still injured all the same. His soul had been broken and I had my doubts that it would ever heal.

However, tonight in the truck, I'd seen a flash of the Lach I'd known before. The alpha that would never tolerate a wolf speaking to him the way I had. I'd grown so accustomed to being the one in charge after Belinda died that I'd almost forgotten how strong he'd once been. For months I'd made him eat and forced him to get out of bed and get fresh air, watching in agony as his body wasted away.

Tonight was the first time in nearly two years I'd seen even a fragment of who he used to be. It was arresting.

And dangerous.

The wolf within me was eager to claim her mate, certain that he was ready. But I knew better. The man was just as much a part of Lachlan as his wolf and the man might never be able to see the truth—that I was his mate. The second mate he would have in his life.

It was extraordinary among our kind to have more than one mate. Though the death of a mate wouldn't kill us right away, the remaining wolf would often wallow in grief until their body gave up. When the spirit was unwilling to continue living, the body would acquiesce.

Lachlan's body was beginning to regain strength, as was his mind. It made me hope for more, which I had no business doing. I couldn't. If I allowed myself to consider that he might one day be able to take another mate, my wolf would wrest control of the situation. I would claim him whether he wanted me to or not.

I couldn't do that to Lachlan. Until he was ready to acknowledge the possibility of a connection between us, I couldn't broach the subject. My yearning for him was too strong and I wouldn't be able to resist the urge to put my mark upon him and make him mine.

Water trickled down from the corner of my eye and I sucked in a deep breath, dropping beneath the surface. I hated crying. It was counterproductive. When I'd mastered the urge, I broke through the water and pulled the plug. As the water drained, I washed my body and hair, taking a moment to rinse off beneath the weak stream of water that the showerhead released. Another reason I preferred a bath to a shower. It was difficult to even get my entire body wet with the lack of water pressure, much less clean.

I dried off, dressed in my pajamas, and brushed my teeth. Though it was barely ten, it had been a long, trying day and I was ready for bed. When I came out of the bathroom, I saw a black duffel bag sitting on the sofa next to a pillow and blanket that must have come from the trunk at the end of the mattress. Lach and I hadn't discussed where he would sleep, but it was clear he'd decided to take the couch. I wasn't going to argue. I'd passed out on it the first night here and it wasn't very comfortable. Though, it was wide and long, big enough to easily accommodate a man Lach's size, the cushions were nearly flat. It would serve him right for showing up here and being bossy.

Lachlan looked up from the sink where he was washing the dishes he'd used. "Feel better?"

I nodded. "Look, I know it's early, but I'm going to bed. If you want to watch TV, go ahead. I'm so tired I'll probably sleep right through it." It was a lie. I'd always been a light sleeper, even worse now that I was here at Darrell's cabin, investigating the death of my parents.

"I'm tired myself. I'm going to take a shower and do the same."

"Okay. Night, Lach."

"Night, Chloe."

Since there was no wall between the sleeping area and the rest of the cabin, I walked over to the far side of the bed and lay down facing the wall, picking up the book I'd bought a couple of weeks ago. I rarely sat still long enough to read, but I found I slept better when I took a little time to unwind before I turned out the light.

As soon as Lach finished washing dishes, he moved to his bag, digging around inside it for a few minutes. Then he disappeared into the bathroom.

When the door shut behind him, I sighed softly and closed my book. I'd been reading the same paragraph since I opened it anyway. I lay on my side, staring at the wall in front of me and listening to the sound of running water as it beat down on the porcelain tub.

Before I realized it was happening, I was asleep.

THE THRASHING SOUND woke me. I lay completely still, forcing myself to breathe slowly and deeply as though I were still asleep, and listened. Had someone broken into the cabin?

Then I heard it again, followed by a low growl that raised a chill on my skin. The growl deepened and grew louder, until it seemed to shake the cabin.

It took me a moment to realize that it was coming from the sofa. When I did, I sat up and saw that Lachlan was moving restlessly.

I climbed out of bed, moving slowly toward him. "Lachlan," I called. "You need to wake up."

He didn't respond. He was too lost in the nightmare.

"Ian!" I shouted.

Nothing except a short break in the growl before it resumed, louder and more vicious than before.

I saw the agonized expression on his face and my heart hurt. I knew he had dreamt of the night that Belinda died for months afterward. Finally after about a year, he'd convinced me that the nightmares didn't come very often any longer.

As I watched him writhe it became clear to me that he'd lied so that people would stop asking him about them.

Bracing myself, I moved closer to him. I didn't want to touch him while he was in the throes of a bad dream. It could result in one or both of us getting hurt, but it was clear that he wouldn't wake up any other way and I couldn't let him continue with that horrible dream.

I reached out, standing just behind his head, and clasped his shoulder, shaking it firmly. "Lachlan, it's Chloe. Wake up!"

Just as I knew he would, he snarled and turned on me in a flash, his body tackling me to the ground. His eyes were open, but he wasn't seeing me, his brain still locked in the past.

His fingers dug into my hips, causing me to cry out in pain. I didn't want to fight him. He was hurting enough and I didn't want to cause more agony. Instead, I lifted my hands and cupped his cheeks.

"Lachlan," I whispered. "You're safe. You need to wake up."

Without thinking, I moved my thumb and it brushed across his lower lip.

Immediately, he stilled. His hands still held me a shade too tightly, but it no longer hurt. His chest moved rapidly as he panted. He was poised between sleep and wakefulness.

"It's Chloe, Lach. You need to wake up and talk to me," I commanded softly.

Slowly, his eyelids lifted and he looked down at me, his eyes glassy. "Chloe?"

"I'm here, Ian."

He collapsed on me then, his body trembling violently as he sucked in deep, broken gasps. I felt the dampness of tears on my shoulder and I wrapped my arms and legs around him, cradling him close. He needed my comfort, however I could give it to him.

"I'm here, I'm here," I crooned softly. "You were dreaming. It's okay."

His hands released my hips and he shoved them beneath me, holding me so tightly I could barely breathe.

"Chloe," he whispered. "Oh God, Chloe."

I didn't ask him what he'd dreamed about because I knew. His nightmares were always about the mate that he'd had and lost. The mate he would have given anything to hold once again.

My heart broke for us both because we were never going to get what we yearned for most—the other half of our soul.

CHAPTER TEN

Lachlan

I CLUTCHED CHLOE tighter to me, my heart pounding so hard against my sternum that I was sure it would break free of my chest.

The dream had begun the same as it always had. Belinda and I were fighting off the wolves that had sided with the Faction. There were too many of them for me to take on alone and there was no way to escape. As I'd ripped at my opponents with teeth and claws, I could see the flashes of light as Belinda fought them with magic.

Just as I'd begun to believe we might win, that she would be safe, I heard her scream. I whirled in time to see a partially shifted wolf lift her in his grasp and give a sharp slash with his claws.

Howling with rage, I'd torn apart any shifters that tried to stop me from getting to my mate. The sight of her blood covering the floor and the wolf that held her drove me to madness. He dropped her body as I approached and bared his fangs at me.

Without hesitation, I pounced on him. In my fury, I raked at him with my teeth and rent his flesh with my claws. He couldn't defend himself against the murderous rage that poured through me. I never felt his blows because I was consumed with madness and the compulsion to destroy him.

When he finally lay motionless beneath me, nothing left of him but blood and bones, I climbed off his body. With shaking hands, I lifted Belinda, cradling her in my lap as I brushed her hair away from her face.

This time the dream was different. The pale features that lay in the crook of my arm didn't belong to my mate.

It was Chloe, deathly still, her body covered in the blood that had poured from her torn throat.

When her voice pierced through the haze of my dream, the emotions that roared through me were indescribable. She was here now, warm and alive, her arms and legs wrapped around me and holding me close.

I felt the tears falling from my eyes but I couldn't bring myself to give a shit. All that mattered was that she was safe.

My body shook with violent shudders as the dregs of the dream faded away, leaving me cold and empty. Slowly, I became aware of the lean muscles of Chloe's thighs where they cradled my hips and the lavender scent of her hair. Unlike the perfume on the note, this fragrance was lighter and carried the undertones of Chloe's own scent.

I inhaled again, my nose brushing her shoulder, letting her presence soothe me.

Suddenly, I realized that my body was reacting to her. My cock began to harden. It had been nearly two years since I felt my blood stir this way.

Shocked, I released her abruptly, which was almost worse. The t-shirt she wore clung to her breasts and without my body pressed against hers, the cool air caused her nipples to harden. Her hair was spread around her on the floor as though she'd been lying beneath me for a very different reason.

"Did I hurt you?" I asked, my voice rough. I sat back, leaning against the bottom of the couch and bending my knees to hide my erection.

"No," she whispered, slowly sitting up.

I wanted to reach out and help her, especially when I saw the way she winced and favored her ribs. Instead, I snapped, "I thought you said I didn't hurt you."

She stared at me, a frown tugging her brows down. "My ribs are a little bruised, but I'm not truly hurt. It'll heal up in a matter of minutes."

"Dammit, Chloe. You know you shouldn't touch me when I'm having a nightmare. Why didn't you yell or call my name?"

"I did," she answered shortly, pushing herself off the floor and to her feet. "You didn't wake up."

"Well, turn on the light or throw something at me next time," I snarled.

She moved to the cabinet next to the sink and took out two glasses, filling them with water from the tap. "Don't worry, I will," she growled back, bringing a glass to me and handing it over with a fierce scowl.

I took the water from her, feeling even more like as asshole. "Thank you," I mumbled.

"You're welcome." She moved over to the trunk at the end of the bed and sipped her own water. "Do you want to watch some TV or something?"

I drained the glass and shook my head. "No. Just go back to sleep, Chloe. I'll be fine."

She didn't speak for a long moment, but I could feel her eyes on me. I tensed, waiting for her to say something, to ask me if I would be okay. To my surprise, she sighed and got up, walking around the bed.

There was a rustle of sheets as she slid beneath the covers and settled. She remained silent, the still air stretching until the quiet vibrated with all the unspoken words between us.

I sat on the floor, my back against the couch, and listened to her breathe until I knew she had fallen back asleep. It was only then that I got up and lay on the sofa, staring up at the ceiling until the moonlight gave way to the rising sun.

THE WHISPER OF the screen door shutting woke me up. It took me a moment to remember where I was and what had happened last night. Grunting in disgust, I sat up on the couch and scrubbed my face with my hands. I saw that there was half a pot of coffee left and the clock said it was just after ten.

I must have fallen asleep after the sun came up, I realized. That surprised me. I usually couldn't sleep again after a nightmare. If I'd been alone in the cabin, I would have turned on every light in the place and paced the floor until dawn. Or I would have gone for a long, punishing run in wolf form. Unfortunately, I could do neither last night.

Getting to my feet, I walked on silent feet to the front door and looked outside. Then I froze. Chloe stood in the front yard with her back to me, naked. Her long hair gleamed in the sunlight, the dark blonde illuminated by the rays until the strands took on a hue of pure honey. Her long body was curved in all the right places and packed with lean muscle.

Unable to look away, I watched as she lifted her arms above her head and gave a cat-like stretch, which should have looked strange on a wolf shifter, but it didn't.

No, it was sexy as hell.

I took several steps away from the door then, backing into the kitchen until I could no longer see her. What the fuck was I doing? Staring at Chloe and thinking she was sexy?

My gut twisted with guilt and horror. I had no right to look at a female with lust. Not after what I had with Belinda. Now that I knew the touch of a true mate, nothing else would fill the void left behind.

A streak of brown out the kitchen window caught my eye and I realized Chloe must have shifted and gone for a run.

The guilt inside me morphed into something darker and uglier—anger. Chloe knew that we were being watched, and possibly in danger, yet she went for a run alone, without telling me.

I let that ire build within me until my temper snapped. Snarling, I tore off the pajama pants and briefs I wore and ran out the door. As I bounded off the porch, I felt my body shifting and changing. Within a few strides, I was running on four paws, following the scent of lavender and Chloe.

CHAPTER ELEVEN

Chloe

A S I RAN through the woods in wolf form, I let the human part of my brain wander back to last night. Remembering things I had no business thinking about.

After Lachlan had calmed down, he'd lain on top of me, just holding me. I'd relished his weight and his heat as his breathing slowed and his trembling subsided.

Then I'd felt it growing against my core. His cock. Whether his mind agreed, his body wanted me.

Part of me wanted to howl in triumph, but I was also terrified. He was still off balance and learning to live once more. His body coming to life again would only make it more difficult for him to cope. He needed more time to come to terms with the fact that his body hadn't died along with his mate before dealing with the demands of his libido.

The furious pounding of paws behind me had me whirling, a snarl peeling my lips away from my fangs.

I relaxed slightly when I saw the familiar figure of a chestnut brown wolf bearing down on me, but it was short-lived. He was growling and baring his own teeth at me, clearly enraged.

Without waiting for him, I shifted back to my human form and put my hands on my hips. "What the hell is your problem?" I yelled.

Lachlan slowed his approach, his ears turning back as he growled at me again.

"Stop with the growling bullshit, shift, and tell me what the problem is or I'm leaving."

Smoothly, Lach's body began to twist and move, the bones lengthening and the fur receding, but he didn't pause in his charge. He leapt in the air, still mostly wolf, but landed in front of me in fully human form.

I often marveled at the ease of his change. While it was painful during the first transition in adolescence, our bodies grew accustomed and it became easier. Alphas found the shift easier than most and some, like Lach, were able to achieve it within a blink of an eye.

"What the fuck are you thinking?" he roared. "You know that it's not safe here but you go out for a run alone or without even telling me where you're going?"

"Lower your voice," I hissed. "I don't think anyone is watching or listening, but even if they aren't, they probably heard you all the way in town."

"Fuck that, Chloe. You put yourself in danger and that is unacceptable. I know you can fight, but you can't take on a bullet."

I wanted to fight, to wrap myself in righteous anger and stand toe-to-toe with him, but I couldn't. Because he was right. After getting that note last night, I shouldn't be running in the woods alone. Especially when no one knew where I was.

"You're right," I sighed. "I should have woken you or waited until you were awake and able to come with me."

"Goddammit, Chloe!" he yelled, shoving his hands through his hair as he turned away from me, pacing wildly.

"What, Lachlan?" I spat back. "You're right. I fucked up. I admitted it. What more do you want from me?"

He turned back toward me. "I'm pissed as hell, Chloe. I can't take it out on you when you fucking apologize," he stated.

If he had been anyone other than my mate, I would have thrown a punch. A good fight would let off enough steam for both of us to calm down. Violence was common in the shifter world, an outlet for our aggressive tendencies or a way to assert our dominance, but I couldn't bring myself to hit Lachlan. I didn't want to hurt him.

Another option would be a hard, fast fuck, but I wouldn't suggest that either. If I had sex with him, I would bite him, mark him as mine, and he would hate me for it.

"What do you want me to do, Lach?" I asked, pitching my voice low in an effort to soothe his ragged temper.

His eyes flashed, the blue turning brighter, and they moved down my body.

I glanced down as well and saw he was fully erect. Aggressively so.

I tore my eyes away from his cock and met his gaze. "I'm heading back. When you've calmed down, we'll talk."

Without waiting for his answer, I shifted back to wolf form and ran back toward the cabin as if the Devil himself were on my tail.

A few moments later, I heard his paws striking the ground behind me, but he stayed several feet back all the way there.

When I reached the cabin, I shifted and walked past my clothes, straight into the house. My body tingled all over and I felt as though I were about to come out of my skin.

If I thought being close to Lachlan at the MacIntire compound was torture, it was nothing compared to this.

I went straight into the bathroom, shutting and locking the door behind me. Even though I'd taken a bath the night before, I turned on the shower and stepped inside. I bit back a curse at the cold temperature of the water but didn't touch the taps. My blood still burned hot, full of lust and frustration.

I scrubbed my skin roughly with a washcloth, trying to dispel the prickling sensation. I gasped when the nubby fabric brushed my nipples, shooting arcs of heat from my breasts to my pussy. Determined to ignore the wild tension within me, I washed myself quickly, standing beneath the chilling spray until I shivered.

Finally, the clamor of my body subsided, leaving me hollow. It was more than a physical feeling of emptiness. After finding my mate in Lachlan, I realized there was a void in my soul. A place waiting within me, aching from the need to be filled. Every day I was in his presence, the throb intensified, demanding action from me.

After I turned off the water, I realized that I hadn't brought any clothes into the bathroom with me. Any other time, I wouldn't have felt the least bit reticent about my nudity. It was just a part of pack life.

But with Lach's presence in the other room and the tension between us, I needed the illusion of protection that my jeans and tank top would afford me. Biting back a sigh, I dried off with a towel and wrapped it around my body. I would just have to suck it up. I'd been doing it for months now, I could continue for a while longer.

I exited the bathroom, glad to see the cabin was empty and the clothes I'd been wearing before I shifted were neatly folded on the bed. Lachlan must have brought them inside. Walking over to the mattress, I turned my back to the open front door and dropped the towel.

I was just shimmying into my jeans when I heard the screen door creak open. I didn't look over my shoulder and bent to pick up my olive green tank top, tugging it over my head. When the fabric was in place, I turned to face Lach.

He looked sheepish and sad, a combination that pierced my

heart and made me want to go to him and give him a hug. I resisted the urge and stood my ground.

"I'm sorry, Chloe," he said. "I shouldn't have…" he trailed off as if he wasn't sure what to say.

"Yelled at me? Gotten angry?" I asked, shaking my head. "I understand, Lach. You don't have to beat yourself up for telling me the truth. I know better than to go for a run alone when there's the possibility of danger. I would have done the same if our positions were reversed." Actually, I probably would have been angrier. Especially with him.

He shoved his hands in his jean pockets. "It doesn't excuse it. I am…was, an alpha. If I can't control myself, how can I control the wolves I lead?"

My grandmother often said something to that effect, which only made my desire to walk over and comfort Lach even stronger. "It's fine. We're good."

God, having a mate was making me soft. If any other male wolf had yelled at me like he had, I would have handed him his balls on a platter.

He studied me for a long moment. The sun poured in through the door at his back, throwing his face in partial shadow. I couldn't read his expression, but I could feel the weight of his stare on my skin.

"Look, about earlier…" he began.

Instinctively I knew he was referring to the erection he'd been sporting during our argument and lifted my hand. "Don't worry about it. I know it didn't mean anything."

He fell silent but the tautness in his body raised a chill on my skin. Finally, he spoke, "Of course not." Lach's eyes never wavered from me. "Have you had breakfast?"

I shook my head.

"I'll make something," he stated, taking his hands out of his pockets and moving toward the stove. "Why don't you call Sophia and give her an update?"

Grateful for a chance to put some space between us, I nodded and grabbed my cell phone from the nightstand. I stepped out of the cabin into the bright light outside and released a long breath.

Just a few more weeks, then this torture would end. I would endure it because I had no other choice.

CHAPTER TWELVE

Lachlan

I STOOD AT the stove making French toast while listening to the rise and fall of Chloe's voice as she talked to her grandmother, Sophia. My mind was back in the woods when I'd been yelling at her earlier. Only the ending of that fight was completely different in my head.

I saw myself tackling her to the ground, flipping her over, and driving deep inside her, fucking her until she submitted.

Even now, the thought had my cock growing hard.

I shook my head in disgust and confusion. What the fuck was happening to me?

Since Belinda died, my libido had been non-existent. I couldn't remember the last time I'd had an erection since then. I scowled down at the pan. If I was going to be honest with myself, I hadn't. Not once had my interest been stirred. Until now.

Then I heard Belinda's voice as though she were standing just behind me, whispering in my ear.

And what I want is for you to live...and to love again.

I growled under my breath as the words from her letter came back to me. In the weeks since I'd read her final words to me, I'd found it easier to get out of bed, eat, bathe, and move. My body grew stronger and my mind sharpened again.

But to fuck someone else? In my mind, it would cut the final tie I had to Belinda and I couldn't bring myself to do it.

Even if I did have sex in the future, it would be nothing more than scratching an itch, sating a hunger. I would never have feelings for the women I slept with and I would never take another mate. *Never.*

I couldn't allow myself to treat Chloe so callously, not after everything she'd done for me. I was certain that I would have died without her. If she hadn't been there every fucking day, forcing me to eat and bathe, dragging me out of my house to run with my wolf, I would have faded away to join Belinda in death.

My phone vibrated in my back pocket and I pulled it out. Then I slid my thumb across the screen and lifted it to my ear.

"Yeah?"

Calder chuckled in my ear. "Is that any way to greet your alpha?" he asked.

"Yes, Master?" I replied.

He laughed louder. "I'm glad to hear you still have your sense of humor. I take it things are going well."

If he only fucking knew. "As well as can be expected," I answered. "We got an anonymous note last night. Chloe thinks it's someone's way of warning us to be careful." I went on to tell him exactly what the note said.

"A threat?" Calder asked.

"No, more like an attempt to help us."

"And you agree?"

I grunted as I used the spatula to scoop out the cooked French toast. "Yeah, I do." I put two more pieces of soaked bread into the sizzling pan. "But I'd still like to talk to whoever wrote it. We need more than vague warnings. We need proof or witnesses."

Calder was quiet for a moment. "How's Chloe doing with this? I mean, this has to be stirring up all kinds of shit for her about the death of her parents."

My body went still at his words and my lungs stopped working. God, I was such a dick. I'd been so consumed with my own pain I'd never stopped for a moment to think about what Chloe might be thinking and feeling. Her parents had died only a few months before Belinda.

I hadn't known them well, but I'd heard enough to know that they doted on their only daughter. The family was close and loving.

"Lach? What's wrong, man?"

I shook my head and cleared my throat. "She seems fine, Calder. She hasn't said anything."

"Yeah, well, keep an eye on her. Grief is a tricky thing. You never know what might set her off."

"I will," I murmured.

There was a loud crash in the background and I heard Ricki yell. "Shit, the pups just took down the TV. I better get in there before Ricki decides to follow through on her threat to neuter me in my sleep. I'll call you in a couple of days."

He disconnected before I could reply.

Slowly, I lowered the phone from my ear and tucked it back into my pocket. The scent of scorching French toast tickled my nose and I swore, flipping the bread. It wasn't quite black, but it would probably taste like shit.

I flicked the burnt mess into the trashcan and started again. I'd already made six slices of French toast and cooked half a pound of bacon, but I knew it wouldn't be enough. Our metabolism burned so hot and fast that it would take more to keep us going until lunch.

By the time Chloe re-entered the cabin, I'd finished making four more slices of toast and had everything warming in the oven as I washed dishes.

I'd also taken the opportunity to get my shit together. It was time for me to focus. I'd let myself wallow in loss for so long that I'd forgotten to think about the people around me. That had to stop now. At least until Chloe found what she needed. There would be enough time for me to retreat back into my head when this was all said and done.

"That smells great," Chloe said.

"Thanks," I said, shutting off the water and drying my hands. I moved to the oven and pulled out two large plates, each holding four slices of French toast and a heaping pile of bacon. "Have a seat." I motioned toward the table, setting a plate in front of her when she settled into a chair.

I'd already put out glasses and silverware, along with syrup, butter, and orange juice.

Chloe grinned as she took in the table. "Damn, I could get used to this. Want a job?"

I smiled back at her. "No, thanks. I can make the basics, but I think you'd get sick of my limited repertoire pretty quickly."

She shrugged, grabbing the syrup and pouring thick ribbons of it over the bread. "Maybe, but you'd be useful until then."

As we dug into the meal, I asked, "How'd your talk with Sophia go?"

"Okay," she mumbled. "She wasn't happy about the note. Unfortunately, she shares your suspicious mind and she wants us to be very careful."

"Did y'all discuss our next move?"

"Yeah. We're going to start with Miss Emma." She forked a huge bite of French toast into her mouth, her eyes rolling up as she let out a little moan. "This is amazing, Lach," she murmured after she swallowed, her tongue coming out to sweep across her bottom lip.

I shifted in my chair, suddenly very aware of the state of my crotch. The abrupt return of my sex drive was already proving to be painful. Literally.

"Uh, thanks," I replied. "What about Miss Emma?" I asked her, desperate to keep her talking rather than eating.

"Well, she said a few things last night that concern me and I think she would be the one most likely to tell me what's really going on inside the pack."

"Will she be in danger if they find out she talked?"

Chloe's expression darkened. "Not if we come down on their asses first. I don't know what in the hell is going on in this pack, Lachlan, but it needs to stop. Wolves should never be so terrified of their alpha that they bow and scrape to his every whim. He's doing something to them and has all of them too frightened to talk. I can't leave them to deal with that alone."

I nodded. "I agree."

"We'll go see Miss Emma today and maybe she can give us a place to start. She's been a member of this pack since she mated with Tom a hundred and fifty years ago. She makes it her business to know everything about everyone."

I studied her as she ate.

"What?" she asked. "Do I have syrup on my face?" She ran her thumb along the edge of her lip, checking for any stray drops of the sweet liquid.

I swallowed hard, suddenly aware of my dry mouth. "Uh, no. I was just wondering how you were feeling about all this."

"What do you mean?"

"Your parents' death. Darrell. Everything. Is this bringing up painful memories for you?"

She cocked her head to the side. "Maybe a little." She shoved food around on her plate with her fork. "The pain of their deaths has faded over the past couple of years. I'm angry more so than anything else. I hate that Darrell has had two years to hurt people I once cared about. And I'm also pissed as hell that he's gotten away with the murder of my parents."

I wanted to reach out and take her hand, but I held myself back. I hadn't thought about how she might be feeling until Calder brought it up and now I felt like a heel.

"Maybe we should get going," I suggested.

"After I finish my breakfast. I meant what I said, Lach. This is damn good and I intend to eat every bit of it. Darrell isn't going anywhere in the five minutes it'll take me to eat French toast. Plus I may need the fuel in case I need to kick some ass."

She had a good point. Though she spoke of anger and grief, Chloe seemed to have accepted the situation for what it was. We ate the rest of the meal in silence and I tried to keep my eyes off her mouth as she savored every bite.

When Chloe finally finished her food and licked her fork clean, I looked down to find my plate empty and my cock as hard as stone. Her obvious enjoyment of the meal had distracted me so thoroughly that I'd eaten every bite of my own breakfast.

"I'm going to go brush my teeth and then I'll be ready to go," she announced, shoving back her chair and carrying her plate to the sink.

When the bathroom door closed behind her, I stood, reaching down to adjust myself with a wince.

We needed to resolve the MacArthur pack issues quickly...before I did something I'd regret.

CHAPTER THIRTEEN

Chloe

M ISS EMMA SMILED broadly when she opened the door.
"Chloe! I'm so glad you came by. I was hoping we'd get more time to catch up before you left."

I returned her grin. "I felt the same way. May we come in?"

Without replying, she stepped back and allowed us inside. As I walked into her cool, bright living room, I found myself instantly transported back to my childhood. My mother often brought me to Miss Emma's when I was younger. I remembered the two of them talking and drinking iced tea while I played on the living room floor. The house hadn't changed much. The walls were still painted white and hung with all sorts of landscapes and photographs. The wooden floors gleamed. The couch was of a different style, but still the same dove grey color. I bit back a laugh. Only Miss Emma would buy a new couch in exactly the same color as her old one.

A large multi-colored rug was spread out beneath the couch and chairs that were arranged to face a huge flat screen TV. Now that was different. The last time I was here, Tom was still watching ball games on his behemoth, fifty-inch television that weighed a ton. This one was even larger, but with it anchored to the wall, the living room seemed even bigger and brighter than before.

"You have a lovely home, Miss Emma," Lachlan murmured behind me.

The she-wolf turned her huge smile toward him. "Thank you, Ian."

I felt rather than saw his slight flinch. Miss Emma was just as perceptive.

"Would you prefer I called you Lachlan?" she asked quietly.

"Please. Or Lach."

She nodded. "Why don't you both have a seat while I get us something to drink?"

"Oh, Miss Emma, there's no need to bother—"

"Hush, child. I don't get many visitors, but when I do, I offer them a cool drink and a snack."

I relented as the older wolf left the room. With a sigh, I sat down on the couch, crossing my arms over my chest. To my surprise, Lachlan sat down next to me so that our hips and shoulders brushed. The sensation made my stomach tighten and brought a rush of heat to the points of contact.

When I saw Miss Emma returning, carrying a tray laden with a tea pitcher, glasses, and a plate full of finger foods, I used that as a means to escape Lach's proximity. I jumped to my feet and took the tray from my former teacher.

"I may be older than you, Chloe MacArthur, but I'm perfectly capable of carrying that tray," she stated tartly.

"I know that, Miss Emma, but my mama raised me to be help-ful to my elders." I hesitated. "Now, where do you want me to put it?"

She laughed and pointed to the coffee table. As I set the tray down, she perched on one of the armchairs facing the couch, leaving me no choice but to return to Lachlan's side.

He now had his arm thrown along the back, his ass firmly planted in the middle of the cushions, leaving me very little room.

When I sat next to him once again, his arm came around me, pulling me against his side.

Miss Emma took us in, smiling happily. "Oh, Chloe. I can't tell you how wonderful it is that you've found your mate at last." I nearly choked at her words, the sound of my throat closing covered by the sudden ringing of her telephone. "Oh, please excuse me. I need to answer that."

She rose and went into the kitchen, where an ancient rotary phone hung on the wall. As soon as I heard her speaking to whoever was on the phone, I nudged Lachlan with my elbow.

"A little space, please," I grumbled, keeping my voice pitched low so that Miss Emma wouldn't hear my words.

His mouth rested against my ear and, God help me, I couldn't suppress the shiver that went through my body. It took me a moment to understand the words he murmured.

"We're pretending to be mates, remember?" His voice was a low rumble and I felt it reverberate through my body, tightening my nipples and making my thighs press together.

I elbowed him again, this time with more force. "You're in the doghouse though because you rejected me."

He chuckled against my skin, the tip of his nose tracing the curve of my ear. The motion made my heart flutter because it was affectionate and sweet, two things I never would have expected from Lach. "Yes, but any alpha worth having would be pushing his boundaries."

"I'm afraid you're going to have to grovel before you'll be forgiven," I retorted.

His nose trailed down my neck, his lips barely brushing my skin, and my body went haywire. My heart was no longer fluttering, it was beating a rapid tattoo against my breast. When he replied this time, I felt his lips moving against my throat. "Alpha wolves don't grovel."

Vaguely, I heard Miss Emma hang up the phone. This time when I jabbed my elbow into his ribs, it was with enough force to make him grunt. He straightened, his hand rubbing his torso as he grumbled, "Ouch."

When Miss Emma returned to the living room, her face was pale and her features pinched.

"Everything okay?" I asked her, watching her expression carefully.

"Not really," she replied, dropping into the chair she'd vacated earlier.

"Is there anything I can do to help?"

Miss Emma's eyes narrowed on me. "First, I want you to tell me something. Are you really here because of a lovers' quarrel?"

Lach's hand tightened on my shoulder, gripping hard. I ignored the warning and answered honestly. "No."

Miss Emma nodded. "I didn't think so. So you're not mates then?"

I shook my head, hating the way her face fell in disappointment. "I'm sorry I lied to you, Miss Emma, but we needed a good cover story. Given Lachlan's history, we thought this would be best."

The she-wolf waved a hand at me. "Don't worry about that. You were right to lie. I'm guessing you're here about your parents?" she asked.

"At first, yes, but after last night, I think there's a lot more at stake here than finding those responsible for the death of my parents."

Tears shimmered in Miss Emma's eyes. I started to move toward her, but she lifted her hand again, stopping me. "No, no. I'm fine. It's just…you don't know how long I've wished for someone strong enough to come and help this pack."

"What's happening?"

She took a shaky breath, releasing it slowly. "Darrell and his—" she paused, as if searching for a word.

"Shitheads?" Lachlan supplied.

I growled at him under my breath, but Emma laughed a little.

"That's the best word to describe them," she stated, her voice quavering. "They keep this pack under their thumb."

"How so?" I asked.

She picked up a glass, poured tea into it, and handed it to me. Then she repeated the gesture for Lach and herself. Finally, she answered, "They take our money. Our things." She sipped her tea before whispering, "Even our daughters."

My body went rigid. "Are you saying..."

She nodded. "If one of the younger she-wolves catches the eye of Darrell or his men, well, she either goes along with what they want or they make an example out of her."

"Are they killing pack females?" I asked, my voice vibrating with rage.

"No, though I worry that's the next step. They will beat them until they agree. Or threaten to go after their mothers and sisters."

"And the mated females?" Lachlan interjected.

Miss Emma shook her head. "They haven't messed with the mated females yet, but I know it's coming. Things are going to get much worse before they get better."

"No, they're not," I stated. "Because I'm going to put a stop to this bullshit as soon as possible." I studied her for a moment. "What about Carter?"

Emma shook her head. "He doesn't do the...things his father and his cronies do, but he's weak. There's no way he can wrest control of the pack from his daddy and he knows it."

"What about Chloe's parents?" Lachlan asked. "Do you know what happened to them?"

A change came over Miss Emma's face, one that caught my

attention and held it. It was agony, but also guilt.

"Miss Emma?" My voice shook. I wanted to believe it was from sadness rather than fear, but I was lying to myself. Her expression made me afraid. Very afraid.

She cleared her throat before taking a sip of tea. "That's long done," she murmured.

"Not that long," I argued. "Why didn't you tell me what you knew before Darrell became the leader of the pack?"

Her eyes shimmered with tears once again. "Trina was still living at home two years ago, Chloe. Darrell knew he couldn't trust me not to go straight to you or your grandmother. He made it very clear that he could get to her at any time. He also explained, in great d-detail, what he would do to her when he did." Miss Emma stuttered over that single word, betraying how afraid she'd been for her youngest child.

As much as it angered me, I also understood. Miss Emma had to protect her daughter. From what she'd told me of Darrell just moments ago, I couldn't blame her for doing whatever it took to keep the leader of the pack away from Trina.

"Can you tell us what happened now?" Lachlan prodded.

Though his tone was light and gentle, the hand he'd curved over my shoulder gripped me so tightly I knew I would bruise. Without thinking, I laid my hand on this knee and squeezed lightly. The muscles in his thigh grew hard as a rock before they gradually relaxed beneath my touch. His hold on my shoulder eased as well.

Miss Emma nodded. I knew Trina was off at school, over a thousand miles away, a distance that was likely intended to protect her from Darrell.

"If you promise me that you'll stop him before he hurts anyone else," she muttered.

"You know I will."

She took a deep breath and began. "Your parents weren't killed by rogues. They weren't even killed with the claws and fangs of the wolves that betrayed them," she explained. "That coward shot them in cold blood."

CHAPTER FOURTEEN

Lachlan

C HLOE'S HAND CLUTCHED my leg, her nails digging into the flesh beneath the denim of my jeans.

I barely even noticed, too shocked by Miss Emma's words.

"Sh-sh-shot?" Chloe stuttered. "Darrell shot them?"

The older she-wolf nodded, sniffling into a tissue she tugged out of her pocket. "Yes, child. Shot with a hunting rifle. He knew he was too weak to win a challenge against your father. Even if he got lucky, your mother would have turned right back around, challenged him, and torn him limb from limb. So he killed them as a human would."

In the shifter world, if a wolf used any weapon against another, it was the gravest insult. Claws and fangs, the weapons nature bestowed upon us, were the only acceptable way to fight one another. Guns and knives might be used when fighting vampires or other supernatural creatures, but not against other shifters.

"Do you have proof?" Chloe asked, her words barely a growl in the back of her throat.

Miss Emma shook her head, tears trickling down her cheeks, dripping onto her shirt.

If she had been able to offer physical evidence, we could have taken it to the Tribunal and Darrell would be removed as leader of the pack and imprisoned.

"But I know who does," she whispered.

"Carter," Chloe breathed.

Miss Emma nodded. "He knows everything his daddy does. And he watches more than Darrell thinks. I'm not sure what his plan is but I know that he has one."

"But will he talk to us?" I asked when Chloe fell silent.

Emma's eyes shifted to me. "I think so, but there are eyes and ears everywhere in this town. If you're not very, very careful, word will get back to Darrell and he'll snatch up Carter before you can get what you need."

"I thought the pack members hated Darrell?" Chloe questioned. "Why would they turn us in?"

"Fear," I answered for Emma. "They're afraid of what he'll do to them or to their children. They wouldn't dare go against him in case he found out."

Chloe snarled. "Then how do we convince Carter to give us what we need?"

"He'll come to you," Emma interrupted. "When the time is right. He and I talked last night at the picnic."

"I wish I could trust your word, Emma, but I'm not sure I can," Chloe stated.

It was the first time I'd heard her drop the prefix from Emma's name. The older she-wolf noticed it too and winced.

"Who do you think contacted your grandmother, Chloe Mac-Arthur?" Emma asked indignantly.

"You were the anonymous tip?" Chloe seemed incredulous.

Emma shook her head. "No, not back then. I was still too scared. It was Carter. He wasn't in the position to challenge Darrell at the time, but he knew what was happening and hoped your grandmother could stop it. Unfortunately, that business with the Faction prevented you from investigating and Sophia couldn't leave her pack."

Chloe's head bowed. "I'm sorry, Miss Emma. This situation has thrown me for a loop. I'm beginning to wonder who I can trust."

"You'd be stupid not to wonder," Miss Emma replied. "And I know you're not."

Chloe's eyes snapped up and Miss Emma froze. "Yes, but I've known Darrell all my life. As did my parents. Just like I've known you all my life."

"I would never harm you, Chloe," the older she-wolf stated. I could smell the truth in her words and I knew Chloe could as well.

"Thank you, Miss Emma," Chloe murmured.

"Tell Carter we wish to speak to him," I instructed Emma, getting to my feet and bringing Chloe with me. "As soon as possible."

Emma rose from her chair, nodding as she did. "Of course."

"Lach, I want to talk with Miss Emma a little more," Chloe began.

"No. We've been here long enough for a pleasant visit with an old friend. They're watching us and they'll get suspicious if we stay too much longer."

"He's right," Emma agreed.

Chloe exhaled, but didn't argue, probably because she knew I was right. "Fine, but I would like to see you again soon, Miss Emma," she insisted.

The older wolf came forward and hugged Chloe tightly. "I would like that too, Chloe."

I gritted my teeth over what I was about to say because I hated to keep the women separated when they obviously cared so much for each other. But it still had to be said.

"I'm sorry, Emma, but I think you and Tom need to leave the town for a little while. A few weeks at least. You'll be safer if you aren't in immediate reach."

Chloe shot me a sharp glance out of the corner of her eye but still kept her mouth shut, a first since I'd known her.

But Emma wasn't going to let it go. "Lachlan, I think Tom and I will be perfectly safe here—"

"Like Nadine and Matthew MacArthur were?" I asked.

She fell silent and didn't respond.

"Is there somewhere you can go that won't make them suspicious?"

"My oldest daughter is about to have her third pup. It's been a complicated pregnancy. They'll understand if we have to leave to help her," Emma answered.

"Then make your calls and arrangements. Tell Carter to find a way to get in touch with us."

Chloe and the older she-wolf hugged again, and then they both plastered bright smiles on their faces and made a big show of saying good-bye on Miss Emma's front porch. Chloe managed to keep her expression chipper until we left the city limits, and then she scowled fiercely.

Before she could cut loose and call Darrell Whelby every foul name she could think of, I asked, "Do you think Carter was the wolf that left that note?"

She stared out the window as the open fields whizzed by. "I think it's very likely," she stated cryptically.

"What will you do if he gives you proof that his father killed your parents?"

Her head swiveled slowly toward me, the expression on her face one I'd seen just before we battled the Faction. She looked fierce, cold, and frighteningly beautiful. An angel of death waiting for her moment to claim those who she deemed worthy of punishment.

"I'll send it to the Tribunal," she replied. Just as I began to relax, she continued, "Then I'll rip Darrell's fucking heart out."

CHAPTER FIFTEEN

Chloe

THE NEXT DAY, I received a call from Miss Emma. She apologized that she wouldn't be able to spend any more time with me while I was in town, but she had to leave because her daughter needed her.

Before she hung up, she said, "Carter will be in touch in a few days to see if you need anything. I'm afraid he's too tied up to call you right now, but you'll hear from him soon."

It was clear that the call was to cover her tracks. I wondered if Darrell had gone so far as to bug pack member's phones. If he had, he would only hear old friends saying good-bye to one another and the promise that someone in the pack would be contacting us.

I wanted Miss Emma to stay safe. She'd risked a lot in sharing what she knew with us.

Even though I believed her completely, I was having difficulty reconciling the Darrell Whelby she described with the man I'd known my entire life. Darrell had always been quick to smile, generous with his time, and always snuck me candy when I was a child. I'd never sensed darkness within him, which was unusual for me. My parents worked hard to teach me how to look beyond the surface of what people wanted me to see, to sniff out lies of omission or evasions.

The idea that we'd all been utterly fooled rubbed me the wrong way.

"I'm going to take a shower," Lachlan stated, breaking me out of my reverie. "Then we need to talk with your grandmother and Calder."

I nodded. We wanted to call the night before, but neither of them was available.

Lachlan disappeared into the bathroom and a few moments later I heard the water come on. Immediately, the sound conjured up images in my mind that I shouldn't entertain. Visions of water pouring down over naked skin and sculpted muscles.

Shaking my head, I stood up and carried the coffee I'd been drinking out on to the front porch. I needed to put distance between us. As I settled on a rickety chair, propping my feet on the railing that surrounded the porch, my cell phone rang.

When I saw the name on the caller ID, I smiled and answered, "I knew you missed me."

"Yeah, you and my sanity," Ricki snarked. "You both left at the same time."

I chuckled. "How are the pups?"

"They're trying to kill each other on a daily basis, but other than that, they're good." Ricki's tone was indulgent and affectionate, as if spending time with three homicidal shifter toddlers was her favorite thing to do.

I couldn't blame her for thinking that because the little devils were adorable. I still remembered the look of shock on her face, and Calder's, when they realized they weren't having one baby, but triplets. As soon as they'd arrived back at the compound, Calder had hidden in Lach's house because Ricki was pissed at him for "knocking her up with a litter."

"How are things going with you?" she asked. "Have you

learned anything?"

"More than I bargained for," I sighed. "We found out that Darrell did kill my parents."

"What? Why?" Ricki had heard of Darrell, though she'd never met him. I'd told her all about my childhood.

"I don't know why," I replied. "But I intend to find out."

Ricki was silent for a long moment. Finally, she spoke, "How's Lach doing?"

"He seems better than he's been in over a year. He's eating more and gaining weight."

"He was really upset when you left," Ricki stated softly. "Especially since you didn't say good-bye."

Grateful she wasn't close enough to smell the lie, I answered, "I didn't think he'd notice I was gone."

"That's bullshit and you know it," she retorted. "You ran away because he's your mate."

Every muscle in my body froze, locking into place. "What did you say?"

"Lachlan is your mate, isn't he?"

There was no way I was answering that question. "Why do you think that?"

"Don't do that," Ricki snapped. "Don't answer my question with a question. Calder and I both noticed how you reacted to him. Well, I noticed and mentioned to Calder that I thought you had a crush on Lach. He started paying attention then and told me that you were acting like a she-wolf with her mate."

I couldn't say anything. All these months I thought I'd been hiding my feelings, but Calder and Ricki both knew.

"Why didn't you tell me, Chloe?" Ricki asked.

I stared blindly into the trees that surrounded the cabin, unable to answer. If I started speaking, it would all come out in a flood and now wasn't the time.

"Chloe?"

"Because it wouldn't make any difference," I stated. The words hurt as they escaped my tight throat. "He'll never see me that way."

"You don't know that," Ricki replied. Her voice was so gentle that tears pricked the backs of my eyelids.

"I do. Even if he recovers enough to want a female, it won't be me. He's never been interested in me sexually. Hell, he treats me like a little sister."

Ricki was quiet for a few moments. "I think you're wrong."

"I know I'm not."

The silence stretched between us for a long time before she finally said, "I just want you both to be happy."

The tears that threatened moments before returned, spilling out onto my cheeks. I sucked in a ragged breath. "I want to be happy, Ricki, but I don't think it will be with him."

"We'll see," she said cryptically. I heard a loud crash in the background and three little voices calling out for their mama. "Shit. I gotta go. I love you, Chloe. Be safe."

"I love you too, darlin'. Call me again soon."

When she disconnected, I got to my feet and turned to go back into the cabin, freezing when I saw Lachlan watching me from the other side of the screen door. He wore nothing but a pair of jeans and a few stray droplets of water. I'd been so distracted by my conversation with Ricki, I hadn't been paying attention to my surroundings, which was a good way to get killed considering the danger we were in.

"Hey, I didn't hear you," I commented, moving toward him.

I opened the screen door and squeezed by him, trying to ignore the way my breasts tingled when they brushed his naked chest. I carried my coffee mug to the kitchen and set it in the sink.

Lachlan stood only a few feet from me when I turned, his expression concerned. "You've been crying," he declared, the sentence sounding more like an accusation than a statement of fact. "Who were you talking to?"

His tone made my hackles rise. "A friend," I answered. "And it wasn't their fault I was crying."

Lach's expression softened. "What's bothering you?"

Shit, I couldn't tell him the truth. I'd faced down my own death several times in the last thirty-five years. I'd been afraid more times than I could count, but nothing struck bone-deep terror in my heart as much as the thought of telling Lachlan he was my mate. Despite Ricki's beliefs, I knew that his response would be one of shock, gentle rejection, and very likely, pity.

Instead, I told a half-truth and prayed he wouldn't be able to smell it. "It's just being here and seeing people from my child-hood…it brings back old memories. It reminds me of what I've lost."

When I said the words, I suddenly realized they weren't a lie. They were true. However, having him here somehow made it bearable.

Before I realized what was happening, Lach's arms closed around me, pulling me against his chest. In my bare feet, my forehead fit against the curve of his neck as though the spot were created just for me. He held me close, one hand cupping the back of my head and the other wound around my waist.

The sensation of his bare torso against my body was over-whelming. I'd never allowed myself to imagine that he might hold me like this one day—as if he truly cared about me. Cherished me.

"It's okay, Chloe," he murmured against my temple. "Let me take the burden. Just let go."

My arms went around his waist and I closed my eyes, feeling another tear trickle down my cheek. Then I did as he said.

I let go.

I let myself feel the heat of his body against mine. I relished it. When I relaxed, giving him more of my weight, he did exactly as he said he would. He took the burden, holding me up. With each inhale, I drew in his scent, knowing that it would permeate my clothes and stay with me the rest of the day.

I let myself imagine what it would be like if he held me like this every day for the rest of my life.

That was when reality returned. There would be no embraces in the kitchen every day. No kisses or declarations of love from Lachlan. Because he still loved his mate, a woman who died protecting him.

There was no future for me with Lach and though I thought I'd accepted it, I realized a small seed of hope was still there.

But with this embrace, he'd managed to achieve what I had not. He shattered that seed.

I took a few moments to gather myself and, when I was certain my eyes would remain dry, I opened them.

Then I once again did what he commanded. I let go.

Of Lachlan.

CHAPTER SIXTEEN

Lachlan

I WATCHED CHLOE as she washed the breakfast dishes and I mulled. Something was different. *She* was different.

Yesterday, I'd been surprised by the anger that rose up inside me when I heard her say, "I love you" to her friend on the phone. I'd been sure she was talking to a male wolf. I had to tamp down on the urge to walk outside, yank the phone from her hands, and throw it as far as I could.

The strength of my reaction surprised me. I had no right to be upset if she was involved with another male.

At that thought, my own wolf growled deep within me. A warning. While my human side understood that Chloe was allowed to have a relationship with anyone she wanted, my wolf hated it.

Then, when I saw her tears, my anger grew even more. Though she never told me whom she was speaking to, I couldn't resist the urge to comfort her. For the first time in our acquaintance, she needed me. This strong, dangerous she-wolf needed someone else to shoulder the burdens for a short while.

Considering she'd dragged me back from the brink of death, a hug seemed like an inadequate repayment.

Even now, a day later, the memory of how she'd relaxed against me, letting me take her weight and her troubles, was thrilling. The wolf within me wanted to howl in triumph over her surrender. He wanted her submission. Craved it.

However, when she stepped back out of my embrace, her attitude…changed. She withdrew, the warmth that once sparkled in her hazel eyes was dulled. She was no longer the Chloe I'd known for the last few years.

As I watched her rinse the last dish, I knew that I needed to get to the root of whatever was bothering her. I needed her focused and alert. I'd come to understand Chloe fairly well and physical exercise seemed to be the best way for her to work through her problems. After she pushed herself through a punishing workout, she often seemed lighter when she was done. Especially when she sparred with the other wolves. Fighting was the best medicine for Chloe MacArthur.

"We should spar today," I suggested.

She glanced at me in surprise. "Sparring? I don't think that's a good idea. You're still not back in top shape."

Her words were a challenge that I couldn't let slide. I may have struggled the past nineteen months, but I was a goddamn alpha wolf, even if she seemed to have forgotten that.

Maybe it was time to remind her.

"All the more reason to work out," I retorted. "I need to regain my strength and speed in case we find ourselves in a situation that we need to fight our way out of."

She studied me for a long moment, drying her hands on a kitchen towel. "You're right. You do need the exercise." Tossing the towel aside, she crossed the cabin to the dresser. "Let me change and we'll get started."

A few minutes later, Chloe led me through the trees to a clearing behind the cabin. We were both barefoot and she wore skintight black pants and a black sports bra. She'd woven her hair in a tight braid down the back of her skull to keep it out of the way. She looked exactly like what she was: a strong, deadly she-wolf.

I'd changed into a pair of loose athletic shorts, pleased to see that they didn't hang off my hips as they had just a few weeks ago.

When we reached the clearing, Chloe tossed her water bottle and phone onto the grass at the edge and moved toward the center. I did the same with my phone before heading toward her.

"Do you need to warm up?" she asked. At my expression, she shrugged. "Just checking. No need to frown at me."

Though we hadn't yet begun, I could already see the energy and the tension emanating from Chloe. She was gearing up for the fight, her body growing loose and balanced, poised on the edge of action.

Without a word, I lunged toward her and the fight was on.

We hadn't had the opportunity to spar often before the Faction had attacked the pack and killed my mate. Chloe parried my punches and kicks, her eyes intent. I knew she was taking in my movements, analyzing the best way to gain the upper hand.

She held back her blows, her fists and feet barely meeting my flesh. I'd watched her train with the pack often enough to know that she was pulling her punches more than usual and it pricked my temper. I wasn't a fucking invalid.

I crowded her, moving quickly, and swept her legs from beneath her. In a blink, Chloe rolled to her feet, a few pieces of hair falling out of her braid to frame her face.

"So it's like that," she stated, her eyes narrowing.

I nodded. "Stop holding back. I know you can hit harder than that."

She came at me again. This time her punches and kicks were harder and faster. Sweat broke out on her skin, gleaming in the sunlight.

When I blocked a particularly brutal combination, she stepped back and studied me with surprise and admiration in her eyes.

"You're getting stronger."

My only response was to lunge at her and take her to the ground. I discovered almost immediately that it was a mistake. Chloe was a damn good fighter standing on her own two feet, but she was nearly unbeatable when it came to grappling.

As we twisted and rolled in the grass, I grunted and cursed as she seemed to slip from my grasp, her body twisting in ways that should have been impossible.

The bout ended when Chloe managed to get me into an arm lock, her body perpendicular to mine, my wrist clasped in hers and her legs across my neck and chest. I tried to escape, but she clung to me. Finally, I had to tap her thigh, signaling that I gave up, as black dots danced in front of my eyes.

She released me and rolled to her feet. I got up as well, watching as she walked over to pick up the water bottle she'd brought. While my human pride stung that I'd just had my ass handed to me by a female I outweighed by seventy-five pounds, the wolf inside me felt surprisingly different. He didn't like to lose any more than I did, but he wanted the strength and the fire that Chloe possessed. A she-wolf like her would bite and claw, demanding as much as she gave in return. And when she finally grew pliant, her capitulation would be all the sweeter.

My cock ached at the images and thoughts that I shared with my wolf. The shorts I wore did nothing to disguise the state of my body when Chloe returned to the center of the clearing, but she didn't seem to notice.

"Are we done for the day or do you want to go another round?"

Her nonchalance and her indifference burned. It set off a chain reaction in my blood. I didn't want to fight. I craved the chase. "I want you to run, Chloe."

She frowned at me. "Run?" Her eyes flashed. "Why, so you can chase me?" Her tone was biting.

"Yes," I hissed.

Crossing her arms over her chest, she cocked one hip and glared at me. "I don't think so, Lachlan. I don't run away from anything."

"Don't you?" I retorted.

Her eyes narrowed. "What the fuck does that mean?"

I inched toward her. "It means that you ran from the MacIntire pack, Chloe. What I don't know is why." I'd been asking myself that question for weeks, unsure why I cared. But I did. Not only did I care, but her leaving the pack, *leaving me*, pissed me off.

Her face changed then, but I couldn't read her expression. It was as if she had shut me out completely.

"Fine, Ian. You want me to run, I'll run. But good luck catching me," she declared before turning on her heel and sprinting into the woods.

Chloe MacArthur might be the best fighter I'd ever met, but she was about to discover that I could track anything or anyone.

"You'll never catch me if you keep standing there," she taunted from the woods, the wind carrying her voice to me.

"Oh yes I will," I growled.

I ran toward the trees where she'd entered the woods, inhaling her scent as I went. My blood pumped wildly in my veins. This was what I wanted.

As I sprinted through the underbrush, one question echoed in my mind.

What would I do when I caught her?

CHAPTER SEVENTEEN

Chloe

I FOUGHT TO control my breathing as I moved through the trees and underbrush. I heard the slight rustle of leaves, but that was my only warning that Lachlan was on my trail. The man barely made a sound as he followed me through the woods. No matter what I did, I couldn't shake him.

I spotted a flash of grey out of the corner of my eye and turned my head to look. There was nothing there.

Adrenaline surged through me and I took off in a dead run. Lachlan had been stalking me for nearly a half hour. Every time I thought I caught a glimpse of him, he would disappear. When the wind shifted, I could smell him, so I knew he was nearby, but it was disconcerting not to be able to see or hear him.

Suddenly, he was right in my path, his eyes brilliant even in the shadows beneath the trees. I turned, skidding a little in the leaves that littered the ground, and tried to dodge him, but it was no use.

Lachlan lunged for me, his arms closing around my waist before I could get more than a couple of feet away from him. I twisted against him, bracing my hands against his shoulders in an effort to leverage myself free. Before I could decide the best way to get loose, my back hit the trunk of a tree, the bark scraping the bare skin of my shoulders.

"Lach, what are you—" The expression on his face made the words die in my throat. Any thought of fighting him vanished.

His eyes gleamed beneath his lowered brows and his hands gripped my thighs, opening them so his hips fit in between. I felt him then, rigid against my pussy. He was hard and long.

I stared up at him in shock as his hand wrapped around my braid, tugging my head back.

"Lachlan," I began.

He snarled at me, a warning. My heart sped up in my chest, thumping so hard and fast that I knew he could hear it.

Lachlan lowered his head, his nose nudging my neck. "You could never hide from me, you know that?" he murmured in my ear. He inhaled deeply. "Peaches and honey. I'd recognize your scent anywhere."

I shivered as his words rolled through me. He growled, grinding his hips against mine, and I trembled again. I turned my face toward his neck and drew his smell into my lungs. He smelled...aroused.

Lifting my face, I pressed back harder into the tree trunk. "Lachlan," I repeated, trying to get through to him. He was in the throes of something I couldn't comprehend and he was dragging me with him. My skin heated as I drew more of his scent into my lungs. His desire ignited my own, feeding the fire within me.

Once again, he stopped me before I could say anything else. This time it was with his mouth on mine.

I was utterly lost.

The sensation of his mouth against my own, his tongue sweeping across my bottom lip, it was like something out of one of my dreams. I couldn't resist the temptation to discover if the reality lived up to the fantasy.

As our tongues tangled, my hands moved up to cup his head. I missed his long hair and beard, but I loved being able to see his face. Lachlan's hands left my thighs, one winding behind my back to wrap around my hips and the other moving up my torso to knead my breast through the thin fabric of my sports bra.

I gasped into his mouth, winding my legs around his waist and gripping tightly. He groaned, rocking against me. My hips jerked instinctually as I felt a tug on the material binding my upper body and heard it tear. Then his palm was against my skin, his fingers rounding over the curve of my breast. My nipple beaded tightly as he massaged my flesh.

Lachlan released my mouth and hefted me higher. I barely felt my back scraping against the tree as he closed his lips around one of my nipples, sucking me deep. I cried out, my head falling back as he tugged and laved at the tip of my breast before moving on to the other.

I felt his hands yanking at my hips and heard another ripping sound. My fingers dug into his shoulders as he tore the top of my leggings away from my body. The strength went out of my legs and they loosened until I slid down his body a few inches.

Lachlan growled against my breast, his teeth sinking into the inner curve just deep enough to surf the edge of pain. His hands came back to my hips, keeping me aloft after my thighs weakened.

Feverishly, my palms moved over his bare skin, touching his pectorals and trailing around his ribs to his back. When his finger slid inside my pussy, I shuddered and dragged my nails up his back.

He growled and yanked me away from the tree. In a blink I was on my hands and knees in a bed of leaves with his body draped over me. The skin of his chest was scorching as it rubbed against my shoulder blades and I trembled. His hand returned between my legs and he slid two fingers inside me, his thumb circling my clit in quick, firm circles.

I threw my head back and moaned. It felt as though fire spread through my body from every part of me that he touched. Heat coursed through my veins and sweat broke out on my skin. My muscles clenched around his fingers as he stroked deeper and I knew I was close to coming.

As I careened toward my release, he stopped and removed his hand. I twisted my head to snarl at him, my body aching with desperate need. He stared at me, his eyes nearly feral, as he yanked down his shorts. Then I felt the head of his cock glide over the flesh between my legs and I bit my lip. Once he was in position, he thrust inside me, deep and fast.

I shook violently. Every dream I'd had about him, every fantasy I'd entertained, paled in comparison to how his cock felt inside me. I moaned and struggled to keep my upper body braced up by my arms. Lachlan leaned over me, wrapping my braid around one hand and placing the other on the ground to hold his weight.

Then he moved. In and out, hard and fast. When I tried to move with him, to match his pace, he growled, tugging a little on my braid. I never thought I would like for a male to pull my hair during sex, but as everything else Lachlan did, it felt deliciously dark and sexy.

I moved again, seeking my climax, and his growl grew louder, rumbling from his chest into my back, spreading throughout my body. Then I felt the edge of his teeth in my shoulder. Not hard enough to break the skin, but just enough that I knew he was close to losing control.

My pussy spasmed at the sensation but the rest of my body relaxed instinctively. I gave in to the feeling, letting him have control. When I did, he growled again, this time in approval. He released my hair and let go of my shoulder, his right hand reaching around my hip to find my clit.

All I could do was take what he gave me, which was everything. Though he no longer held my hair, I kept my head arched back, desperately seeking relief for the tension that wound tighter and tighter within me. As his fingers circled my clit rapidly, my thighs shook. My climax built beneath his touch until I could no longer contain it.

My body tightened as the waves washed over me, growing in intensity until I cried out and my arms collapsed beneath me. Lachlan's hands gripped my hips, holding up my lower body he pounded into me. A few moments later, he slammed into me a final time and his body shuddered as he came.

We stayed in that position for a long while, our lungs heaving as the clamoring of our bodies died down. Slowly, Lachlan withdrew from me, collapsing into the leaves on his side. I turned toward him as I stretched out on the ground, keeping space between us.

He had one arm thrown over his face as he struggled to catch his breath. I could see the pulse in his neck and reached out to put my hand on his chest, wondering if his heart was thundering as hard as mine.

As soon as my fingers touched his skin, he tensed. A new scent drifted into the air between us, one I recognized even as it made my heart ache.

Regret.

I pushed myself into sitting position, refusing to let myself think or feel. If I allowed the emotions to push to the forefront, I would break. I removed my shoes and socks, tugging off my ruined leggings. It was unnerving, my sudden modesty around Lachlan. Somehow, his presence made me feel more naked than before.

"Chloe," he murmured behind me.

This time it was my turn to interrupt him. "We can talk about it later," I stated, proud of the steadiness of my voice. "Right now, we need to get back to the cabin."

Without turning to look at him, I gathered my ruined clothes, leaving the tatters of my sports bra on my shoulders. I stood, aware of the twinge between my legs, and walked back toward the clearing where I'd left my phone and water bottle.

After I retrieved them, I turned and found Lachlan standing near me. Though I knew what he was going to say and I wanted nothing to do with this conversation, it seemed I would have to endure it anyway.

"I'm sorry, Chloe."

Unable to stand the idea of listening to him give me all the reasons why what we'd just done was a mistake, I tried to speak. "It's okay, Lach. I—"

He lifted a hand. "Let me finish," he demanded.

I clutched my clothes tighter to my chest and bit back my angry response.

He moved closer to me, his expression unreadable. "I shouldn't have behaved that way with you. I…" he trailed off for a moment. "I lost control." His voice lowered. "I could have hurt you."

"I'm fine, Lachlan."

He nodded. "I know."

"Look, you don't have to explain anything to me. We were both running on adrenaline and we did something we regret. It shouldn't have happened."

Lachlan didn't respond. He put his hands on his hips and lowered his head to stare at the ground.

Without waiting to see what else he might have to say, I set off back toward the cabin.

Once I was inside, I went straight to the bathroom and locked myself inside. I dropped my clothes on the floor, turned the water on, and climbed inside the tub before it was even warm.

As the bathtub filled, I curled into a ball, wrapping my arms around my knees, and I cried.

CHAPTER EIGHTEEN

Lachlan

I COULD HEAR water running in the bathroom when I entered the cabin. I moved to the door and listened, but there was no other sound.

I'd managed to fuck things up royally and I wasn't sure how to untangle it all.

As soon as I'd emptied myself inside Chloe, I'd wanted to do it again immediately. Over and over until I was too exhausted to move.

And that scared the shit out of me.

Then sanity returned and I realized that I'd just fucked Chloe. Chloe, who'd taken care of me when I was in the throes of grief. The she-wolf I considered a good friend and someone I cared about deeply.

And she'd let me. I didn't know what to think about that.

My mind was chaotic, my thoughts snarled and twisted. I walked away from the bathroom door and took a bottle of water from the fridge. As I drained it, I went outside onto the front porch and plopped down on one of the chairs.

As upset as I was by what happened, hearing Chloe call it a mistake made me angry. It hadn't felt like a mistake at the time. It was only after that the guilt crept in.

I leaned back in the chair and closed my eyes, trying to shut out my conflicting feelings. Yes, I felt guilty, but that didn't stop me from wanting to repeat the experience. It was all so fucked up.

Let me go, my love.

My eyes snapped open as Belinda's voice drifted through my mind, repeating the words from her letter.

"I can't, Bee," I whispered.

But she wouldn't leave me. Wouldn't let it go.

Don't deny yourself happiness because I am gone. Release yourself from the pain and the grief. It is time.

"How?" I asked her, feeling like a crazy person for talking to someone who wasn't there.

Her.

"Chloe?"

My only answer was the sound of the breeze moving through the trees. I thought I felt a light, cool touch on my cheek, but I barely had a chance to register the sensation before it disappeared.

I remained in the chair for a long time, even after I heard Chloe exit the bathroom and the rustle of her clothes that let me know she was dressing. I stayed outside until I heard the quiet whoosh of the screen door opening.

"Lachlan," Chloe murmured. "Please don't do this. Don't beat yourself up over what happened."

I looked up at her. "I'm not." Her eyes hardened and I continued. "I mean, I was, but then..." I hesitated. I couldn't exactly tell Chloe that I was hearing the voice of my dead mate telling me that it was okay for me to have sex with another female. She would think I was insane. Instead I stated, "I was thinking of the letter Belinda wrote me."

Confusion filled Chloe's face. "Belinda wrote you a letter?"

"Before she died. She made arrangements for it to be delivered to me..." I hesitated. "After." Chloe moved to the chair beside me and sat down, but she didn't speak, so I told her the rest. "It arrived not long after you left the pack. Belinda knew she was going to die, you see."

Chloe covered her mouth with her hand. "She did?" she asked, her voice muffled.

I nodded. "She did. I always wondered why she resisted mating with me as strongly as she did. She didn't want me to die with her."

Chloe's eyes were sad as she watched me. Slowly, she lowered her hand and clasped it around her opposite wrist. "Did she say anything else in the letter?"

"She wants me to let her go. To move on with my life."

"And what do you want?" she asked hesitantly.

Hearing her quiet question and seeing the reticence on her face made something in my chest twist into a knot. "I want that too," I answered. "But I'm not sure how to do it."

She remained silent.

I took a deep breath and went on. "Will you help me?"

"What?" Astonishment filled her voice.

"Will you help me figure out a way to move on?"

"How?" she asked.

"Just be here. With me. Until this is all over."

Her eyes narrowed. "I've been here with you for the last few days."

I rubbed my hands over my face. "That's not what I mean."

"What do you mean?" Her voice was getting stronger, her hesitancy vanishing.

"I want to spend time with you, Chloe. To get to know you. For the last nineteen months, you've taken care of me, learned things about me. Right now, I'd like to learn about you."

"And when this is over?"

"We can decide what's next when the time comes. Are you

willing to do that? To try?"

With her hands folded in her lap, Chloe stared at me, considering my question. If she said no, I wasn't sure what I would do. For reasons I didn't understand, I needed this time with her.

"I think I'd like that, Lachlan," she stated.

I smiled.

Before either of us could speak, her cell phone rang. Chloe shot me an apologetic look before she jumped to her feet and ran inside to answer it. I was glad for the interruption because I wasn't sure what I might have said anyway. I was relieved and...happy that she agreed to spend time with me, yet I didn't trust myself not to suggest we go inside and break in the mattress.

A few moments later, Chloe returned with her phone in her hand. "That was Carter. He's going to meet us in the woods not far from here. He sent me the coordinates."

All thoughts of spending the afternoon in the cabin vanished. "Do you think it's a trap?"

She tapped the phone against her palm. "I don't believe so. Miss Emma never would have suggested we talk to him if she thought he would hurt me."

"She didn't give you all the information about your parents' death, either," I pointed out gently.

Chloe frowned, staring down at the screen on her phone. "I know, but I didn't smell a lie on her when she talked about Carter. I think everything she said was the truth." Her eyes lifted to mine. "Still, we should be prepared for anything."

CHAPTER NINETEEN

Chloe

LACHLAN AND I remained silent as we walked through the woods. We'd discussed our plan before leaving the cabin. After we determined whether or not Carter was alone, Lach would hang back in the trees, watching, as I talked to Darrell's son. In my gut I felt that Carter truly did intend to help us, but it would be stupid not to take precautions.

I lifted my head and inhaled as we drew closer to the area where Carter directed us. I could smell another wolf in the vicinity, but just one. Glancing at Lachlan, I gave him a nod and we split off, moving as silently as possible through the brush.

After circling the area, we met on the other side, far enough away from the clearing that Carter wouldn't hear us.

"He's alone," Lachlan stated.

"I hoped he would be."

"I'm going to move back around to wait. I'll be watching and listening. Give me a couple of minutes before you go out to talk to him."

I nodded. He disappeared through the trees, his feet making no sound in the leaves. The wind changed and I could smell Carter once again. That meant he wouldn't be able to scent Lachlan's location at the moment.

When enough time had passed, I walked toward the clearing and emerged from the trees, not bothering with stealth.

Carter's face was turned toward me as I appeared. He looked a great deal like his father, tall and lean with dark hair and eyes. He inclined his head when he saw me.

"Chloe." He looked around. "Where's Lachlan?"

"He's waiting for me in the woods," I answered simply.

A small frown pulled at the corners of his mouth before it quickly cleared. "I suppose that was a smart move. I'm an unknown element."

I nodded. "There are not many children who would turn on their parents."

The frown returned, morphing into a scowl. "Then their parents haven't done what my father has. Someone has to stop him, but I'm not strong enough."

Moving slowly, I walked closer. "What has your father done, Carter?" I asked softly.

His eyes focused on me, dark and haunted. "You know he killed your parents. Emma said she'd told you."

"Yes, she did."

"He's done so much worse," Carter murmured. "And he encourages his friends to do the same."

"Has he always been this way, Carter?" I asked.

"Yes. Always." My surprise must have shown on my face because he released a harsh bark of laughter. "My father is many things, but first and foremost he's a talented liar and manipulator. I don't know how he does it, but no one can ever smell his lies."

That explained how he managed to hide his inclinations from my parents. "What else has he done, Carter?"

"Emma said she told you everything," he replied. I could smell the frustration and the anger emanating from his pores.

"She told me about the females of the pack, and about the

stealing. Is there more?"

Carter nodded, his shoulders slumping. "He's killed others. Males and females who defied him or tried to report him to the Tribunal. He's not alpha enough to hold the pack according to our laws, but he'll use any means necessary to circumvent losing his position. He has no honor."

"Do you have proof?" I questioned. "Any evidence of his actions?"

"No, but I know where to find it. My father..." he stopped and swallowed hard before he continued. "He likes to take pictures so he can look back and remember. He also records everything. He's gotten complacent over the last two years. Somehow he's convinced himself that he's untouchable."

My stomach twisted at Carter's words. "Pictures? Of my parents? And the girls?"

"Of everything," he reiterated.

Disgust and triumph mingled within me. "Where?"

"In his office in town. There's a hidden safe. I've wanted to go inside and get them so many times over the years but the building is never empty and he has cameras everywhere. Not just inside, but all over town."

My skin crawled at the idea of a pack leader watching the lives of his wolves, learning their habits and perhaps choosing his next victim.

"Well, you aren't alone anymore, Carter. Lachlan and I can help. And my grandmother."

At the mention of Sophia, his eyes shifted to the side.

"I know you called her, Carter," I stated gently. "And I'm glad."

His gaze came back to me. "I just wish you'd come two years ago."

Guilt ate at my gut. "I do too, but we were all under attack then, not just this pack."

"I know," he admitted, his eyes never leaving mine.

I sensed Lachlan's presence and turned my head. He walked into the clearing, moving cautiously. One look at his face and I knew that he felt guilty as well. I'd spent the last eighteen months dragging him away from the brink of oblivion while this pack suffered. I jerked my head, a short, single shake. This wasn't his burden to take on.

Carter noticed Lach's presence then and turned toward him. "Lachlan," he greeted. He squared his shoulders. "Thank you for coming."

Though Emma said that Carter was weak and he'd admitted as much a few minutes ago, I noticed he had little trouble meeting my eyes or Lachlan's. If he were truly a beta wolf, he wouldn't be able to maintain eye contact with us for such a prolonged period. The mystery of Carter Whelby deepened. He was clearly stronger than he let everyone else believe. Why wouldn't he challenge his father?

Then I realized that he was just trying to survive. His father was surrounded by wolves that wouldn't hesitate to kill him by any means necessary if they believed he was a threat. If Carter were removed, there would be no one brave enough or strong enough to take on Darrell and his officers.

"Can you get me specs for the police department?" Lachlan asked Carter. "And a map of the town with the locations of the cameras?"

Carter nodded. "Yes, but it'll take me a few days to get it."

"Be careful, Carter," I said.

His mouth curved into a grim smile. "I'm always careful. That's why it will take me a few days. With Darrell watching every move his pack makes while you're here, we're all walking on eggshells."

I winced inwardly at the idea that the pack was terrified by my presence.

"We'll need your help creating a plan," Lachlan declared, bringing our attention back to him. "Are there any wolves here you can trust to help us?"

Carter's expression was sad when he shook his head. "They're too frightened of what Darrell might do to them. Or their children."

I bit back a growl. Only a monster would threaten a child. "Gram will find a way to help us."

Lach glanced at me. A look that clearly stated *we'll talk about this later*. It seemed he wanted to keep some of our plans separate from Carter.

"I can't stay any longer," Carter said. "It'll raise questions if I'm unreachable for any length of time. I'll call you when I get what we need. Just sit tight."

I waited until he was a few feet away before I called his name. He stopped and turned back toward me. "Thank you, Carter. For calling my grandmother and helping us now."

His jaw tightened and his entire face changed. He no longer looked weak or beaten down. Carter Whelby was strong, determined, and smart—an alpha wolf forced to hide to save the shifters he cared about. He chose to do what was necessary to help his pack rather than allowing his pride to dictate his actions. He could have easily challenged his father, ending up buried beside my parents and leaving his pack unprotected and isolated.

"I'm only doing what's right," he replied before turning and disappearing into the trees.

When the sound of his footsteps faded, I looked at Lachlan and opened my mouth. He shook his head, lifting a finger to his lips.

"Not here. Let's go back to the cabin."

We moved through the trees at a quicker pace this time since we weren't trying to muffle the noise we made. When we reached the cabin, I followed Lachlan inside.

He grabbed a bottle of water from the fridge and asked, "Want one?"

When I nodded, he tossed me the one in his hand and withdrew another. After he took a deep drink, he spoke. "Carter is no beta wolf," he stated.

"I know."

"He's fighting his instincts to protect his people," he continued.

I sipped my water and shrugged. "Isn't that what a good alpha does?"

Lachlan sighed. "Yes."

"Do you believe him about Darrell?"

He eyed me. "Do you?"

I nodded.

"So do I," Lachlan admitted.

"Why didn't you want to talk in front of him then?" I queried.

"Because he's in a dangerous position. If his father finds out what he's doing, he'll do whatever it takes to find out what our plans are. It's better if he doesn't know until later."

I saw the logic in that and agreed. "So we should call Gram and tell her we need help, then."

Lachlan shook his head. "I'll call Calder. The pack is closer."

"No, Lach. I'm not dragging the MacIntire pack into this. They're still recovering from our battle with the Faction and the devastation of discovering so many traitors in their midst. And Calder and Ricki have pups now. They can't afford to go to war. There's too much at stake."

"And there isn't for your grandmother's pack?" he asked, arching a brow.

"It's different, Lachlan. She's a thousand miles away from here. If we don't succeed, Darrell can hardly declare war from Oklahoma. Calder is too close to this."

"We won't fail," Lachlan stated darkly.

"I don't want to pull Calder into this," I reiterated.

"He's already in it, Chloe," Lachlan declared. *I'm here.* Darrell knows why you're here, how much of a stretch do you think it is before he realizes that I'm not here because we're mates?"

My heart skipped a beat when he said the word mate. But he was right. Darrell might be a sociopath, but he wasn't stupid. He probably already suspected that we were lying.

"Fine, but I don't want Calder or Ricki here unless it's absolutely necessary," I growled. "Their pups need them whole and healthy."

"Agreed."

Surprised at his capitulation, I sank into the chair at the small kitchen table. "All we can do right now is wait," I sighed. "Fuck."

Lachlan nodded. "We wait and we plan." He sat down across from me and we drank our water in silence for a few minutes.

"I feel like this is my fault, Lach," I admitted.

"Don't. You had no way of knowing what was happening here."

"I should have come back two years ago," I argued.

Lach's eyes sparked with anger, the scent of it tingeing the air. "We wouldn't have been able to beat the Faction without you, Chloe. If we failed, how long do you think it would have been before they spread from Texas and the surrounding areas to the rest of the country, then the world? You were needed in Dallas. This pack would have been fucked whether you were here or not because it would have only been a matter of time before the Faction corrupted this area too."

"Maybe you're right," I conceded.

"I know I am." He surprised me by leaning forward and taking my hand. "And, Chloe, *I* wouldn't be here without you. If you hadn't been there, refusing to give up on me, I would have died too. I wanted to die for a long time. You were the only thing standing between me and the Underworld."

"Calder wouldn't have let you pine yourself to death, Lachlan," I whispered. Something in my chest twisted, as if my heart were tying itself in a tight knot.

Lach shook his head. "He couldn't get through to me. Only you could," he insisted, gripping my hand tighter. "If you're going to blame someone for this situation, blame me. If I hadn't needed you, you could have come here a long time ago and saved this pack a multitude of pain."

I shook my head. "Don't say that. This isn't your fault," I stated.

"It isn't yours either," he replied quickly. "But you can help them now. And you will. We both will."

I nodded and Lachlan squeezed my hand tighter, but he didn't release it.

We sat at the kitchen table, holding hands, as the afternoon faded to evening.

CHAPTER TWENTY

Lachlan

A S WE ATE dinner, Chloe covered her mouth several times as she yawned widely. I knew how she felt. The day had been exhausting.

We washed the dishes together and when they were done, she mumbled, "I'm going to change and go to bed."

I nodded, drying my hands on a towel. She gathered up some clothes and disappeared into the bathroom, emerging ten minutes later, her face scrubbed and smelling of peaches and the minty toothpaste she used. The scent made my mouth water.

After our meeting with Carter, we hadn't continued our discussion of what happened following our sparring session earlier. Hell, the day had been so long it almost felt as though it had happened a week ago rather than just a few hours before. While I'd been relieved to have a reprieve from the conversation, it also meant that I couldn't make assumptions about changes in our sleeping arrangements.

Chloe pulled back the blankets on the bed and settled beneath them with another jaw-cracking yawn. Without a word, I went into the bathroom to brush my teeth and slipped on the loose shorts I'd worn to bed every night I'd been here. I preferred to sleep naked, but for some reason I'd felt compelled to wear them. I'd originally chalked it up to the possibility that we might be attacked in the middle of the night, but now I realized it was to hide my body's reaction to Chloe.

When I came out from the bathroom, I turned off the lights and moved toward the couch. While it was actually big enough to accommodate me, the cushions were old and provided no support or comfort. I was grateful for my body's ability to heal quickly because a night on that monstrosity would cripple a human man.

Chloe's voice floated out of the darkness. "You don't have to sleep on the couch."

I turned toward the bed, looking at the outline of her body in the shadowed room. Clouds had moved in, covering the moon, so very little light came through the windows. All I could see was her upper body propped on an elbow, her head turned toward me. Her face was still shrouded in the dark.

Then she reached over and pulled the covers back on the opposite side of the bed. "Come sleep with me, Lach. That couch can't be comfortable." I saw the faint gleam of her teeth in the shadows. "And I'm too tired to pillage you, so you're safe."

I smiled a little at her words, even as a slender shaft of disappointment pierced my chest. "If you're sure…" I trailed off, giving her one more chance to change her mind.

"Did you mean what you said earlier about spending time with me? Learning about me?"

I nodded.

"Then come sleep beside me," she murmured. "I think I'd like that."

My feet carried me to the bed and I climbed in beside her, lying on my back and staring at the shadows of tree limbs that the dim moonlight cast on the ceiling. After a few moments I twisted my head and saw that Chloe was lying on her stomach next to me, her face turned toward me. Her arms were tucked beneath the pillow and her hair trailed down her back. Her eyes were already closed, her face peaceful. I'd never seen her so still. She looked beautiful.

Though my brain understood there would be no sex, my body had other ideas, my cock already semi-erect. I tore my eyes away from Chloe's tranquil face and looked back up at the ceiling. Then I closed my eyes and focused on my breathing, hoping it would help me relax.

WHEN I WOKE, I wasn't sure how much time had passed, but the cabin was still dark. In our sleep, Chloe and I had changed positions. She was on her side, facing away from me, and my body was pressed against her back. One of my thighs lay between hers, pulled high so I could feel the heat of her pussy against my bare leg through her thin cotton shorts. My left arm was beneath her head and the other was wrapped around her waist, my hand beneath her shirt and cupping her breast.

My cock was so hard that it hurt. My hand flexed instinctively against her breast and she moaned softly. Her hips rocked against me, grinding her pussy against my leg harder.

I buried my face against her shoulder, running my lips against her hot, soft skin as I closed my fingers around her nipple and tugged.

She gasped then, her body tensing, and I knew she was awake. I pulled lightly at her nipple once more and she moved against my thigh, her hips jerking. "Ian," she breathed, her voice barely audible.

At the sound of my name on her lips, my dick hardened even more. I always hated my first name, but there was something about the way she said it that turned me on.

Wrapping my arms around her, I rolled over, bringing her body with me so that she sprawled over me with her back against my front. Then I hooked my thumbs in the waistband of her shorts and panties, jerking them down her body. Chloe's hands helped me push the material over her legs until they fell onto the bed.

Her head fell back as I hooked my knees on the inside of her thighs and spread her legs apart, baring her pussy. When my hands went to her top, she yanked it over her head and dropped it on the pillow beside me.

I swept her hair to the side, gripping it to pull her head back against my shoulder. She stretched out over me, her body completely naked and exposed to my hands. Though I couldn't see her face in this position, her ass rubbed against my cock as she squirmed on top of me, telling me she liked what I was doing. Releasing her hair, I covered both of her breasts with my palms, running my fingers lightly over her flesh, trailing them over her nipples.

I could feel her heart beating beneath my touch and her chest moved rapidly as her breath came in pants. Her body writhed against mine again as I toyed with her nipples. I pinched them lightly at first then harder, listening to her reactions to see what she liked.

She cried out, the scent of her arousal intensifying, when I tightened my grip and tugged. Her back arched, rubbing her ass harder against my dick. I closed my mouth over the curve of her shoulder where it met her neck, scraping my teeth over skin, and she moaned louder.

I released one of her breasts, moving my hand down her body to dip into her pussy. She was wet and tight and her clit pulsed as the tips of my fingers passed over it.

Her hands reached back, gripping my hips, as I pushed my fingers inside her slowly. I stroked in and out, feeling her muscles clamping down on my hand.

Suddenly, she lifted her hips and reached between us, pulling down the waistband of my shorts until my cock was free. I released her and brushed her hands aside, angling my erection so that it rested between her thighs and against her pussy, the head gliding over her clit.

Chloe shuddered against me, her hips bearing down on my body as she squirmed on top of me. I moved my hips, gliding my cock over her clit as my hands moved back to her breasts. She groaned, her legs tightening against mine, and I used my knees to force them wider.

Then her hand slipped down over my dick, her palm rubbing against the tip and I hissed. "Fuck."

"Yes," she whispered. "Fuck me."

I wanted see her face and nearly turned her around but her fingers wrapped around me before I could act.

She gripped my cock and guided it inside her, angling her pelvis so that I slid deep. When her ass rested against my stomach again, I was fully seated within her and I felt her muscles spasm around me.

I nipped her neck with my teeth as I rubbed her nipples with my thumbs. She was so tight and wet that I wanted to flip her onto her hands and knees and pound into her as I had that afternoon, but I resisted. She deserved better than another hard, fast fuck. My wolf and I wanted her weak and begging, submitting to our every demand.

At the sensation of my teeth on her skin, I felt her body relax against me, trembling, and I knew she'd let go of her control.

"Touch yourself." I whispered into her ear. "Make yourself come," I demanded before sucking the lobe into my mouth.

Chloe whimpered, but her right hand moved down her body, gliding past her clit to touch my cock as it slid slowly in and out of her pussy. Her left hand covered my fingers as they tormented her breast.

"Chloe," I growled as her touch drove me closer to the edge. "Rub your clit for me. I want to feel you come on my dick."

Her fingers left my cock and began to circle her clit in slow, firm circles. Her body tightened around me, clenching my cock hard as I thrust into her. As we moved, I decided that the next time we did this, I would make sure I could see everything. While this felt better than good, being able to watch her bring herself to orgasm on my lap would probably blow my mind.

I released her breasts and gripped her hips, bringing my knees up so I could fuck her harder. Her back arched, her head twisting toward me so that her mouth fastened on mine.

As her tongue slid into my mouth, I groaned at the taste of her. Peaches and honey. I wondered if her pussy was as sweet as her mouth. Next time, I would find out.

Her hips rolled against me, her fingers moving faster on her clit, and I wished again I could see what she was doing. I nearly stopped, intent on telling her to turn to face me so I could watch her come, but her breathing was harsh and wild and her pussy fluttered around me. She was close. I slammed into her hard, yanking her hips down as my body crashed into hers.

She cried out, a wordless sound of pleasure, and her body trembled wildly over mine. I moved inside her, fast and nearly brutal, until I came so hard that white bursts of light filled my vision.

Chloe sprawled over me, her legs limp on either side of my knees and her hands lifted to grip my head. Our mouths barely touched as we caught our breath. I wrapped my arms around her waist, holding her, until Chloe wiggled against me.

"I need to clean up, Lach," she whispered.

I released her, listening to her soft gasp when my cock slid out of her body, and watched as she walked naked into the bathroom, shutting the door behind her. I got out of the bed and removed my shorts, using them to wipe my come and her wetness from my dick.

Naked, I crawled back into the bed, not bothering with the blankets. The tiny air conditioner in the window barely cooled the cabin and my skin was still damp with sweat.

Chloe came out of the bathroom and moved back toward the bed. I watched as she stopped by my side and retrieved her tank top. Before she could walk away, I reached out and grabbed it.

"What are you doing?" I asked.

I couldn't read her expression in the dark room, but her body tensed. "Getting dressed."

I snatched the shirt from her hands and shoved it under my pillow. "No."

Her stance changed, her hands going to her hips. "Excuse me."

"I want you naked."

"Well, you're shit out of luck then," she retorted, holding out her hand. "Give me back my shirt."

My mouth curled into a smile. This was promising to be an interesting night. "No."

I could feel her eyes moving over me, taking my measure. To my surprise, instead of arguing with me, she turned and walked toward her bag. When she bent to reach inside, I jumped to my feet and wrapped my arms around her, pulling her away.

"Lachlan," she growled. "What the hell?"

"Why do you want to get dressed?" I asked. "I've known you long enough to know that you don't usually wear clothes to bed." I nuzzled her neck. "Besides, I'd like to be able to slide inside you if I wake up again later."

Chloe's body went rigid against me and her anger was palpable.

"Chloe?" I asked, confused by her reaction. Why was she pissed all of the sudden?

"I'm not sure I want to have sex with you again, Lachlan," she muttered.

"What? Why?" I didn't understand. Not only was she angry, she was hurt. There was a hint of it beneath the scent of her ire.

She twisted in my arms until I loosened my grip and she faced me. A small beam of moonlight caught her face and I saw the hurt shimmering in her eyes as well. "You can't stand to look at me when you fuck me, can you, Lach?"

I frowned down at her. "What in the hell are you talking about?"

She drew in a shaky breath, her voice calmer when she spoke again. "Both times you've fucked me, you've made sure I'm facing away from you. You barely even kissed me." Her eyes shuttered, hiding the hurt that I smelled. Her anger was completely gone now, leaving only pain behind. She shook her head. "I shouldn't have let this happen," she whispered.

I reached up, brushing her hair back from her face, and cupped her cheeks in my hands. Tipping her head back, I stared down at her. "That's not how I feel," I stated. When she opened her mouth, I growled low in my throat. "Will you stop fucking interrupting me all the damn time?"

Her brows snapped together and she glared at me, but she didn't speak.

Glad to see that her usual feistiness was returning, I continued, "I want to look at you, Chloe. I want to watch your face when you come and taste your pussy and your mouth. I also like to fuck you from behind because I fucking love it. I can touch your body and make you come that way and I can fuck you hard. That's the only reason. I'm not trying to pretend it isn't happening." I studied her face. "And I'm not pretending you're someone else."

I knew I'd hit on what was really bothering her when her body tensed infinitesimally. If I hadn't been watching her so closely, I would have missed it.

I kissed her lightly then, just a brush of my lips against hers.

"I meant what I said, Chloe. I want to know *you*. I want to talk to you. And I want to fuck you." I smiled a little, hoping my next words would lighten the mood. "And let you kick my ass then chase you through the woods too."

Her mouth quirked at my statement and the tension in her body leeched away.

"Now, you wore me out and I'd like to go back to sleep. Preferably with you naked."

The heaviness left the air and she pinched my waist. "*I* wore you out? You're the one who attacked me while I was asleep."

"You still started it," I teased, guiding her back toward the bed. "What's a wolf supposed to do when he wakes up to find a she-wolf's ass rubbing on his dick?"

Her only reply was to smack me in the head with her pillow.

CHAPTER TWENTY-ONE

Chloe

THE NEXT MORNING, I woke up with my face smashed against Lachlan's chest. We were both lying on our sides, face to face. His arms were tight around me, one beneath my head and the other circling my ribs. His right leg was between mine, his thigh nudging my center.

Though my body stirred, I rolled away, moving to the edge of the bed. Despite his words the night before, Lachlan hadn't woken me up again. Getting to my feet, I lifted my arms above my head, arching my back, and stretched my muscles.

I heard a low growl behind me and glanced over my shoulder to find Lach lying back on the pillow, his eyes roving over my body.

"Good morning," he rumbled, his voice rough. He sounded sleepy and extremely sexy.

"Good morning," I replied, turning to face him. Once again, when his eyes moved over me, I was intensely aware of the fact that I was naked. However, this time I liked that he was looking. I wanted him to see what his attention did to my body.

Another growl sounded, but this one came from my stomach. Lachlan laughed and bounded to his feet. "I guess you worked up an appetite last night," he teased, his eyes sparkling with humor in the morning light.

My breath caught in my chest at the sight of him. He looked younger and carefree. I'd never seen him smile like that or laugh with such openness.

I covered my reaction by teasing him back. "Since it's your fault I'm in this state, I think you should do the cooking."

His grin widened. "In the mood for pancakes?" he asked.

"I'm always in the mood for pancakes," I retorted.

Lach's smile grew positively wicked. "Good. Then you can eat them naked."

I rolled my eyes. "You've seen me naked plenty of times, Lach," I scoffed.

"Yeah, but I didn't have all these ideas about syrup then."

Unbelievably, I blushed, which only made him laugh again. "Maybe I should go take a shower," I mumbled.

He shook his head. "No, no. You'll just have to take another one later."

For a moment, I was confused then I remembered what he said about syrup and shivered. A playful Lachlan definitely had some interesting ideas.

"Fine, I'll make coffee," I conceded, ignoring the way his eyes locked onto my tight nipples.

When he went to his bag and pulled out a pair of loose shorts like the ones he'd worn to bed last night, I sputtered, "Hey! If I can't wear anything, neither can you."

He lifted his brows at me. "That's different. I'm going to be cooking bacon and pancakes. My delicate areas need to be protected."

I laughed at his comment, but didn't say anything else. I wouldn't want to fry bacon in the nude either. Shifter or not, grease splatters hurt, even if they healed within seconds.

While Lachlan put the bacon in a pan and mixed the pancake

batter, I brewed a pot of coffee. Once I'd made us each a cup, he grabbed me around my waist and sat me on top of the counter, far enough away from the stove that I wouldn't get hit with grease as the bacon spat and sizzled. I inhaled sharply at the coolness of the laminate under my butt.

"Ian, seriously. I'm bare-assed naked, sitting on this counter, and we prepare food in this kitchen. It's not sanitary," I protested.

He roared with laughter then. "Just stay there. I'll let you disinfect the kitchen later." He winked at me. "But you should know I have plans for the table too."

Unwilling to ruin his good mood, I stopped arguing and sat on the cool countertop, drinking my coffee as I watched him make me breakfast. He was done quickly, flipping bacon and pancakes with skill that spoke of experience in the kitchen.

When I hesitated by the chair at the table, he chuckled again and pulled me into his lap. I ignored his teasing and forked up my first bite, the sugary syrup melting on my tongue, followed by the buttery, rich flavor of light, fluffy pancake. I couldn't hold back the moan of appreciation. Pancakes were my absolute favorite meal at breakfast so I hadn't been lying to Lachlan when I said I was always in the mood for them.

I ate a few more bites, savoring each one, before I shifted on his lap to look at him. "These are amazing, Lach." My tongue darted out to sweep up a drop of syrup on the corner of my mouth.

His eyes focused on the movement and I realized they were hot and a little wild. Then I felt the hard length of his cock against my ass.

Without a word, he shoved our dishes to the side and lifted me up so that I sat on the table in front of him, his chest between my thighs. Based on his expression, I expected him to fuck me then and there.

Instead he reached out and grabbed my fork, cutting off another chunk of pancakes. Then he lifted it to my lips. I opened my mouth and took the bite, my eyes never leaving his as I chewed.

He fed me, one bite at a time, until the food was nearly gone. Then, as he lifted the fork again, a small stream of syrup dripped onto my skin, running down my chest and following the slope of my breast. Hot blue eyes followed the path of the sweet liquid as it clung to my nipple.

The fork in his hand crashed to the floor as he dropped it and I cried out as his mouth latched onto my nipple, sucking me deep. Then the flat of his tongue followed the trail up my chest until it reached my collarbone.

With one hand he jerked down his shorts and the other dipped into the puddle of syrup in my nearly empty plate. I leaned back, bracing my weight on my hands as his fingers circled the tip of my breast. Then he gathered up more syrup and repeated the process with the other.

My head fell back as he devoured the sticky sweetness from my breasts, his groan vibrating against my sensitive flesh. Then his fingers pressed against my lips, urging me to open my mouth. I laved them with my tongue as I sucked every bit of the sugary liquid.

When his fingers were clean, he pulled them from my mouth and sat back down in his chair, shoving my legs open then yanking my ass to the edge of the table. I lifted my heels, resting them against the tabletop next to my ass to support my legs and gasped when the tip of his tongue ran down my inner thigh.

My clit throbbed as he repeated the caress on my other leg, stopping just short of my pussy. Using his thumbs, he opened me up to his gaze. Then his mouth was on me, devouring me with uncontrollable urgency. My hips jerked on the table, my legs clenching around his face. He put his palms to my inner thighs and shoved them back apart as his lips and tongue consumed me.

My upper body fell back, my head dangling over the edge of the table on the other side, and I gave myself up to the sensations. My hands clutched at his skull as his lips closed around my clit, sucking hard as the tip of his tongue flicked. I cried out and arched against the intensity of the pleasure. He took my hands, hooking them behind my knees, urging me to hold my legs up.

When I did, his left hand moved up my body to pluck at my nipples before pinching one and tugging hard as he plunged two fingers of his right hand inside me. The table shuddered and groaned beneath me as I writhed on top of it, unable to keep still beneath his mouth. Then he pressed the tips of his fingers against a spot deep inside me that made me see stars.

As he rubbed that spot firmly, his tongue moved rapidly over my clit, and my entire body jerked. Seconds later, I screamed as I came, my back arching so hard that only my ass and head touched the table beneath me. Black spots danced in front of my eyes as his mouth continued to work me, drawing out the spasms until I was begging him to stop.

I heard his chair crash to the floor as he stood, sweeping me off the table and carrying me to the bed. As soon as my back hit the mattress, he was on top of me, the rigid length of his cock already sliding inside my body.

"I was right," he growled. "Your pussy tastes even better than your mouth."

His arms shoved beneath my back, his hands clasping the nape of my neck to hold me still as he pounded inside me. Incredibly, the friction brought my orgasm to life again and I wrapped my legs around his hips, crying out from the wild trembling that wracked my body. My nails dragged down his back, breaking the skin.

"Fuck," he growled, his thrusts losing their rhythm before he rammed into me one last time and came.

He lowered his head, his cheek brushing mine. We were both breathing hard, our chests pressed so tightly together that I could feel the hard thump of his heart against mine. My arms were loosely wrapped around him and my ankles were hooked at the base of his spine.

As our bodies calmed, I ran my hand over the back of his head, enjoying the prickliness of his short hair and pressing a kiss to the skin beneath his ear. He shuddered against me, which created an echoing shiver in me when his cock twitched.

He chuckled against my shoulder. "I think I'm going to make you pancakes every morning," he said, flicking my earlobe with the tip of his nose. "Though I'd probably be too exhausted to do anything else the rest of the day."

"Hmmm," I mumbled, my mind too hazy to form a reply.

"Is that a yes or no?" he asked, lifting his head to look down at me.

"That's an *it's fine with me*," I replied, my voice hoarse. "Now quit talking. I need a recovery nap."

"Nope," he teased. "You have to go disinfect the kitchen and the table."

I closed my eyes. "Meh. Who cares? We're shifters. We can't catch diseases."

He laughed, rolling to the side without releasing his hold on me. After a few moments of fidgeting and my accidental elbow to his gut, Lachlan lay on his back with my body tucked against his side, my head on his shoulder.

Convinced I was now boneless, I lay against Lachlan, drowsy and satisfied. I stroked his chest with my hand, enjoying the feel of hard muscle covered in hot, smooth skin and a light dusting of hair.

His fingers moved over my scalp, sifting through the strands of my hair.

When he spoke, I could feel the vibration against my cheek. "Why did you leave without saying good-bye, Chloe?" he asked.

My hand stilled and I closed my eyes. Shit, why did he have to ask me that right now? There was no easy answer. No believable lie that I could give him.

"Chloe?" he asked when I didn't answer at first.

I focused on the slow, steady beat of his heart against my palm for a moment. I could give him the truth. Just not the whole truth. I wasn't ready for that conversation and neither was he.

"I didn't want to say good-bye to you," I murmured. "Because I knew if I did, I wouldn't want to leave."

It was his turn to still, his fingers tangled in my hair. "Why?"

Grateful I wasn't looking into his eyes, I answered, "I care about you, Ian. A lot more than I realized. But I needed to come here. I just didn't expect to feel guilty about it."

He moved then, turning us so that I lay on my back and his face hovered above me. "Why did you feel guilty?"

Fighting to keep my expression neutral, I replied, "I felt like I was abandoning you. You were still so deep in your grief."

He stared down at me, his face unreadable. "Do you pity me, Chloe?"

"Absolutely not," I declared. "But I know what losing a mate does to a wolf. I saw what happened to Gram when my grandfather died." I lifted a hand and cupped his face, my thumb tracing the bottom curve of his lip. "I knew I could help you through it."

He stared down at me, his blue eyes taking in my face. "I didn't realize how much I liked having you around until you were gone," he admitted softly. "I never thought I would want another female again in my life, but when I found you here, it was as if I was seeing you for the first time. I don't know what will happen when this is all over, but I want you to promise me you won't leave again without saying good-bye."

A crack formed in my heart at his words. From that tiny opening, a seedling of hope sprouted. His words weren't an admission that he recognized me as his mate, but maybe, just maybe, he wasn't completely blind to it after all.

"I promise, Ian," I whispered.

He made a noise, something between a chuckle and grunt. "I always hated my name," he mused, his hand tangling in my hair. "Until you said it."

As his mouth covered mine, the small seedling of hope in my heart bloomed.

CHAPTER TWENTY-TWO

Lachlan

TWO DAYS LATER, I woke before Chloe yet again. As I had the past couple of mornings, I put a great deal of effort into rousing her. It wasn't until I saw her smirk that I realized she was faking sleep.

I smacked her ass sharply in retaliation, which led to a wrestling match that we both won.

As we had for the past two days, we ate breakfast after working up an appetite. Though I wanted pancakes again, Chloe nixed the idea, insisting that our exercise should come in the form of a run and sparring rather than breaking in the kitchen table.

After breakfast, Chloe dressed in another pair of leggings and a tank top.

"Let's go to the clearing," she suggested. "We've barely left the house in days and you need to get back into top shape."

For the next hour, we sparred. She won, again.

"You should practice your tracking skills," she suggested.

I grabbed the towel I'd brought from the house and wiped the sweat from my face and chest. "You mean you want to practice your evasion skills."

She grinned. "That too."

A few moments later, she disappeared into the woods. I waited for a while before I followed. Immediately, I picked up her trail, both in scent and sight. My she-wolf could kick ass in a fight, but she sucked at covering her tracks.

Shaking my head, I followed the trail, stopping every so often to listen for telltale sounds that would give her away. When I ascertained her location, I crept around behind her, careful to stay downwind, and pounced before she even knew I was there.

"Dammit, I didn't even hear you this time," she complained. "And it took you less than ten minutes to find me."

"That's because you don't cover your tracks," I explained.

"But if you can follow my scent, why should I bother?"

I stared at her. "Didn't anyone ever teach you how to throw false trails? Sure, your scent will give you away, but if you do it right, it will take a good tracker a lot longer to figure out which way you went. By that time, you could be long gone or set up a defense. A mediocre tracker might never be able to figure out where you went."

Chloe tilted her head to the side. "Show me."

For the rest of the morning, I instructed her and, with her razor sharp mind, she picked it up quickly. The final time I found her, it took me thirty minutes and my stomach was growling loudly by the time I realized she'd climbed a tree.

Standing at the base with my hands on my hips, I looked up at her grinning face. "Good call with the tree."

When my stomach rumbled again, she leapt down, landing lightly on her feet. "Hungry?"

"Starving. You need to feed me."

She scoffed. "Me? You're a big boy, feed yourself."

Slinging my arm around her shoulders as we walked back to the clearing, I said, "I made you breakfast. It's your turn to make me lunch."

She laughed as we gathered our things and strolled through the woods toward the cabin, my arm still holding her close to my side.

Just before we emerged from the tree line, I stopped her. "Someone's at the cabin," I whispered. We were upwind of the little house, which was why I hadn't smelled them earlier, but I saw a vehicle parked in the driveway.

"It's Darrell's SUV," she explained.

Something about the situation struck me the wrong way, but I couldn't put my finger on it.

Before we could discuss it further, the screen door to the cabin flung open and Darrell came outside, his head turned toward the trees where we were hidden.

"Are you two coming in or what?" he hollered. "I brought lunch and the food is getting cold."

"Shit," Chloe mumbled. "I don't like this."

"Just stay alert and don't hesitate if things go wrong."

"You too," she directed.

We stepped out of the cover of the trees, my eyes moving quickly around the perimeter as I looked for any men who might be with Darrell. He appeared to be alone, which surprised me.

Since the note was left in the truck, Chloe and I had checked the area surrounding the cabin twice a day for any visitors who might be watching, but there was nothing.

It made the skin between my shoulder blades itch. If Darrell really knew why we were here, the fact that he hadn't sent some-one to keep an eye on us seemed suspicious.

Darrell grinned when he took in our rumpled state as we skirt-ed his car in the drive. "Been out for a run?" he asked.

Chloe nodded. "I'm glad you brought lunch. We're both starv-ing."

Internally, I applauded her intelligence. Her words sounded friendly but didn't require her to lie, an action Darrell might smell. Lies had a distinct perfume and it had been my experience that the dishonest were the most adept at picking it up.

"I also brought visitors," Darrell explained, looking chagrined. "I know I should have called first, but they insisted it should be surprise."

As we followed him up the steps, I caught a scent that made my back snap straight. They couldn't have come at a worse time.

Inside the cabin, I saw Brian and Brayden Kirkpatrick sitting on the couch. Brian looked relaxed and pleasant, just as he had in Dallas. Brayden, however, scowled fiercely, his eyes trained on the bed.

When Darrell opened the screen door, allowing Chloe and I to enter first, Brayden's gaze snapped toward us. When his eyes met mine, I saw the barely restrained rage burning in them and the white-hot hatred. I half expected him to lunge at me then, but he clenched his fists tightly in his lap and held back.

I forced myself to focus on the words coming from Darrell's mouth.

"I'm working on an alliance agreement with Brian and when I mentioned my niece, Chloe, was visiting, he realized it was you and wanted to say hello."

Darrell and Brian both grinned at Chloe and I marveled at how easily the two of them lied. A tendril of foreboding curled inside me. Though I smelled no duplicity on either of them, everything about this situation seemed wrong.

I did pick up the dark, stinging scent of Brayden's rage and hatred. It filled the small cabin.

Once again, Chloe handled the situation perfectly. "How unexpected to see you, Brian," she said, stepping forward to shake his hand. "How are you doing?" Her gaze shifted to Brayden. "Hello, Brayden."

Her words were the truth, since neither of us expected to see the Kirkpatrick's, but she said them in such a friendly tone that they seemed warm rather than offensive.

"I'm fine, Chloe," Brian answered. "Though I have to say I was surprised to hear you mated." His eyes drifted down to her shoulder and his brows lifted at the absence of my bite mark on her skin.

She laughed. "Lachlan has a lot of work to do before I'll take him as a mate, Brian."

I realized that was my cue to speak. Taking a page from Chloe's playbook, I decided to keep my words as close to the truth as possible. "I didn't want to take another mate," I explained. "Then Chloe left and I realized how much she means to me."

Brian nodded, his expression grave. "That's understandable, son. It's a horrible thing to lose a mate." Then he smiled a little. "But there are few who are so lucky as to be granted another by Fate. I'm glad you didn't throw away your chance."

"That's good advice," I replied, earning a wider smile from the older wolf.

Brayden shifted on the couch, as though he were having trouble restraining himself. Calder and I had been right to worry about the wolf. It was becoming clearer that he was unstable.

I also didn't like the way he was looking at Chloe. It was a combination of lust, fury, and jealousy. The wolf inside me took note of it and his hackles raised. No one coveted what belonged to us.

When Darrell's phone rang, he apologized and went outside, lifting it to his ear as he opened the door.

Somehow, Chloe managed to make small talk with Brian, leaving me able to listen to Darrell's conversation. Unfortunately, he was speaking too softly for me to hear everything, but I heard enough.

A few moments later, Darrell returned. "Brian, Brayden, I'm very sorry, but we're going to have to cut our visit short. There's a problem back in town and they need me." He looked at Chloe. "Darlin', you and Lach enjoy the food we brought and we'll all have lunch together some other time."

"Of course, Uncle Darrell," she agreed.

I wanted to lunge forward and rip his arms off when Darrell gave her a quick hug and a peck on the cheek, but I managed to suppress the urge. Brian and Brayden were smarter. They merely nodded at her, though I did see Brayden's fingers twitch and lift as though he wanted to reach for Chloe.

The most difficult part was enduring handshakes with Darrell, Brian, and Brayden. Darrell and Brian kept their clasp firm but brief. However, Brayden gripped my hand and squeezed as if he intended to grind my bones to dust.

Biting back a growl, I stared into his eyes, openly challenging him, as I bore down hard. I felt the bones in his hand move, giving under the pressure, and felt the snap as one of them cracked.

He made a noise between a snarl and a whimper, jerking his hand from mine. Brayden glared at me, his body vibrating as he dropped his hands to his sides. He wanted to tear my throat out. It was in every line of his body and leaked from his pores.

Brian broke through when he placed his hand on Brayden's shoulder. "Come on, son. Darrell needs to get back to town."

Suddenly, the barely leashed animal that had been staring at me became docile, lowering his head and following his father outside.

It wasn't until they climbed into the SUV and drove away that I realized Brayden hadn't spoken a single word the entire time they were in the cabin.

The inherent wrongness of the visit crashed over me again. My eyes traveled over the interior of the cabin and what I saw made my instincts twang.

When Chloe turned to me, her mouth open as though she were about to speak, I shook my head and talked over her. "It's a

beautiful day. Why don't we eat our lunch outside? Have a picnic?"
I kept my voice light and as normal as I could manage.

Immediately, she understood that I didn't want to discuss what
just happened inside the house.

"That sounds great," she agreed, moving to the table to pick up
the bags of food that Darrell brought. She also took two bottles of
water from the fridge.

Neither of us spoke as we left the cabin. Chloe followed my
lead as I walked several hundred feet from the structure, making
sure to remain downwind so the sound of our voices wouldn't
carry.

When I stopped, Chloe said, "They bugged the house, didn't
they?"

"I'm almost certain. There were some small things out of place
and I know I left the bathroom door open this morning before we
left. When we returned it was shut."

A closed door didn't necessarily mean anything. Any one of
them could have taken a piss and shut the door behind them, but
combined with the fact that there were so many other things
moved inside the house, it seemed likely.

"They bugged the bathroom?" she asked, a look of disgust on
her face.

"Probably," I answered with a shrug. "I know I would."

"Ew."

Though the situation was serious, her adorable reaction made
me chuckle.

"I don't find it very funny, Lach. Every time I use the toilet, I'll
be wondering if they're listening." She shuddered. "Or watching."

"You're right, it isn't funny," I replied, the smile fading from
my face at her declaration. It reminded me of something Carter
said. Darrell liked to take videos and pictures. It was his fetish. He
wanted mementos.

"What?" Chloe asked.

"They probably did place cameras," I explained. "Remember what Carter said about his father's tendency to take photos and videos."

The disgust on her face morphed into rage. "I'm going to enjoy killing that sick motherfucker," she growled. "I may even keep a memento of my own."

"You'll get your chance," I stated. "If I don't get to him first."

She blinked, the anger draining away. "What about Brayden?" she asked. "When you told me he seemed off in Dallas, I thought he was being his usual creepy self, but if he was like he was today, I can understand why you and Calder freaked out. I've never smelled anything like it before. It was as if he were angry, jealous, and horny all at the same time." She paused. "But when he looked at you, all I could smell was hate."

"I don't think what he feels for you is a harmless crush, Chloe. It's almost as if he's obsessed."

Chloe rubbed her arms and I saw goose bumps break out on her skin. "And did you see how quickly he shut down when his dad touched him?" she asked.

I nodded.

Chloe stared off into the trees, her eyes unfocused as she thought. "I feel like there's something bigger happening here, but I can't figure out what it is. My instincts are telling me it's all connected; the death of my parents, Darrell's sick hobbies, and the Kirkpatricks, but I just can't see how."

"I agree. Something big is brewing. When we see Carter again, we'll ask him what he knows about the Kirkpatricks."

She glanced over her shoulder at the cabin. "I hate the idea of him watching us."

"I do too. We may not be able to remove the cameras without tipping him off, but we should be able to figure out a way to impede the view of one or two once we know where they are."

"But he'll still be able to hear us," she said, pacing and rubbing her arms. "Fuck, I hate this. I hate waiting. I hate not knowing if Carter is going to double cross us or not. And I hate the fucking idea that Darrell is going to watch us and listen to us, probably while he's jerking off, the sick bastard."

I stepped in front of her and put my hands on her shoulders, my thumbs stroking the sides of her neck. "Just a few more days, maybe a week, and we should have the evidence to take to the Tribunal. I know that they'll rule to take Darrell and his officers into custody and try them for their crimes. Once that happens, this will be over and we can go back to Dallas."

She stared at me for a moment, biting her bottom lip. "You're right. I'm just so angry I want to beat the shit out of something." She kicked the bag of food she'd dropped on the ground, knocking it over. "And I'm hungry as hell but I refuse to eat the shit Darrell brought."

"Well, at least there's something I can do about that," I said, wrapping my arms around her. I told myself the hug was meant to comfort her, but, in truth, it was for me.

CHAPTER TWENTY-THREE

Chloe

LACHLAN WAS RIGHT about the cameras. We found three. One was in the bathroom, hidden behind a picture on the wall. There was no way to cover it. The lens faced the door rather than the toilet and tub, but I hated knowing it was there.

The second was in the kitchen, inside a fake plant on a shelf that contained someone's poor attempt at making the place homier. Since I'd cleaned the cabin several times after my arrival, I made a show of complaining about how everything got dusty in the country and using a cloth and polish on all the wooden surfaces in the little house. When I dusted that particular shelf, I made sure to turn the plant away.

The final camera pointed directly at the bed. It was concealed in the lamp on the table by the sofa, just feet from the foot of the mattress. When I realized it was there, it pissed me off to no end. Darrell could have hidden the camera in other places in the room that would have encompassed the entire floor plan. Instead, he'd hidden three, one with the intention of filming us doing whatever we did when we were in that bed.

The angle of that camera was conveniently changed when I "cleaned" the cabin, pointing toward the kitchen and dining area rather than the bed.

The most difficult part of the situation was watching everything I said and did. It put me on edge, my mind in a constant state of awareness. Though shifter senses were sharper than a human's, we still needed our downtime. Keeping my guard up twenty-four hours a day would wear on me.

When my phone dinged that evening, I was relieved to see it was a text from Carter's burner phone. It contained the same coordinates that he sent me for our first meet and the word *midnight*.

Forcing a smile on my face, I walked over to the couch where Lach was stretched out, watching a video. "Aw, look at the picture Ricki sent of the pups," I said cheerfully.

Lach's eyes flicked over the screen, taking in the text. From where he lay, the cameras wouldn't be able to catch the words on the screen or his short nod. "They're getting bigger every day," he replied.

I glanced at the time on my phone and saw that it was nearly eight. Only four more hours until we could meet Carter and put an end to all of this.

As if sensing my restlessness, Lachlan reached up and snagged my hand, pulling me down onto the couch with him. "Let's watch a movie."

In the end, we watched two movies. Though I was still distracted by our upcoming meet with Carter, I found myself relaxing against Lach. He lay on his back on the wide couch, with me tucked against his side next to the rear cushions. I wondered how many more chances I would have to sprawl across his body like this. I tucked my nose against his chest, inhaling his scent. He talked about both of us returning to Dallas earlier today, but I wasn't sure if he even realized what he was saying. Or if he truly meant it.

After our conversation about Lachlan getting to know me, I'd allowed myself to hope that perhaps our relationship would develop into something more. But when he told Brian that he didn't want to take another mate this afternoon, I knew he was telling the truth by his smell alone, never mind the sincerity that rang in his words.

Right now, with the two of us lying together quietly, I rarely thought about mating. But each time Lachlan and I had sex, I had to fight my urge to bite him. To mark him as mine.

As we spent more time together, the instinct would only grow stronger until I would either have to mate with him or leave him forever. Even without the mating mark, I sensed that I would pine for him until I withered away into nothing.

When the second movie ended, I saw that it was nearly eleven-thirty. Tonight was cloudy again, which meant the woods would be almost completely dark. It would take us at least twenty minutes to walk to the clearing without the moon to light the way. Probably longer.

I rolled over Lachlan, getting to my feet and stretching my arms over my head. He watched me from his position on the couch, his eyes warm as they moved over me.

Deliberately, I moved into the line of the camera lens and stripped my shirt over my head, making sure to hold it in my left hand. I would need it later. "I have an idea," I said, trailing my finger over the waistband of my jeans. "Let's go for a walk. It's a beautiful night."

Lachlan understood what I was doing immediately. He growled playfully. "Maybe I don't want to go for a walk. Maybe I want to fuck you right here."

My mind working quickly, I taunted, "If you want to fuck me, you have to catch me first."

Turning on my heel, I darted out the front door and around the house toward the tree line. I heard Lach's heavy steps behind me. I made sure that I didn't stop until I was hidden in the trees. As I waited for Lachlan to join me, I pulled my shirt on and sniffed the air. Someone had been here recently. Maybe a few hours ago, but their scent had faded too much for me to recognize it easily.

When Lachlan appeared beside me, I knew he smelled it too.

"Someone was here," I whispered. "Do you recognize the scent?"

He shook his head. "Whoever it was has been gone for hours."

"We should check the perimeter, make sure there's no one here now."

Quickly, we circled the house, finding signs that someone had been in the woods, just far enough away that we wouldn't notice them, but they were gone now.

A chill crept down my spine, even though the night was warm. I'd been here for days now, and no one had bothered with me except Darrell. Now we were being watched via cameras and by other wolves. Whatever they were planning would happen soon.

Lachlan and I met up where we started and headed deeper into the forest. I let Lachlan take the lead since his sense of smell was better than mine. I focused on making my steps silent in the darkness, keeping my head up so I could sniff the air and my eyes moving constantly along the shadows.

A short while later, we approached the meeting place. Lachlan stopped abruptly, still hidden by the darkness and underbrush. That was when I smelled it.

Blood.

I craned my neck, looking around Lachlan's shoulder toward the clearing. It was empty.

Lachlan turned toward me, putting his mouth directly against my ear. When he spoke it was barely audible. "I want you to follow right behind me. Step where I step and stop when I stop."

I gave a single nod of agreement.

Lachlan turned away from me then, moving slowly and stealthily through the brush and trees, circling the clearing. I put my feet in his footprints and watched him closely in case he stopped.

When he did, I peered around him, my eyes widening when I saw a heap leaning against a tree nearby. In the faint light from the stars, I could see Carter's bloody face. His body was utterly still.

I swallowed the sound that wanted to escape my throat when he gasped, his chest rising in a deep, ragged breath. His exhale ended in a low sigh.

Lachlan crept closer, still silent, and crouched down next to Carter. The wolf looked up at him, blood covering half his face and his right eye swollen shut.

"What happened?" Lach asked.

"I got caught," Carter replied, coughing a little. The sound was painful and I winced at the wetness of it. Then he grinned, revealing teeth stained with blood. "But I also got away."

Lachlan's fingers went to his neck, checking his pulse.

Carter shoved his hand away. "I'll survive. I've taken worse beatings than this before."

"You may have internal bleeding," Lachlan argued.

Carter leveled his good eye at Lach, his stare piercing even in the shadows. "I'm already healing. I'll live." He reached behind him and Lachlan and I both tensed. When he revealed a small backpack, our bodies loosened a little. "Here is everything you asked for."

"Thank you," Lachlan said, taking the bag.

"I didn't tell them about you," Carter stated suddenly. "But they already suspect you're helping me. You need to leave the area tonight. As quickly as you can." With a rough groan, Carter hauled himself to his feet, keeping his back braced against the tree. "Come back when you have a plan and help."

"What about you?" I asked, stepping forward.

He looked at me and once more I was struck by the strength of his personality. Carter Whelby, the alpha, was here tonight, even in his currently bloodied state. "I'm not leaving my pack."

"He'll kill you," Lachlan argued. "You should come with us."

Carter shook his head. "I have a place to hide. I'll contact you when I'm healed. Even if you have help, you'll need me when you return for the evidence."

"Carter," I said quietly. "Come with us."

He shook his head. "No. I'm not leaving h—" he cut himself off. "My pack." He grimaced. "Besides, in my state, I'll only slow you down. You need to go. Now. They'll be coming back soon and you should be gone by then."

I started to argue further, but Lachlan reached out and took Carter's hand, shaking it. "Thank you for the warning. If you ever need us, the MacIntire pack will be here for you."

Carter nodded. "You're welcome."

I tried to resist when Lach took my arm, looking back at Carter. He leaned heavily against the tree and shook his head at me. "Go," he commanded.

I loathed it, but I did as he said. Lachlan slung the backpack over his shoulders as we walked away, moving quickly through the trees.

"We need to run," he muttered to me. "If they know he's gone, they'll be coming for us next."

Without a word, I picked up my pace. The darkness slowed us down, but only a little. Adrenaline sharpened my night vision and soon I was flying through the trees, my feet barely touching the ground.

Within a few minutes, we reached the edge of the cabin property. The house was still dark. I looked around as Lachlan scented the air.

"There's no one here yet," he commented. When he turned to look at me, I realized I was seeing another side of Lachlan. Yes, he was an alpha, but he was also a strategist. As good as any warlord. "When we get to the house, you go inside and get our bags. We'll take the truck since it's a 4x4. If they planted cameras in the house, it's also likely they put a tracking device on our vehicles. I'm going to look for it. We need to drive out of here in five minutes."

There was a reason I never wanted to be the alpha of my own pack, and this was it. I could win almost any fight, one-on-one, but strategy and battle planning weren't my strengths. I also lacked the patience necessary in a good leader.

Lachlan appeared surprised when I nodded in agreement without a word of argument. Rather than questioning his good luck, he grabbed my hand and we ran toward the cabin. He released me as he headed toward the truck, dropping to the ground and pulling out his phone to use the flashlight capabilities.

I dashed into the house and scooped up the few personal items we left lying around. For the most part, Lachlan and I both kept our bags packed for this very reason.

As I shoved things inside, an odd feeling washed over me. They had put cameras all over the house, so maybe they'd done something to our bags as well. Moving quickly, I unpacked everything once again and ran my hands on along the exterior and interior of our bags. Sure enough I found a tiny device tucked into the lining of each bag. I repacked everything as quickly as possible, leaving the tracking devices lying in the middle of the bed.

I grabbed our phone chargers, some water and food, and walked back out the door. It took me longer than expected, but I was surprised to see that Lachlan wasn't waiting on me.

When I returned, I found a tracking device on the ground next to the truck, but Lach was rummaging around in the cab of the pick-up as though he were looking for something.

"What are you doing?" I asked.

Without stopping, he answered, "I found that one within sixty seconds. It was almost as if Darrell wanted it found. Since he's not stupid, I'm betting he planted another one..." Lachlan trailed off as he bent to look beneath the passenger seat.

He shoved the seat back as far as it would go and reached beneath, cursing under his breath. I smelled the metallic tang of blood in the air when he swore again and pulled his hand free. Between his index and middle finger, he held a slim disc, barely the size of a quarter. Blood trickled from the small cut on his hand.

"Found it," he said triumphantly, dropping it on the ground. Taking the bags from me, he tossed them in the storage space behind the seats. "Let's go."

"I found two devices in our bags too," I informed him as he gestured for me to get in.

"Shit. Are you sure that's all there was?"

"I think so," I answered.

He nodded and walked around the front of the vehicle.

I climbed into the passenger seat, shutting the door just as Lach got inside and turned the key. I'd barely buckled my seatbelt when he put the truck in gear and shot down the driveway. He didn't bother with the headlights, trusting his shifter night vision to guide us to the main road. When we reached it, I looked to the right and saw headlights in the distance, coming from town.

"They're coming," I murmured. "I think they're too far away to see us with the lights off."

Lachlan peeled out of the driveway, turning left. He floored it, the speedometer in the dash quickly shooting up to eighty miles per hour. The road veered to the left. The trees would hide us from view if they intended to pursue us. Quickly, Lachlan turned right down another small country road, followed by a left, then another right.

"Do you know where we're going?" I asked.

"Yes," he answered shortly. "I memorized the route before I came. If we take a few more turns, the roads will lead us to 412."

"Where are we going?"

"I don't know."

I grinned. "I do."

He glanced at me. "What?"

"Gram arranged for me to have a house under an assumed name. No one knows about it but the two of us. We should be safe there."

"Where is it?" Lachlan asked.

"Twenty miles from here," I answered. "But in the opposite direction."

"Shit."

"That's okay," I said. "We can take the scenic route."

CHAPTER TWENTY-FOUR

Lachlan

I PARKED THE truck in front of the small house and shut off the engine. It was nearly four in the morning and Chloe and I were exhausted.

"We need to check the place out," I stated tiredly.

"I know," she answered, her voice quiet.

In agreement, we climbed out of the truck and Chloe gestured to the right. I went left. We circled the house, finding no evidence that anyone had been there. Not even humans.

When we met back at the truck, I pulled our bags out of the cab. "Come on, let's get to bed."

She dug the keys out of her bag and unlocked the door. I followed her inside, my nose twitching from the dusty smell of the house. She walked through a compact living room and down the short hall. A door stood open to our left that revealed a bathroom. The door at the end of the hall was open as well and Chloe went inside. I followed her, discovering a spacious bedroom. Against the far wall was a king-sized bed.

Chloe gestured to a chair in the corner. "You can stick the bags there. Are you hungry?" she asked.

"It can wait. We need sleep."

She sighed. "That sounds good. I'm going to go turn on the air then we can go to bed."

I dropped the bags in the chair, grabbing the phone chargers out of mine. In her rush, Chloe had stuffed them both inside. Then I stripped out of my clothes, letting them drop to the floor as I walked to the bed.

I heard the air conditioner kick on and felt cool air blowing into the stuffy room. When Chloe returned a few moments later, I was already in bed. She removed her own clothes, disappeared into the bathroom for a minute, then came back to slide into bed, sighing as she settled against me.

I slid my arm under her head and exhaled as her cheek hit my chest. In the last few days, I'd grown so accustomed to having her in bed with me that I wasn't sure how I'd ever sleep alone again.

If I hadn't been so tired, the thought probably would have scared the shit out of me. As it was, I could barely keep my eyes open.

"Do you think Carter will be okay?" Chloe asked suddenly, her voice sleepy.

I rubbed my hand over her shoulder. "Yes, I do. He's a survivor."

"He should be alpha of the pack," Chloe stated.

"You don't want the job?"

She chuckled against my chest, rubbing her nose on my skin. She had a habit of doing that at night before we went to sleep, as if she wanted to make sure that my scent was the only thing she smelled in her sleep. "Hell, no," she replied. "I don't have the temperament."

Now that I knew her better, I was inclined to agree. Still, I was impressed that she understood that about herself. A lot of wolves, male or female, would assume that their fighting prowess meant that they would make excellent pack alphas. Often times, they were wrong.

"He should change the name of the pack," she said idly. "I don't think it will be led by MacArthurs ever again."

"What about your children?" I asked.

She shrugged. "I doubt I'll have any."

"You never know when you'll meet your mate," I pointed out, ignoring the shaft that pierced my heart when I uttered the words. I shoved the feeling away. I cared about Chloe, but she wasn't my mate. My mate was dead.

"I already have," she whispered, her body going lax against me. "He doesn't want me."

Every muscle in my body tensed at her words. "What?" I asked.

She didn't answer. She was already sleeping.

I lay awake until the sky was tinged with pink, unable to stop thinking about the mate that hadn't wanted Chloe. I couldn't wrap my head around it. Any male would be lucky to take Chloe as a mate. I could have the she-wolf with me for the rest of my life and never regret it.

I cursed myself, because I knew if Chloe had a mate and he returned for her, she would leave me behind.

THE SMELL OF coffee and bacon woke me up the next morning. I sat up, throwing my legs over the side of the bed and rubbed my forehead with my hands. A glance at my phone showed that it was nearly noon.

Hoping a shower would clear the fuzziness from my head, I walked into the bathroom, emptied my bladder, and climbed into the tub.

"Fuck me!" I yelled when the water came out ice cold. The showerhead was low, the nozzle pointed at my chin rather than raining water over my head. I got a face full of frigid liquid.

I heard Chloe's chuckle on the other side of the shower curtain, stepped out of the spray, and stuck my head outside to see her put a cup of coffee on the counter. "I see you've discovered the horrible plumbing."

"Jesus Christ, you could have warned me," I complained.

She grinned at me. "But where's the fun in that?"

I gave her a look that promised retribution, which only made her smile widen.

"Will I be forgiven if I tell you I made breakfast?" she asked sweetly.

"Maybe," I mumbled, ducking back into the shower and reaching for the shampoo. She must have gotten it out of my bag while I slept. I stared at the bottle in my hand, a testament to her thoughtfulness, and once again my mind wandered to the mate that refused her.

His loss would be my gain, I decided. At least for now.

I heard Chloe leave the bathroom as I washed my hair. When I finished my shower and dressed, I came out of the bedroom to find a huge mound of bacon and waffles waiting for me. There was even orange juice.

"Did you go shopping this morning?" I asked.

She shook her head. "No, I had all this in the freezer. I left some things here. I planned to come back for a week or two after this was all over. It's not the best meal we'll ever eat, but at least we won't go hungry today."

My stomach rumbled as I looked over the food. "Looks good to me. I'm so hungry I don't really give a damn how it tastes."

We sat down and ate, Chloe asking me what I wanted to eat for the next few days as she made a list. In the midst of chaos, the simple domestic task seemed blessedly normal.

"We'll have to go shopping this afternoon. It's probably a good idea to grab things that we'll eat for the next few days. If we have to leave again, we can put what's left in the freezer."

"We need to call Calder and your grandmother today," I reminded her.

She looked at me. "I know, but we also need to eat, so food comes first. We can go into town after breakfast and make the call when we come back."

The trip to the grocery store revealed another facet of Chloe's personality to me. She marched through the aisles as though she were on a mission, working her way through the store with swift precision. She rarely lingered over choices, selecting products after a quick perusal of ingredients and price.

Within twenty minutes, we'd gathered what we needed, paid for the items, and were back in the truck, heading out of town. I noticed Chloe checking her mirrors, making sure we weren't followed as she drove. I'd been doing the same and it seemed we were safe for now.

Once we were back at the house, the groceries put away, Chloe and I opened the bag that Carter had given us last night. Inside we found everything he promised—a map of the city, blueprints of the police station, and something he hadn't promised, his father's habits, schedule, and, best of all, the combination to his safe. Then we called Calder and her grandmother, Sophia.

Quickly, I explained what had occurred over the past two days. Calder and Sophia remained quiet as I spoke, neither saying a word until I was done.

"You don't know where Carter went?" Sophia asked, her tone displeased.

"No, I don't, but I trust him."

"Yes, well, my son trusted Darrell and look what happened."

"Gram," Chloe interrupted. "Lachlan did the right thing. Carter got us everything we need to break into his father's station and get proof of everything he's done. Including proof that he murdered Mom and Dad."

Sophia was silent.

"How many wolves will you need?" Calder asked.

"Four, maybe five," I answered.

"That many?"

I sighed and rubbed my forehead. "There's a complication." When Calder didn't speak, I continued. "Brian and Brayden Kirkpatrick are here."

"What?" Calder's voice was loud enough to make me wince. "What in the hell are they doing there? They were just in Dallas a few weeks ago."

"I don't know but it definitely gives me a bad feeling."

"Me too," Calder murmured. "So do you think they're there to see Chloe?"

I glanced over at her and knew she'd heard Calder's question. Her eyes were intent upon me and full of questions. "Yeah, I do."

"Fuck, I really don't like this. Okay, so four or five wolves. Do the Kirkpatricks have any of their pack with them?"

"Not that I know of."

"Maybe I should send more than five," he stated.

"It's your call," I agreed. "Either way, we'll need to wait a few days and give Carter a chance to heal before we attack. If you send Mason and Shane, plus two others, the six of us should be able to handle it. None of them are as strong as our weakest wolf."

"Seven of us," Chloe corrected me. "Unless you were planning to stay behind because I'm sure as hell not." Her tone held a warning.

"I'm not sure how effective Carter is in a fight," I explained. "Even if he's healed, it's doubtful he'll be at his full strength for weeks."

Chloe tilted her head. "I think he'll surprise you," she drawled.

"But a few days' wait will give them time to get ready for us," Sophia argued.

"Maybe, but Carter said we'll need his help to get in and I believe him," I replied.

"I'll tell them to get ready to leave tomorrow. It will give you time to formulate a plan and get them up to speed," Calder offered.

"Sounds good." I glanced around the house. "Tell them to be prepared to rough it. There are only two bedrooms and a damn tiny couch."

Calder chuckled. "They've slept in worse places, I'm sure."

We talked for a few minutes longer before hanging up.

"What did you mean by the Kirkpatricks being here for me?" Chloe asked.

I stared at her, unsure how to explain the feeling in my gut every time Brayden Kirkpatrick looked at her, or the way his eyes flashed whenever he heard her name. I had no proof, just a deeply seated sense that something was wrong.

"Lach?"

"I'm trying to figure out how to explain it," I answered. "It's nothing concrete, just a feeling I have about Brayden. His body language and the look in his eyes when you're even mentioned gives me..." I trailed off, searching for the best way to describe it.

"The creeps?" she injected.

I huffed out a laugh. "For lack of a better word, yeah."

"He doesn't give me the best feeling either, especially after seeing him yesterday," she agreed, surveying the papers spread on the kitchen table. Chloe rubbed her hands together. "Well, we should probably get to work," she stated, changing the subject.

I could sense the agitation in her. She wanted to end this, the sooner the better. She really hadn't been lying when she said patience wasn't her strength.

"It's just a few more days, Chloe," I said quietly.

She looked up at me, her hazel eyes bright. The green stood out in her amber irises, a clear sign of her frustration. "I want him to pay," she growled and I realized she wasn't thinking of Brayden Kirkpatrick anymore. She was focused on Darrell. "With his blood and his bones. Because that's what he took from me."

"He will. I promise."

CHAPTER TWENTY-FIVE

Chloe

SINCE LACHLAN COOKED dinner, I washed the dishes. The day had been a long one. The simple task allowed my mind to calm and wander. God knew I needed it.

I couldn't believe I'd told him that I'd found my mate. When he'd mentioned children and never knowing when I'd meet my mate, my tired mind didn't have the energy to filter my thoughts and the words had slipped out.

Still, he hadn't mentioned it, so I hoped that perhaps he'd been asleep and hadn't heard me.

I rinsed the last fork and put it in the drain board. Once I let the water out of the sink and wiped down the counters, I turned off the light in the kitchen and walked into the living room. Lachlan was sprawled on the sofa, his feet flat on the floor and legs spread wide as he watched me pause in the doorway.

"Come here," he murmured, lifting a hand to beckon me forward.

Recognizing the gleam in his eyes, I moved toward him. When I was between his outstretched legs, I knelt to the floor. His gaze followed the motion, his lids lowering, hooding his eyes.

I put my hands on his knees, curving my palms over the top of each one. Then I slid them up his thighs until they met in the center. His tongue darted out to wet his mouth as he watched me, but he didn't move. Though we'd been intimate several times now, he always stopped me when I tried to use my mouth on him.

There would be no stopping me this time.

Without taking my eyes off his face, I unbuckled his belt, slipped the button free, and lowered the zipper of his jeans. My knuckles brushed his cock as I loosened his clothes and I felt it growing harder as I spread the denim. He wore nothing beneath them.

He lifted his hips up and let me jerk his pants down his legs and over his bare feet. As I tossed them aside, he reached back over his head and grabbed the fabric of his t-shirt, pulling it over his head.

I knelt before him, fully clothed, as he leaned back on the couch, his nude body burnished by the golden light of the lamp. He looked like an erotic work of art, his hard cock lying against his firmly muscled stomach.

I reached out and circled him with my fingers, lifting his rigid length up so I could stroke him with my hand. He sucked in a sharp breath, his arms flexing at his sides, but he didn't move.

Still staring into his burning blue eyes, I leaned forward and opened my mouth, flicking the head with my tongue. He twitched in my hand, growing harder. Smiling at him, I licked him again, starting at the base and dragging my tongue up to the tip.

Lachlan's eyes never left my face as he watched me run my lips and tongue over the smooth, hot skin of his cock. Even as his hands clenched and opened at his sides, he didn't touch me. Without direction, he knew that I wanted him to lie still and let me touch him.

It wasn't until I closed my lips around the tip of his cock that his hips jerked against the couch and his hands lifted so he could bury his fingers in my hair, sweeping it back from my face.

Stroking my hand up and down his length, I sucked and licked the crown, his hands growing tighter with each pull of my mouth. When he stiffened beneath me, I lowered my lips, taking him deeper until I could handle no more.

Lachlan groaned deep in his chest and he broke eye contact as his head fell back on the couch. I squeezed him tighter with my hand and my mouth, sucking harder and deeper. He guided my motions with his hands, but never shoved my head down or forced me to take him too far.

His body grew taut beneath me and I knew he was close. I pushed him harder, my head bobbing and my fingers moving in long strokes, and he came, spilling down my throat.

I swallowed, drinking him down, taking every bit of the salty, slightly bitter liquid. When I gave him one last lick, he flinched. "Fuck," he gasped. "That felt fucking amazing."

I smiled up at him, my lips feeling swollen. He leaned forward and kissed me. His hands tangled in my hair and tugged my head back.

Against my mouth, he whispered, "But next time, you're going to be naked and you're going to touch yourself while you do it."

I shivered at his words and watched as his pupils dilated.

"You like that idea, don't you?" he asked.

"Yes," I whispered.

His hands moved from my hair, down my neck and over my breasts, stopping at the hem of my tank top. He tugged it up, pulling it over my head. My bra hit the ground only a moment after the fabric.

He urged me to stand up, hooking his hands in the waistband of my shorts and underwear so he could yank them down my legs. When I stood naked before him, his fingers slid over my pussy, dipping inside me.

"God, you're so fucking wet," he muttered. "Did sucking me

off turn you on?" he asked, his eyes lifting to meet mine.

"Yes," I whispered, watching as he lifted his fingers to his mouth and slid them inside.

My legs went weak and collapsed when he grabbed me, pulling me down until I straddled his lap. He kissed me then, his tongue tangling with mine. Grabbing my hair again, he positioned my head where he wanted, baring my neck to his mouth. His teeth scraped down my throat as he bent me farther back, lifting my breasts to his lips.

Curved in an arch over his lap, I cried out as his tongue and teeth teased my nipples, tugging and flicking at my flesh until it ached from the pleasure. I felt his cock then, fully erect against my ass. I shifted my hips, lifting them until our bodies lined up. He reached one hand between us and guided himself inside me.

"That is the sexiest fucking thing I've ever seen," he groaned as I sank down on him, my head still positioned at a sharp angle as he held my hair.

"I want to see," I said, fighting against his hold.

He released me and I looked down to watch as his cock slid inside me until my ass rested on his thighs. I gasped at the sensation of being filled, lifting my hips and lowering my body again. I reached out behind him, closing my hands over the back of the couch as I moved. Our motions were slow and with each stroke I felt as though he was going deeper. He sucked one of my nipples into his mouth, working at the tip of my breast until I couldn't take the sensation any longer and begged him to stop.

My body was clamoring for orgasm and I gasped as my hips moved faster.

"I'm close," I whispered, throwing my head back when his thumb hit my clit. "Ian!" I cried out as the climax burst inside of me, fire flooding my veins.

As I convulsed on top of him, his mouth went to the curve

where my neck and shoulder met and he bit me. Not the playful nip of a lover, but the deep bite of a wolf marking his territory.

I screamed as every muscle in my body locked in ecstasy. I would have bitten him then, marking him as my mate, if he hadn't grabbed a fistful of my hair again. I cried out again as he sucked the wound, feeling the sensation in my clit.

Finally, his mouth released me and I fell on top of him. Our chests bumped and I heard the echo of my heartbeat roaring in my ears. Then I realized the echo was his heart hammering against mine—pounding in perfect unison with my own.

What in the hell had he just done?

CHAPTER TWENTY-SIX

Lachlan

CHLOE'S HEAD DROPPED onto my shoulder, her heart pounding against my chest. I smelled blood and realized the bite on her shoulder was still oozing a little. I ran my tongue over the wound.

She winced and sat up. Moving slowly, she climbed off of me and walked out of the room without a word. Water ran in the bathroom and I knew she was cleaning up. Feeling strangely content, I got to my feet, slid on my jeans, and followed her.

The bathroom was empty when I entered. Grabbing the damp washcloth she'd left in the sink, I rinsed it out and cleaned myself off. I heard the rustle of fabric in the bedroom and found her yanking a t-shirt over her head. The expression on her face froze me to the spot.

She looked tortured and incredibly sad.

"Do you realize what you've done?" she asked, her voice shaky and thin.

"You mean the bite?"

"Of course I mean the bite!" she yelled. Chloe drew in a deep breath, shoved her hands in her hair, and turned her back to me.

I watched her fight for control over her emotions. When she won the battle, she faced me again, her eyes still overcome with sadness.

"You marked me, Ian. Not just a love bite but a claiming mark. If I'd bitten you..." she trailed off, shaking her head.

The peacefulness within me faded. "I know," I replied, crossing my arms over my chest.

Her eyes widened. "You know? You did it intentionally?"

With my jaw clenched tightly, I nodded.

"What in the hell were you thinking?" she asked, her voice growing louder. "You said yourself you don't want to take another mate yet *you fucking marked me*! You didn't discuss it with me, you just did it. If I'd bitten you in return, we would have been mated and there would be nothing either of us could do about it!"

She had a valid point. I hadn't thought, at least not about what she might want. Since she'd mentioned the mate who rejected her, all I could think about was that he might change his mind and she would be gone. I knew it was entirely selfish, but I wanted Chloe to myself. *For* myself.

"If you're worried about your mate—" I began.

"I don't give a fuck about that right now, Ian. What I care about is that you did something that affects both of us without so much as asking me how I felt about it. You know there's no going back once the bond is in place. There's no changing your mind."

She stopped speaking, her chest heaving with emotion, and her eyes filled with tears.

"Shit, Chloe. Don't cry. You're right, I wasn't thinking about what you wanted. All I cared about was what I wanted."

A tear trickled down her cheek and the wolf within me whined. He wanted to go and comfort her. Hold her until she no longer felt sad or afraid.

"Do you even know what you want?" she asked softly. "Truly? Because I know I couldn't take it if you decided after all was said and done that you made a mistake."

God, I'd completely fucked this up. I took a step toward her but she lifted her hand to stop me.

"No, don't touch me right now. Think about my question and answer it. For yourself." She brushed by me, heading toward the door. "I'm going for a run. We'll talk when I get back."

The implication that I was too weak to know my own mind stirred my own anger. "Are you worried about what your mate will say when he sees the mark? If he ever does?" As soon as the words left my lips, I regretted them. I opened my mouth to apologize but she'd already turned toward me.

It wasn't ire sparkling in her eyes but utter dejection.

"I told you, Lachlan. He doesn't want a mate. He probably never will. This isn't about him. It's about you and me."

Without another word, she slipped out the front door, closing it quietly behind her. I stood in the hall, staring after her, my mind sifting through everything she'd said and the hurt in every line of her body.

She was wrong. I did know what I wanted—her.

I took a step to go after her, but stopped. She asked me to think about what I truly wanted. She wanted me to be sure.

But not once had she said she didn't want to be tied to me.

My fear that she would leave me for the mate who rejected her had driven me to do something drastic, but that wasn't my only motivation.

I wanted Chloe. For a week. A year. A lifetime.

I would never have that soul deep bond I'd shared with Belinda, but it didn't matter because I loved Chloe.

There was no version of my future that didn't have her in it.

Determined, I went to the front door and walked outside. I would shift and track her down. When I found her, I only hoped I could make her understand.

Before I reached the edge of the porch, something sharp

pierced my back. I whirled, facing my attacker. My entire body was on fire, my muscles convulsing uncontrollably as I fell to the wooden planks beneath me.

The pain subsided for a moment and I looked up at the shadow looming over me. He crouched down, his face coming into focus.

Darrell Whelby's dark eyes stared back at me. "Thanks for saving me the trouble of coming in to get you, son." He held a black device in his hand, his finger twitching on the trigger.

Once again, my body was seized by unending waves of pain that continued until I slipped into unconsciousness.

WHEN I CAME to, I was lying on my side, my body swaying. I cracked my eyelids open, hoping to get an idea of where I was. I saw the metal shell of a van and realized that my body was swaying because the vehicle was in motion.

Then I focused on the lump in front of me, my blood running cold when I realized that it was Chloe. I tried to reach for her, but my hands were caught tight behind me, bound in chains and thick shackles.

The van slowed to a stop. I tilted my head back to look toward the driver's seat. Darrell stared back, his eyes grim. He lifted a black handgun, pointing it straight at my chest. I barely had a chance to register his intentions before he pulled the trigger.

When the tearing pain never came, only a sharp pinch, I looked down and saw a silver dart sticking out of my chest. My head swam as it dawned on me that he'd drugged me.

"You don't get off that easy, Lachlan," Darrell muttered as I fought the effects of the sedative. "You have a lot to answer for."

I couldn't keep my eyes open any longer. As the darkness

claimed me one more time, I whispered, "Chloe."

CHAPTER TWENTY-SEVEN

Chloe

I LAY PERFECTLY still as the van rolled to a stop, keeping my eyes shut. I knew without looking that Lachlan was beside me and he was awake as well. We'd only been on the road for a short time and I wondered if we'd already reached our destination. Then I heard a soft whooshing sound and Darrell's voice.

"You don't get off that easy, Lachlan. You have a lot to answer for."

I lifted my lids slightly to look at Lach, but his eyes were rolling back in his head, a silver dart sticking out of his chest.

"Chloe," he whispered.

My wolf rose up within me, enraged to see our mate in pain, but I fought the urge to howl. If Darrell knew I was awake, I would get the same treatment as Lach.

I listened as Darrell put the van in gear and we moved back onto the road.

When I'd left the house earlier, my heart breaking after seeing the look on Lachlan's face, my only thoughts had been of outrunning the pain. By the time I'd smelled Darrell's scent in the air, it had been too late.

There was another wolf up front with Darrell, one of his officers from the Prater Police Department. The rest were following behind us in an SUV marked PPD. Six against one were shitty odds, but I had no choice.

There was no doubt in my mind that once they got Lach and I to our destination, they were going to kill us. I had no choice but to try and fight my way out of the situation.

As I told Lachlan before, strategy wasn't my strong suit. I couldn't even feign weakness in hopes it would lower their guard. These wolves knew my reputation and me. They'd taken no chances, chaining me to the floor of the van just as they had Lachlan.

My only hope was to let them think that I was unconscious when they removed me from the vehicle and lash out when they least expected it.

Thirty minutes later, the van turned, going over several bumps, before rolling to a stop. I controlled my breathing, keeping it deep and even, as Darrell shut off the van.

"You and the boys grab him. I'll get the she-wolf."

My ears strained as they climbed out. A few moments later, there were footsteps and the doors at the rear of the van swung open. I desperately wanted to open my eyes and take measure of how many men were there, but I couldn't risk it. I would only have one shot at escaping. With Lachlan unconscious, I would have to find a way to get him out of here too, but I needed to take one step at a time.

I hoped they would remove me first because then all I would have to do was grab the keys and drive the van away with Lach inside, but those thoughts were dashed when I felt the bed of the van dip as one of the wolves climbed inside. The jingling of keys told me they were unchaining him from the floor. The van jostled more as they slid him out, the two wolves barely grunting as they took Lachlan's weight.

When hands grasped my ankles to turn me over, I fought the

urge to kick. My wolf raged inside me, wanting to fight. To kill. But I forced her back.

Not yet.

Someone clambered up into the van, standing over me. From his scent, I knew it was Darrell. He stood there for a long time and I felt his stare on me. Then the chains holding me to the floor loosened and my body slid toward the open doors.

Darrell threw me over his shoulder, my skull crashing against his lower back. I swallowed a groan as my head swam. The drugs he'd given me were wearing off, but not quickly enough. I risked a peek around us through the curtain of my hair, but all the other wolves had gone inside.

It was time.

Moving quickly, I looped the chains that connected my hands around Darrell's neck, snapping them tight. He grunted and dropped me, which was a mistake. As I fell, I dragged him with me, turning us so he hit the ground face first.

Slamming a knee into his back, I gripped the chains and yanked hard. I heard a high whine escape from his mouth as the pressure around his windpipe increased.

He thrashed beneath me, his body bucking. My head spun dizzily, but I fought to hold on. Gathering my strength, I pulled back on the chain, tilting his head at an unnatural angle. All it would take was one good yank to break his neck.

Nausea roiled in my gut and bright multi-colored lights burst behind my eyes. Now that I was upright, the side effects from the drug were making it difficult to remain conscious.

I bit my lower lip so hard that I tasted blood, the pain bringing me back from the edge. I had to save Lachlan.

Darrell's feet kicked wildly and his hands scrabbled at the chain, jerking against it. I took a deep breath, preparing for the final strike, when I heard a familiar whoosh.

Something sharp pierced my shoulder and I cried out. Immediately, my limbs felt sluggish and my head spun, but I kept a death grip on the chain. Rough hands grabbed me. I snarled and bit, fighting with everything I had, but the sedative was weakening me.

Finally, a fist crashed into the side of my face and I could fight no longer.

WHEN I CAME to, the throbbing in my skull was so intense that I gagged. Somehow I managed to keep from throwing up, probably because there was nothing in my stomach.

I fought to control the heaves, taking deep breaths until the urge passed. I opened my eyes and hissed as the bright light pierced my retinas. Squeezing them shut, I focused on keeping the nausea at bay.

When my body finally calmed, I opened my eyes again, squinting against the light. My forehead rubbed against cold, metal and my gaze focused. I realized my face was pressed against steel bars. I was in some sort of cell.

Turning my head, I looked toward my hands. They were tied with thick rope, spread out to my sides so that my upper body formed a T shape. A quick glance down confirmed that my ankles were tied down to the anchors in the floor so that I was spread-eagled. The front of my torso rested heavily against the bars. I had some room to move, but not much. I was glad to see that I still wore the t-shirt and panties I'd thrown on back at the house.

A groan caught my attention and I looked up. There was another cell next to mine. On the opposite wall of bars, Lachlan was trussed up in a similar fashion, only he was facing me and he was still shirtless. His head lolled forward and he groaned again, his body straining.

I knew he was probably fighting the same nausea and pain I had when I awoke.

"Just breathe slow and deep," I murmured to him, my voice catching on the last word. "It'll pass in a moment."

His eyes opened and he stared at me blindly for a moment. I watched as awareness took hold and his eyes focused.

"Chloe," he choked.

"I'm here."

"I'm sorry," he whispered.

"Me too."

"Oh, how touching," a voice drawled from behind me.

I twisted my head and watched as Darrell sauntered into the room. I realized he'd brought us back to the Prater police station when I saw the familiar desks behind him as he came through the door.

"I'm glad you're both awake because we have some things to discuss," he said. The cell doors were open, so he entered the second cell, standing between Lachlan and me. "Now, I'm going to ask you nicely the first time and give you a chance to answer my questions without using pain as an incentive." He turned to look at me. "I'd recommend you answer truthfully because we can all smell lies. If you lie to me, I'll be forced to find other ways to gather the truth. I find that my imagination when it comes to you, little Chloe, is extremely creative."

I stared at Darrell, taking in the changes to his demeanor. His hair was still the same dark brown, his shoulders still broad and strong, but he looked nothing like the man I knew as a pup. His brown eyes were glittering malevolently in the light and the muscles of his face seemed to tighten, thinning his mouth and lifting his jaw.

This man was cold, calculating, and cruel.

Even his scent was different, sharper and almost painful when inhaled. He might be a shifter, but the real monster lived inside his mind and it had long ago devoured his soul.

"What do you want to know?" Lachlan asked.

Darrell smiled, the expression feral rather than showing amusement. "Ah, I'm glad to see one of you is feeling reasonable."

When he turned his head, I saw the thick band of purple bruises around his neck and upper chest and felt a surge of glee at the knowledge that I'd caused them. Even a shifter would take days to heal from wounds like that.

"Where is Carter?" Darrell asked Lachlan.

His gaze steady, Lach replied, "I don't know."

Darrell growled. "This is your last chance. Answer me honestly or…" In a blink of an eye, he stood in front of me and thrust his hand through the bars. His fingers tangled in my hair, jerking hard. "I show you exactly how creative I am when it comes to hurting people who piss me off."

I glared at him out of the corner of my eye, the warning snarl rolling up my chest and throat and out of my mouth.

Darrell glanced down at me, smirking. "Threaten me all you like, Chloe MacArthur. We both know you aren't getting out of those ropes."

He was right. In the position that Lach and I were tied in, we couldn't claw or chew at our bindings without hurting ourselves. We couldn't shift either because our arms and legs would be dislocated. By the time we healed enough to fight or run, it would be too late.

Darrell yanked my face against the bars, my forehead hitting them with a thunk. "Answer me!" he yelled at Lach.

"I don't know. He wouldn't tell us. We offered to let him come with us when we ran, but he refused. The last time we saw him was in the forest near the cabin." Lachlan's eyes narrowed on Darrell and the muscles in his arms and legs bunched. "Let her go."

As swiftly as he'd grabbed my hair, Darrell released me. "See, that wasn't so hard, was it?" He turned toward me, crouching down so we were at eye level. "Now you. How much does Sophia know about the situation?"

I couldn't help it. I laughed in his face. He scowled at me, his hand shooting through the bars to grab my chin.

"What the fuck is so funny?" he asked.

"Y-y-you," I answered, taking a shaky breath as I struggled to control the hysterical giggles bubbling up inside me. "Who do you think sent me here, Darrell? She knows *everything*. In fact, I don't think it will be long before she and her allies descend on this town and put you all down like the sick animals you are." I wiped the smile off my face, my gaze boring into his. "And I think you know very well what Gram will do to you when she finds out you've killed me."

I saw a shimmer of real fear in his eyes before he blinked and it was gone. My reputation as a fighter was well known in the U.S., but the hushed rumors whispered about my grandmother spread all over the world. Sophia MacArthur was the first female alpha to hold her pack against all challengers for over a hundred years. She was fair and generous to the wolves under her protection, but anyone who crossed her would quickly find out that she was merciless. There would be no hiding from Gram once she realized what he'd done, and Darrell knew it.

The door to the front area of the police department slammed open. Darrell and I both twisted to look at the newcomer.

"Get your hands off her," Brayden Kirkpatrick snarled.

Carefully, Darrell released me, lifting his hands up to show his palms as he backed away.

"No one touches my mate but me," Brayden continued, stalking forward. His voice sounded rusty, as if he used it so little it no longer worked correctly.

I watched him warily as he entered my cell, walking up behind me until I could no longer see him. I felt his hand stroke my hair and fought the instinct to shudder in revulsion.

"Leave, Darrell," Brayden commanded. When Darrell hesitated, Brayden growled low in his throat. Though he was creepy as hell, he was more dominant than Darrell Whelby and they both knew it.

"I'll be back later," Darrell threatened, his eyes darting from me to Lachlan.

Brayden remained utterly still behind me as the older wolf left the room, waiting until the door clicked shut before he moved again. His hands whispered over my hair, down to my shoulders and back. I wondered what he was doing, my body tensing. When his palms came up to squeeze my breasts, Lachlan and I both growled.

"Don't touch me," I commanded, my voice so low that the words were little more than a rumble in my throat.

Without a word, Brayden grabbed the front of my t-shirt and ripped it from collar to hem, his hand coming back up to twist my nipple in a punishing grip.

I couldn't bite back the yelp that emerged from my throat at the pain. Lachlan howled, throwing the weight of his body against his bindings, straining to get free.

Brayden leaned against my back, pressing my naked torso into the bars as he twisted my nipple again. "You're my mate and I will touch you however I like," he hissed.

When I turned my head and tried to bite him, he backed off quickly, releasing my breast. His hand flew up and connected with my cheek in a sharp slap. Though it wasn't pleasant, I'd been hit harder in sparring practice by adolescent wolves. I snapped my teeth at him again.

"You're weaker than most of the pups I train." I hissed.

He hit me again and I laughed, which only made his rage boil higher, but I didn't care.

"I'm not your mate," I stated, leveraging against my bonds in order to face him more fully. "And I never will be."

His only reply was to tear my ruined shirt from my body and shred my underwear. A tendril of fear unfurled inside me as he stripped me naked. He pressed his nose against my shoulder and inhaled, letting me know that he smelled my trepidation. His eyes glinted with malicious amusement. He wanted my fear. He liked it.

Just feet away, Lachlan fought the ropes holding him like a mad creature, snarls and nearly unintelligible threats falling from his lips, but Brayden ignored him. I didn't dare look in his direction and draw Brayden's attention away from me.

He brushed my hair aside, his hands nearly gentle, revealing the bite mark on my neck. The mark that Lachlan had left there just hours ago.

His body crowded mine and I swallowed down the bile that rose in my throat when I felt his erection grind against my ass. "You shouldn't have let him bite you, Chloe," he whispered in my ear.

I tensed and strained against the ropes when his hands moved around my thighs, his fingertips trailing up over my hipbones and belly to my breasts. He cupped them, stroking my nipples. I gagged and bucked, trying to dislodge him, but he merely pressed his weight more firmly against my back, pinning me to the bars. With his cheek brushing mine and his chin resting on the bite, Brayden stared at Lachlan.

"For marking what's mine, you will die, Ian Lachlan," he stated. "But first, I'm going to make you watch me claim my mate while you're powerless to stop me."

His hands released my breasts, one moving up to fist in my hair and angling my head to the side, his grip so tight that tears sprang into my eyes. With my neck bared to him, he struck, his teeth sinking deep into the muscle of my shoulder. Growling low in his throat, he shook his head, tearing into the flesh and destroying the mark that Lachlan had put on me.

I screamed in agony, my back arching hard in an attempt to escape the pain. Only then did Brayden release me.

"There," he crooned as blood dripped down my chest and back. "That's much better."

I heard the telltale clink of his belt buckle and I knew what was coming. The constant thud of Lachlan's body hitting the bars behind him as he fought to free himself pierced the haze that pain had cast over my mind. I looked at him, knowing even if we escaped with our lives, neither of us would be able to get past this. Even if I succeeded in killing Brayden, the ghosts of tonight would drive a permanent wedge between us.

Shrieking, I jerked my hands and feet inward, feeling the rope cutting in to my flesh as I strained. The anchors beneath my feet groaned in protest and I felt a flash of hope. The wall of bars holding me up quivered and squeaked as I pulled harder.

Brayden's hands were on me, trying to hold me still, but I was possessed.

"I AM NOT YOUR MATE!" I roared, feeling the muscles and tendons in my arms stretch to their breaking point.

Suddenly, the ceiling above us caved in with an explosion of debris and dust, and Brayden was thrown away from me.

CHAPTER TWENTY-EIGHT

Lachlan

A CLOUD OF dust obscured Chloe and Brayden from my view. My wolf was howling inside me, fighting to get out. I held onto my control by the thinnest thread. If I shifted, trussed up as I was, my arms and legs would be pulled out of joint.

Instead, I focused on my fingers. If I could keep the change only in my hands, I might be able to shred the ropes enough to break them. Eager to join the fray and kill the male who attacked our she-wolf, the animal inside me cooperated. I'd never attempted a partial shift before. It was dangerous and difficult. Only the oldest, strongest wolves mastered the feat, but right now I was willing to try anything to help the woman I loved.

My fingernails lengthened and sharpened, becoming claws. It hurt like hell. The rest of my body wanted to follow, to shift into wolf form, but I couldn't allow it.

I twisted my wrist until I managed to scrape at the rope stretched taut between the bars and my arm. I glanced at the other cell. The dust was settling and I could see Chloe's shadow, still bound to the bars, and two forms battling behind her.

Someone had come to help us. As I cut at the ropes, I sniffed, sneezing when the dust hit my nostrils. I couldn't smell our rescuer, but I had an idea who it might be. If my guess was correct, he would still be weak.

Finally, the rope snapped and my arm was free. Releasing my other arm and my feet was much quicker. I lunged across the cell. Chloe's eyes met mine, hard and cold. She nodded to me as I split the ropes on her wrists. Crouching down, I reached through the bars and freed her feet.

Without a word, she whirled and jumped into the battle that raged behind her. The dust had settled enough for me to catch a glimpse of the wolf that had crashed through the ceiling. It was Carter Whelby.

The door that led out of the holding area flew open, crashing against the wall. Three of Darrell's officers came in, heading toward the cells. Adrenaline cleared the last of the drugs from my system, my vision sharpening and the nausea fading. Leaping to my feet, I charged.

Rather than fight as shifters did, with fangs and fists, the first officer drew his sidearm, pointing it at me with trembling hands. The first shot grazed my shoulder, but I was on top of him before he could squeeze off another. I ripped the gun from his grasp and my hand sliced across his throat. He gaped at me, his hands clutching the torn flesh as he hit the ground.

The other two wolves reached for their weapons as well, their eyes wheeling wildly. I felt a surge of loathing as I lifted the weapon I still clutched and shot them both without hesitation. They were too weak to hold their position with their shifter abilities, so they would die without the respect of a fair fight.

I glanced out the door, found the police station empty, and turned to aid Carter and Chloe in their fight with Brayden. As I faced the group, a body flew at me from the cell, sending us both through the wall. A figure sprinted past us, his clothing torn and bloody.

Chloe ran after him, stopping only when she saw me sprawled

beneath Carter. She stared after Brayden for only a moment before coming over and helping me shift Carter to the floor.

He groaned, clutching his ribs as his head lolled. "Did we get him?"

A smile tugged at my lips, but it was grim. "He got away."

"Fuck," Carter groaned, rolling onto his side and sitting up. "What about Darrell?"

"Gone," I answered, standing and helping Carter to his feet.

Chloe moved ahead of us, checking the open room that held the officer's desks and the reception area. It was empty.

"We need to leave," she said. "Before they come back."

Carter coughed. "No. We have to get to the safe. This might be our only chance."

Though Chloe gave him a measuring look, she didn't argue. "Where?"

I supported Carter's weight as he led us to Darrell's office. He pulled away from me, staggering behind the massive desk in the center of the room. Falling to his knees, he shoved the office chair aside. The floor beneath the desk appeared to be the same tile that appeared in the front part of the building, until he pressed on one of the squares. There was a quiet click and the tile popped up. Moving it aside, he began pulling out stacks of CD's, flash drives, and printed photographs.

"Take these," he commanded me.

"Where am I supposed to put them? In my pockets?" Chloe was still naked and all I wore were my jeans. There was no way everything in his hands would fit in my pockets. I was itching to get out of this place. There was no telling how many wolves would come with Darrell when he returned.

Chloe appeared at my side, a plastic shopping bag in her hand. Without a word she took the stack of evidence from Carter and shoved it inside. Tying the handles together, she moved to Carter, helping him to his feet.

"Let's get the hell out of here," she declared.

"I have a car hidden a few blocks away. Go out the back," Carter mumbled, leaning heavily on her.

The night was utterly still when we exited the building, the first, faint streaks of dawn appearing in the east. I watched Chloe carefully, looking for any signs that she might still be suffering from the effects of the tranquilizer that Darrell had given us, but she was alert, moving swiftly and silently through the shadows despite her burden.

A few minutes later, we were inside Carter's car, driving away from town. His voice was thick and pained as he gave me directions. The fact that he'd managed to take on an alpha wolf in his weakened condition said more about his commitment to helping us than any vow he could have made.

We arrived at an old farmhouse a half hour from Prater just as the sun rose over the horizon. Chloe and I helped Carter from the car.

"Are you sure this place is safe?" I asked him.

He stumbled, nearly falling to his knees. "Yes. No one knows about the house. Not even my father."

Chloe and I exchanged a look over his head. That's what we'd believed as well. We needed to figure out how Darrell had found us in the first place, but now wasn't the time.

I leaned down and scooped Carter in my arms. He groaned in pain but didn't argue as I carried him up the steps to the door.

"Key?" Chloe asked, coming around to open the door.

"My right pocket."

She gingerly fished it out his pocket and unlocked the knob, pushing the door open for us.

As I entered the house, Carter asked, "You gonna give me a kiss while you carry me across the threshold?"

I heard Chloe chuckle behind me. Considering the ordeal she'd just been through, the fact that he made her laugh meant I owed him a debt I could never repay.

"Where's your bedroom?" I asked.

"Whoa, now I am not that kind of girl," he slurred.

"Maybe I should just drop you if you're feeling well enough to joke," I muttered.

"Up the stairs, second door on the left," he replied.

Chloe was still smirking when she followed us into Carter's bedroom, but the smile faded when she got a clear look at his injuries.

"Get me some towels and hot water," I commanded, leaning over Carter's prone body on the bed. "I'm going to get him cleaned up and see what I can do for him."

"I'll heal," he argued weakly. "Just bring me some water and some ibuprofen."

"Ibuprofen thins the blood, you idiot," Chloe retorted testily. "Just let us get you sorted out."

I ripped Carter's t-shirt down the middle, revealing the cuts and massive purple bruises on his abdomen.

"Okay, I'm really beginning to think you have a thing for me. First you carry me into my bedroom and now you're tearing my clothes off."

I prodded the worst of the bruising, making him hiss with pain. "Sure, once you're healed I'll take you out for dinner and dancing."

He rolled his eyes. "You're definitely not my type. Dinner and dancing? When were you born? In the 1940's?"

"Yeah, 1942."

He chuckled harshly. "Damn, you look pretty good for an old fucker."

"How touching," Chloe said dryly as she re-entered the room. "Should I give you two another moment?"

I glared at her. "Just bring me the stuff."

She and I worked together, cleaning Carter's wounds. He tried to refuse when we began licking the worst of the cuts, but we ignored him.

"Shut up," Chloe demanded. "You saved our asses and we're going to help you in any way we can."

He stopped protesting. By the time we were done, his breathing was much easier and the bruising on his abdomen was fading. The internal bleeding had stopped as his body healed itself.

Chloe helped me strip him naked and draped a sheet over him.

As his eyes closed, Carter mumbled, "There's clothes and stuff in the other bedroom. Take whatever you need."

We waited until his breathing was deep and even before we left the room.

As I closed the bedroom door behind us, I said, "I need to see to your injuries, Chloe."

She turned toward me, looking exhausted in the morning light. "They're probably all healed by now."

I glanced at the savage bite mark on her neck and she winced, looking away.

"I'll tend to it," she stated quietly.

"No, I'll do it. I'm going to have to help close the bite with saliva," I insisted.

Her shoulders drooped as she gave me her back and walked into the bathroom. "Just let me take a shower first. I'm covered in blood and dust." Then she shut the bathroom door in my face.

With a sigh, I found the other bedroom Carter had mentioned and rummaged around until I found a pair of men's boxers and a t-shirt. It wasn't ideal, but I thought she might want some clothing between her injured skin and the coarse sheets on the spare bed.

When I entered the bathroom, she was just stepping out of the shower.

"You should get cleaned up too," she suggested. "So I can see if your cuts need treatment as well."

I sensed that she wasn't ready for me to touch the bite wound on her neck yet, so I did as she asked. The water ran black and red as I washed the blood and dirt from my skin as quickly as possible. A few minutes later, I climbed out of the tub and snagged the towel she'd left hanging on the rack for me.

I dried off and slipped on the shorts I'd found for myself. Chloe was no longer in the bathroom, but I found her sitting on the side of the bed in the spare bedroom. Her hair was wrapped in a towel and she was wearing the clothes I laid out for her.

"Thanks for finding these," she said.

I nodded. "No problem." She tensed as I moved behind her. Seeing it, I shifted to the side closest to her injured shoulder but still within her sightline. "I need you to take off the shirt so I can see the bite," I stated, keeping my voice soothing.

Exhaling heavily, she lifted the shirt over her head, taking the towel with it. Gently, I shifted the damp strands of her hair to the side, revealing the ragged edges of Brayden's handiwork. Though it had been hours since he'd bitten her, the wound still oozed blood and the skin was healing in some places, but unevenly. The scarring would be deep and likely permanent.

Rage filled me at the sight. Not just of another male's bite on her body, but the pain it symbolized. Her pain. Swallowing a growl, I leaned forward and slid my tongue along the one side of the injury, then the other.

Chloe made a small sound, shifting slightly away from me. I knew that my ministrations hurt, but they were necessary. With my saliva, the scarring wouldn't be as bad.

I worked as quickly and gently as I possibly could until the bleeding stopped and the marks left by Brayden's fangs were pink where the skin was healing.

When I lifted my head, she immediately put on the shirt she clutched against her chest.

"Thank you," she whispered. Clearing her throat, she looked at me. "What about your wounds?"

I looked down at the bullet graze on my arm. It had already closed on its own, a scab forming on my skin. By tomorrow it would be gone. The rest of my lacerations had been superficial.

"I'm good."

She nodded. "Okay, well, I'm going to try to sleep for a few hours."

"That's a good idea."

She crawled into the far side of the bed, giving me her back. I stared at the curve of her shoulder for a long moment, hating the fact that my fierce she-wolf was so quiet and complacent.

As I stood and walked across the hall to check on Carter, I decided then and there that Brayden Kirkpatrick would die the most painful death I could think of, and I'd had occasion to think of a fair number of ways to kill a wolf slowly.

CHAPTER TWENTY-NINE

Chloe

I LISTENED TO Lachlan leave the room, my heart aching in my chest. When he was gone, I closed my eyes and felt the first tear trickle down my cheek.

The events of the past twelve hours were straight out of a nightmare. With trembling fingers, I reached up and touched the ruined tissues on the side of my neck. I felt a surge of rage. I wanted to kill Brayden Kirkpatrick so badly that it hurt. With the bite he'd left on me, I would be scarred for life. There would be no way to cleanse myself of the stink of his mark.

When he was dead and no longer able to assert a claim on me, I would find Darrell Whelby.

I heard the soft murmur of Lachlan's voice and realized he was talking to Calder. I hadn't even thought about calling my grandmother or Calder. My mind had only been on getting away from Prater and helping Carter survive his injuries.

I couldn't fall apart now. There was too much at stake. When it was all over, I would have time.

Lachlan returned to the bedroom, pulling the drapes over the windows before he climbed into the bed behind me. I stiffened when his arms closed around me, my back to his front. I didn't want another wolf at my back. Not today and maybe never again.

The memory of what Brayden had done to me in that cell, and that he intended to do more, was too fresh.

Then I felt Lachlan's lips brush over the scar tissue rapidly forming on my shoulder and it was too much.

I twisted, backing into the wall against the bed and shoving him at the same time. My breath came in rapid pants as I held my hands out between us.

"Don't," I whispered, holding on to my control by a thread.

The sadness in his eyes was too much. He pitied me and I couldn't take it. I lashed out, my closed fist hitting his shoulder.

"Do not look at me like that," I growled. "Don't you fucking *pity me*." I spat the last words out because I hated the taste of them on my tongue.

I hit him again, rocking his body back on the mattress. Even now, seeing the way he was looking at me, I couldn't bring myself to use the full force of my strength.

Lachlan's hand lifted, curving around my face. When his thumb swept across my cheekbone, I felt the dampness he spread across my skin. I was crying again, the tears burning my eyes and blurring my vision.

"I don't pity you, Chloe. I've never known anyone as fierce or as brave as you." His eyes shone with sincerity as he spoke, his thumb still caressing my skin. "I just want to hold you while we sleep so that I know you're really here." He shook his head against the pillow. "Not want. I *need* to do it. I won't be able to rest without knowing that I have you close."

He didn't try to force me closer, just moved his palm down my neck and curved his fingers around my shoulder, stroking my arm.

"Can we do that?" he asked. "Just lay here together?"

The fight left me then. He spoke of my ferocity and my bravery, but there was nothing left in me at that moment except exhaustion. I knew he wouldn't push me. If I told him no, he'd let it go.

But I didn't want to say no. I wanted to lean on him for a while, to let him be strong while I could not.

Inching forward, I lined our bodies up so that I faced him, my nose pressed against his chest. He didn't try to hold me there. Lachlan bent the arm beneath him, resting his head on his bicep. His other draped lightly over my hips. Not pinning me down, just touching me.

As I inhaled his scent, the wild pounding of my heart began to slow and the terrible tightness in my chest loosened. I could feel my muscles relaxing against him, giving in to my heart's desire to be close to my mate.

His lips brushed my hair tenderly and I bit my lip to keep a sob from escaping. I wondered if this was what he felt all those months ago when our roles had been reversed and he was the weak one that I cared for.

The hurt filled every part of my body, but his proximity was a balm, easing the worst of the pain even if it couldn't remove it completely.

"I'm here, Chloe," he whispered. "You can sleep now. I'll always be here."

I closed my eyes, shutting out the lie as much as giving in to fatigue, and I slept.

LACHLAN'S BODY LURCHED, jolting me awake. Then he was out of the bed and across the room, looking out the window.

"Someone's here," he whispered.

He put an eye to a crack in the drapes then cursed. "Shit. The cavalry has arrived."

I rolled out of bed and crossed to the window. He moved to

the side to let me look. In the driveway, the doors were thrown open in two SUV's and I saw familiar wolves climbing out. I was also surprised to see a vampire among them.

Calder drove one of the vehicles and behind the wheel of the other was Finn, the vampire mate of Ricki's friend, Kerry. Despite Lachlan's words, I was glad to see them.

Until the passenger stepped out of Calder's SUV. Her back was straight and rigid, her shoulder-length honey blond hair lifting in the slight breeze. As if she could sense my eyes on her, my grandmother looked up to the window, meeting my gaze.

My father had often joked that my grandmother and I looked more like sisters, despite the one hundred and fifty year age difference. He'd also stated many times that the reason we fought so often was because we were too much alike. It was strange because the reasons we fought usually became the same reasons we got along. Sophia MacArthur was a formidable wolf, regardless of her age or sex.

I didn't want her to see me in this state, marked by a male I despised. A wolf I'd let go instead of chasing him down and killing him.

Even at this distance, I could see her jaw tighten.

"We'd better go downstairs," I murmured to Lachlan. "Will you check on Carter?"

He nodded, his hand taking mine for a moment, squeezing gently. Then he left the room.

I stood by the window a few seconds longer and took a deep breath, gathering myself for the conversation to come. Once my shield was in place, I went downstairs and opened the front door for the wolves that had come to help us.

My grandmother was already on the porch, waiting by the door. She looked me over carefully, her eyes lingering on the fresh bite on my shoulder. I knew she could smell Brayden's scent emanating from the mark when her lips drew into a thin line.

"The Kirkpatrick's are dead," she muttered.

To my complete shock, when her eyes lifted to mine, there were tears shimmering on the lower lids. She took a deep breath, blinked, and they disappeared.

Then she hugged me tightly and kissed my cheek, surprising me further. My grandmother could be affectionate, but never in front of other wolves, especially those from another pack. It spoke a great deal to the trust she placed in Calder.

"I love you, Chloe." The words were whispered so softly that not even the nearby wolves would have been able to hear them.

"I love you too," I murmured in return, my voice barely audible.

My grandmother's right hand, Nicholas, came up behind her, his black eyes going directly to the wound on my neck and turning hard. "Chloe," he rumbled by way of greeting.

Calder, Mason, Shane, and Finn came up the stairs. Two unfamiliar wolves loitered by the cars and I realized they were from Gram's pack.

Lachlan emerged from the house, shaking hands with everyone. As the ritual of greeting wound down, Finn sidled up to me.

"Hi, Finn," I said, meeting his beautiful amethyst gaze. He was one of the few vampires that didn't raise my hackles. I liked Conner, Lex, and Asher well enough, but Finn had something inherently soothing in his manner. I assumed it came from the Druid magic in his blood because I got the same sense of peace from Kerry, his mate.

His eyes swept over my face, taking in every detail, before skimming down to my shoulder, where the fresh scar was partially covered by the t-shirt I wore.

"Hi, Chloe." He nodded toward my shoulder. "May I?"

I wanted to shy away, to hide the mark, but I squared my

shoulders. I was a MacArthur and I'd be damned if I let myself give in to the urge.

I tugged the material away, watching Finn's face as I did.

His eyes flared, the purple depths glowing from within, as he took in the damage. "May I try something?" he asked. He looked to me for confirmation before his gaze flicked briefly to Lachlan, who nodded in approval.

I frowned, wondering why in the hell he thought he needed Lachlan's okay.

Finn's hand lifted, hovering over my shoulder. He began to chant in a language I'd never heard before. His eyes grew brighter and brighter until I could no longer bear to look at them. The skin beneath his palm tingled, then stung. Heat built beneath my skin and I sucked in a sharp breath at the burn, but I forced myself to remain still.

Then I felt it. Somewhere deep in the muscles of my shoulder and neck, I felt twitching and warmth. It built to nearly an unbearable level, bringing a low whine from my throat.

Lachlan's hand closed around mine and I gripped it tightly, fighting the instinct to flinch from the pain.

"Almost done," Finn muttered softly. "I know it hurts."

I gritted my teeth and held on. Finally, the agony began to fade, the burn settling into a comforting glow.

"There," Finn said, rubbing his hands together. I saw lavender and silver sparks falling from his fingers, disappearing before they could hit the porch.

I lifted my hand, running my fingertips over my neck. Beneath my touch all I felt was smooth, unblemished skin.

Then I did something I never thought I would do. Especially not in front of my grandmother or Calder. Or any other wolf for that matter.

I threw myself at a vampire, wrapping my arms around his neck.

CHAPTER THIRTY

Lachlan

FINN'S EYES MET mine over Chloe's head and I mouthed, "Thank you."

He nodded, just a subtle tilt of his head.

I'd felt the way Chloe tensed when my lips touched the wound this morning while we were in bed. If the scar remained, every time she looked in the mirror, she would be reminded of that night.

I owed the vampire something I could never repay because he'd not only healed the wound, he'd saved Chloe from more pain.

While I held her in the early morning hours, I'd realized why I'd been so desperate to stop what was happening in that cell. I knew she would fight until Brayden killed her before she would submit to a forced mating.

And I could no longer imagine a life without Chloe in it.

At the realization, something stirred within me. An instinct I never thought I would feel again. The urge to mate. To mark her as mine.

As I watched Chloe release Finn, I knew that discussion would have to wait. We had wolves to track and a pack to save.

But when it was all over, we would talk. I only hoped she would listen.

Carter appeared in the front door, still pale and a little stooped, but he looked much better.

"We need to talk," he stated, his eyes taking in the wolves on his porch, pausing on the single vampire in the group. He took Finn's presence in stride without a word, gesturing for us to follow him.

We filed inside and trailed behind Carter into the living room. In one corner a bank of monitors and speakers was set up, showing different camera feeds of Prater.

"Darrell's gone off the deep end," Carter stated grimly, gesturing to the screens. He turned up the speakers and voices began to filter into the room.

I watched in horror as Darrell and two of his deputies dragged a family from their home, mates and their two female pups. One deputy had a tight grip on the little ones' hair, lifting them onto their toes as they walked. Darrell had secured the parents' hands behind their backs but I could see the fear and rage on their faces as they stumbled behind.

Carter pointed to another screen, which showed the ruined cell room in the police department. Two more families waited inside, mates and children. One of the she-wolves was hunched over, but when she straightened I realized with horror that she was pregnant.

"What the fuck is this?" Calder asked, his voice furious and rough.

"He sent me a text message," Carter replied, lifting his phone. "He's taking families that helped me. All this time, he's known and he's just been watching and waiting for me to make a move so he had a legitimate reason to kill us all."

"We have to help them," Chloe said, her eyes intense. Frighteningly so.

My eyes were caught by another camera feed, this one in Darrell's office at the police department.

I pointed to the screen. "What are they saying? Do you have sound for that room?"

Carter nodded, fiddling with the computer he had set up on the table next to the monitors.

Suddenly Brayden's voice filled the room.

"Where is she?" he snarled. "She's my mate and I want her here!"

Brian sat behind Darrell's desk, looking completely at ease. "We'll find her, son. Just be patient a bit longer. With what Darrell is doing, I doubt it will be long before she comes to us."

"She should have been mine already," Brayden growled, shoving his hands through his hair as he paced back and forth in the office. "If you'd let me take her when I wanted to, none of this would have happened."

"People would have talked if she mated right after her parents died, Brayden. They would have suspected that you forced her and we would've ended up in front of the Tribunal answering uncomfortable questions about forced mating."

"Then why in the fuck did we hire Darrell to kill them? Huh?" Brayden stopped pacing, some of the madness leaving his face. "This had nothing to do with what I wanted," he stated with sudden clarity. "It was you. You wanted the pack. You knew you couldn't take it from Matthew MacArthur, so you had Darrell kill him. Now you're letting someone else do your dirty work again, hoping Carter and Lachlan will kill Darrell for you."

The older wolf smiled. "Finally, you're beginning to think the way an alpha should."

My fists clenched and I glanced at Chloe. Her face was pale and her eyes burned with fury. Sophia MacArthur was much better at hiding her rage, but I could smell it as it swelled. Her face gave nothing away, but there was no way she could hide the scent.

"We need to get into town right now," Carter insisted. "I know my father. He's going to start killing wolves until I show up." His eyes were haunted as he looked at me. "He'll start with the weakest."

The pups, I realized with horror.

"We can't just go in there with guns blazing," Sophia argued. "We need a plan."

Carter's eyes fired. "Oh, I have a plan. I'm going to kill the motherfucker like I should have years ago."

"She's right," Chloe stated. "We need a plan." When Carter looked as though he were about to argue, she lifted a hand. "But we'll decide quickly. We have the advantage of strength and numbers. Darrell and his deputies aren't as strong as any of us. Brian Kirkpatrick is just as likely to stand back and watch Darrell die as he is to fight." Her jaw hardened. "And Brayden is mine."

Something like admiration crossed Carter's face.

Chloe glanced down at her body. "I need clothes," she stated. "Something more substantial than boxers and a t-shirt."

"I took care of that," Sophia replied. "Your bags are in the car."

"I'll get them," Nicholas stated, moving silently out of the room.

"Now, how are we going to do this?" Calder asked Carter. "You know the best ways into town, correct?"

"So does Chloe," Carter answered, looking to her.

"Then let's figure out how we're going to get in there without detection and take care of the fuckers," Calder said.

I watched as Finn stepped forward. "I think I can help you with that."

"How?" I asked.

A sly smile crossed his face as he answered, "With magic of course."

FIVE MINUTES LATER, we were crowded around the map of the town that Carter had pinned to the wall.

We agreed to split into three groups. Chloe, Finn, and I would be together. Sophia, Carter, Shane, and Nicholas would enter the town from the opposite side. Calder, Mason, and the two wolves that Sophia brought, Paul and Greg, would make up the final group.

Surprisingly, there was very little arguing over strategy, especially when Finn detailed how he intended to help us.

"I can mask your scent with a spell," he explained. "And another that will make you difficult to see. It's not invisibility exactly and it only works when you aren't moving quickly, but it should be enough to get us into town undetected."

I was beginning to see the variety of advantages that came with having a vampire warlock as a friend.

Chloe and I dressed quickly once the general plan was in place. I shot a look at Carter, concerned about his pale appearance. I worried he wouldn't have the strength to continue.

Finn must have shared my thoughts because he approached the wolf cautiously. "You're too weak to fight in your current state." When Carter bristled, he lifted a hand. "I'm offering to help you. I can heal most of your injuries if you'll allow me."

"Will that affect your ability to cast the spell to hide us?" Carter asked, obviously surprising Finn with his knowledge.

"Normally, yes, but Kerry is sharing her power with me. I will have plenty left if I heal you."

Carter eyed him for a prolonged moment before nodding. "I would appreciate your help then."

"I'll need you to stand completely still for me until I'm done," Finn directed. "And the deeper the injury, the more this will...sting."

"Great," Carter exhaled. I knew that many of his internal injuries were already better, but they weren't fully healed.

"Maybe he should sit down," I suggested to Finn.

Carter didn't even argue. He moved to the couch and lowered himself onto it, leaning back against the cushions. I moved to stand behind him in case he tried to move or stop Finn when the pain intensified. Finn nodded in approval of my position and knelt in front of Carter. Using both hands and starting at Carter's ankles, Finn seemed to stroke the air around the wolf.

A pale glow spilled from Finn's palms and echoing light appeared on different areas of Carter's body. Finn's eyebrows lifted as he took in the size and number of pulsing lights. I realized I was looking at Carter's wounds, both internal and external, and I couldn't believe the wolf was still standing, much less preparing to go into battle.

As Finn moved his palms to cover two areas, he closed his eyes. Carter sucked in a deep breath, his hands fisting at his sides, but he didn't move. He didn't even make a sound.

Until Finn reached the largest area on his abdomen. It was the place where I'd seen the deep bruising and known Carter had internal bleeding. When the light brightened, I squinted.

Carter grunted, his shoulders jerking, but the rest of his body remained completely still. I could hear his teeth grinding together as he endured the pain, but he never moved again.

When it was finally over, Carter relaxed against the back of the couch, breathing hard.

"I don't know if you're a fool or the most valiant wolf I've ever met," Finn muttered, staring at Carter with glowing purple eyes.

"I'd go with the first one," Carter panted, squeezing his eyes shut as the residual pain wracked his body. However, his color was much better, his cheeks no longer white and the fine lines around his eyes vanishing.

"Me too," I agreed.

One of his eyes popped open. "Oh, hey there. You gonna kiss my booboos better?"

"He's definitely healed if he's hitting on me," I stated, rolling my eyes. "Be careful, Carter, or I'll ask Sophia to do it."

His eyes shot to the she-wolf, who bared her teeth. "Uh, I appreciate that, but I'm feeling much better now."

Chloe came forward with a bottle of water. "Drink this. We need to get on the road."

Carter's eyes moved to Finn. "Thank you," he said quietly.

"You're welcome."

Carter drained the water bottle and got to his feet, rolling his shoulders and straightening his spine as if to test his muscles.

Then he smiled, but it was thin and vicious.

"Let's go."

CHAPTER THIRTY-ONE

Chloe

THE TOWN WAS unusually quiet as we approached. Though there were a few hundred residents, there were no cars on the streets and no lights on inside the homes. It was as if the town was sleeping.

Or dead.

I shook off the unsettling thoughts. No one was dead yet. We'd been watching via Carter's laptop. They were waiting for us, but I doubted they realized exactly what they were up against. If they had, it wouldn't just be Darrell, his two remaining deputies, and the Kirkpatricks.

Though we outnumbered them, they were all armed with guns and knives. It sickened me that they were too cowardly to face us with fangs and fists, as was custom in shifter communities. They knew they weren't strong enough to win without them and counted on firepower to replace strength, speed, and skill.

I couldn't see the others or even smell them, but I knew they were there. Finn's spell worked better than any of us had thought it would.

We crept through the streets, moving silently. Finn explained that the spell would be impossible to hold once we attacked as all his focus would need to be on fighting, but it gave us the advantage of surprise.

As we approached the police department, I could hear the shifters talking amongst themselves. The prisoners were scared but trying to keep their children calm. Darrell and the rest were discussing what our possible strategy might be and how to defend against it.

When we reached the rear of the building, I took the key Carter had given me out of my pocket. Finn was up front, holding the spell. He would have to release it when he set off the distraction he had planned. I doubted they would go outside to investigate, but it would at least serve as a chance for us to sneak in the back without gaining their attention.

Carter had checked the roof and the hatch he used the night before was chained shut. He'd merely shaken his head and gone to a house a few streets over. He'd returned with a "borrowed" set of bolt cutters and climbed back up, Nicholas on his heels. Carter insisted that Darrell would go straight for the hostages if he thought he wouldn't be able to escape, and he wouldn't let his father kill any more innocent wolves.

I took a deep breath and waited for the signal. Finn assured us all earlier that he had something special planned. As we stood still, waiting, Lachlan was tense beside me, his body vibrating with ferocity. Even as we faced danger and possibly death, he was more alive than he had been for two years. Whether he wanted it or not, the events in this town had brought him completely back into the land of the living.

Silently, I fit the key into the lock, not turning it, but ready. A loud explosion rocked the building, coming from the parking lot to the side. I twisted the key and cracked the door to peek through. There was no one in the back room.

Lachlan shoved the door open, rushing in before me with Finn right on his heels. I could hear shouting from the front of the building and the screams and sobs of the families in the holding cells.

I followed Lach and Finn down the hall, moving quickly. We didn't want to get caught here when they realized we were coming. It would be too easy to shoot down the hall and take us all out.

Lach crouched at the mouth of the hall, his eyes toward the front. Finn moved to the other side of the doorway and peered through as well. When Lach motioned us forward, we stayed low and crept through the file room.

I nearly laughed when I looked out and saw all the wolves standing near the front windows. They'd made themselves perfect targets.

Except for Darrell.

He edged back, toward the room where we waited. He might not be strong enough to take be a true alpha, but he was cunning. Darrell knew that the fireball that had enveloped his car was just a distraction.

We stayed out of sight as he backed up a few more steps before turning and heading straight for the file room where we waited. As soon as he stepped through the door, Finn was on him.

I watched in surprise as the vampire's eyes glowed a brilliant purple. Darrell slumped in his grasp, unconscious. Without a word, Finn dragged him to the door at the rear of the room. When he opened it, I saw cleaning supplies. After he stuffed Darrel inside, Finn shut the door and waved his hand over the knob. I knew without asking that he'd locked the door to anyone but himself.

Lach shifted beside me and I looked out toward the front room again. My mouth dropped open when I realized that Darrell's two remaining officers were exiting the front door, their guns drawn. Brian and Brayden Kirkpatrick clutched their own weapons, two shotguns.

I wondered if it truly was going to be that easy, shaking my head at their stupidity.

As soon as the thought crossed my mind, all hell broke loose. I heard the gunfire exploding outside as Calder, Mason, my grandmother, and her men, Paul and Greg attacked. Brian Kirkpatrick turned, heading straight for us.

Unfortunately, Lach didn't move out of sight quickly enough and Brian raised his shotgun and fired. The pellets hit Lach, blood spreading on his shoulder and chest. Then Brian turned, fired a shot out a side window, and dove through.

I glanced up front, but Brayden's attention was riveted to the window his father disappeared through. I leapt to Lachlan's side, ripping his shirt open to examine his injuries. My pounding heart slowed a little when I realized he'd only been hit by a few pellets.

"Thank God," I whispered under my breath.

I looked back to see Finn brushing pellets off his shirt as well. A few had entered his skin, leaving dots of blood behind, but it appeared as if the rest had been halted by an invisible shield around his torso.

"He okay?" Finn mouthed.

I nodded.

The sound of crunching glass brought my attention to the front of the department again, just in time to see Brayden Kirkpatrick disappear out of the same window his father had used.

"Like hell," I murmured.

The sound of gunshots outside stopped abruptly and I knew that Darrell's two officers were down. Without hesitation, I jumped to my feet and sprinted after the Kirkpatricks.

I heard Lachlan call my name but ignored it. I would *not* let either of the Kirkpatricks get away with what they had done. Not only had Brayden tried to force me to mate him, but, for reasons I still didn't understand, they'd arranged for the death of my parents. I wanted to know why. Then I fully intended to kill them both.

I paused at the edge of the parking lot, inhaling deeply. Brayden's scent was the strongest so I followed his trail. Wherever he went, his father would only be a few steps ahead.

As I followed the scent, I cursed the fact that it was broad daylight outside and we were in town. I felt exposed as I darted down the street, my eyes moving from side to side.

The trail disappeared into a copse of trees on the edge of the city limits. I glanced back for a moment but didn't see anyone behind me. I hesitated. I knew I should wait for the others. It was the smart thing to do.

Then I remembered the horrible pain of Brayden's bite, the way he'd touched my body as if he had every right, and I knew I wouldn't wait. I couldn't.

Sniffing the air one last time, I followed the trail Brayden left behind.

CHAPTER THIRTY-TWO

Lachlan

I GROANED WHEN Chloe ripped my shirt open, tiny points of fire prickling along my shoulder and chest. I saw the relief in her eyes when she realized I wasn't gravely injured.

Then, before I could stop her, she was gone.

"Chloe! Chloe, wait! Fuck, Finn, grab her!" I yelled. "Don't let her go alone!"

He was too late. She'd climbed out of the same window as the Kirkpatricks and she was gone.

I hauled myself to my feet, Finn appearing beside me.

"I'm sorry, Lachlan," he apologized. "I couldn't reach her in time."

"Goddammit, I hate getting shot," I gritted out through clenched teeth. "It hurts like fuck."

Finn studied my injuries for a moment. "You've got a bleeder there," he said finally. His hand moved over my shoulder and I could almost feel the energy focusing on the point where one pellet had entered my body. I grunted as it popped out of the hole. It hit the ground with a ping and rolled away.

Then I felt the heat and clenched my jaw against the pain. A few moments later it subsided. Finn waved his hand over my flesh again and I flinched as the rest of the pellets slid from my skin, the sound of them hitting the ground like rain.

"I can't heal the rest of your wounds," Finn stated apologetical-ly. "There are others who need me more and I don't want to take too much power from Kerry."

I nodded. "I appreciate it. Tell the others I'm going after Chloe. Calder should be able to track me."

Finn nodded and I felt his eyes watching me as I launched myself through the window and immediately found Chloe's trail. I traced her steps through town and paused at the edge of the trees. I sniffed the air, and then crouched in order to get my nose closer to the ground. I smelled a combination of scents. Chloe, Brayden, and Brian.

My mate was out there alone with two armed wolves. I growled low in my throat and followed. The Kirkpatricks had hurt her enough. I wouldn't allow them to do it again.

I tracked them through the woods, stopping to listen or exam-ine a footprint.

The only warning I got of his presence was the sound of a shotgun ratcheting. I barely had time to ascertain where the sound originated before the first shot went off. I managed to dive behind a tree trunk. I could hear the pellets as they hit the trees and brush around me.

I heard the pump again and lunged behind another tree, this one larger than the last. He shot at me as I moved, but he missed again.

That was two shots. I wondered if he had reloaded after he ran from the police department. Even if he had, it was likely he only had three left. Maybe four if the gun held six shells.

Either way, I didn't intend to get shot again. Once a decade was enough for me. There was another pump of the shotgun and I could hear him shifting around, trying to find a better position, but he was downwind of me and I couldn't get a lock on his scent.

Swearing silently, I glanced around the edge of the trunk. Pellets splintered the bark near my shoulder.

"Fuck," I hissed as pieces of bark and splintered wood rained down on me.

There was another pump, then silence. The nearest tree was nearly ten feet away, and though I had shifter speed, so did Brian Kirkpatrick. Leaves rustled and I could hear him suck in a quick breath. He was moving again.

I needed to distract him, throw him off until he ran out of shells. There was no chance I could work my way to him without getting hit otherwise. The trees were too far apart, letting the sunlight pierce the canopy. I wouldn't be able to hide my movements. My only choice was to divert his attention and get him to take shots at me until he was out of shells.

"You do realize you're going to die today, right?" I asked him, keeping my tone conversational. "Even if I don't kill you, one of the other wolves will."

"If they can find me before I get to Houston. Not even Sophia MacArthur would trespass on my pack territory."

I snorted. "Wouldn't she? You arranged to have her son killed and helped Darrell kidnap Chloe for Brayden. I think she'd rain hellfire down on your pack, consequences from the Tribunal be damned."

He was silent and I knew he was mulling over my words. He knew they were true. I leapt behind another tree, but no shot followed. He was off balance and this was my chance.

From my new vantage point, I could barely see the side of his face. He was still looking toward the tree where I'd been, unaware that I'd moved. The wind shifted, carrying my scent away from him, and I smiled.

Moving noiselessly through the trees and underbrush, I crept closer.

"I still can't let you live, Lachlan," he called. "Otherwise I won't have any chance of surviving myself."

I was only a few feet from him now, praying that the wind wouldn't change again and give away my position. He lifted the shotgun, still aiming toward the tree where I'd been hiding moments ago.

"If you come out now, I'll make it quick and as painless as possible."

Before he could react I was on him, my hand coming down on the barrel of the shotgun. The gun went off, but it was too late. I had him in my grasp. Jerking the weapon out of his hand, I hit him with my right fist, using every bit of my strength.

He sprawled on the ground, his eyes glassy and unfocused.

"I can't promise you the same," I said. Then I brought the butt of the shotgun down on his temple.

I pulled my cell phone out of my pocket and turned it on, noting that Calder had called several times. I tapped the screen, calling his number.

"Where are you?" he demanded.

"In the woods, southwest of town. About a half-mile in."

"Were those shots you?"

"Yeah. I've got Brian here and he's unconscious. I need one of you to get here quickly. I have to go after Chloe."

"I'm on my way," Calder replied. I could hear the sound of his running feet through the phone. "I'll be there in less than five minutes."

I glanced down at Brian Kirkpatrick. I couldn't wait. If he woke up and managed to escape before Calder got here, then I would just track him down again. Right now, my priority was Chloe.

"I can't wait for you. You'll pick up my trail on Hedgecoxe Drive. Follow it and you'll find Brian."

"Lachlan, wait—"

"Chloe's on her own and going after Brayden, Calder. I will not let my mate die again."

"Mate?"

I growled. "I don't have time for this. I'm shutting off my phone."

Without waiting for a response, I disconnected and turned off my phone. I did take the time to secure Brian's wrists together behind his back with the twist ties Carter had given me. Then I bent his legs, using several more ties to attach the bands around his ankles to those on his wrists. I didn't want to waste precious time, but I also wanted to make sure that it wouldn't be easy for the wolf to sneak up behind me as I tracked Brayden and Chloe.

With that done, I walked back to the place where I'd last scented Chloe.

When I picked it up, I began running. I would not lose another mate. I couldn't survive it.

Then I heard the sound of another shotgun blast and I ran faster, the taste of uncontrollable fear on my tongue.

CHAPTER THIRTY-THREE

Chloe

I COULD HEAR Brayden breathing as I followed him. I was grateful for those days that Lachlan tracked me. I'd learned a few tricks that were serving me well right now. Only this time I was the hunter rather than the prey.

I stopped moving when Brayden paused and looked behind him. He was panting and I could smell the fear from where I squatted behind underbrush. The idiot was so concerned about looking behind him that he never noticed me to his left, just out of range of his peripheral vision. I'd been hiding the best I could, but the trees weren't as dense as the forest around Darrell's cabin. If he turned his head at just the right time, he would spot me.

Brayden started moving again. He was trying to be quiet, but he sucked at it. I shook my head as I took another step, moving behind a tree.

A shotgun blast made us both pause. Brayden looked behind him again, turning his back completely to me. Now was my opportunity.

I crept closer, using the sound of the next shot to cover my movements. I was almost on top of him when the third blast sounded. He must have sensed me because just as I pounced, he turned.

His eyes widened and he lifted the shotgun, but I was too close. I knocked the gun to the side, free of his hands. My ears rang and I smelled the powder when the gun went off so close to my head, but there was no time to worry about it.

He recovered quickly, shoving me back and making a dive for the weapon. But he underestimated the strength of my fury. The strength of *me*.

I grabbed his shoulders, jerked him back, and kicked the shotgun as hard as I could toward the trees. It disappeared into the underbrush ten feet away.

Brayden whirled on me, his teeth snapping. When my fist crashed into his nose, annihilating the bones and cartilage, I felt fierce satisfaction. I followed that blow with two more, one to his gut and the other to his jaw.

Shaking his head, Brayden stumbled back. He clutched his abdomen where my fist had sunk into his belly. Then he reached for his knife.

I bared my teeth at him. "Coward," I snarled. "You're too weak and spineless to fight me claw and tooth the way a true alpha would. How you thought you were strong enough to be my mate, I'll never know. I would have chewed you up and spit you out the moment you let your guard down."

He screamed at me, lunging forward. He might have been a coward and an idiot, but it quickly became clear that he knew how to use the knife he wielded. I evaded his slices and thrusts, looking for my opening.

He was a decent fighter, fast and strong, but he lacked the ability to observe his opponent dispassionately. He also wasn't as fast as me. Though my blood burned with rage and the desire to kill him, I controlled it. Then I watched and took note of his movements as he attacked.

My father had drilled that into me from childhood—always

fight with your head first. Emotions could easily blind you and make you sloppy.

Finally, I saw my opening. Brayden lunged again, swinging the knife in an arc. Instead of evading, I stepped into it, my hand lifting to grip his wrist. Then I used his own momentum to throw him to the ground, his wrist still in my grasp.

I heard the bone snap just before he screamed in agony. I smiled as I took the knife from his limp hand and threw it toward a tree. It pierced the bark, the blade sinking into the wood halfway to the hilt.

Brayden scrambled away from me on his back before jumping to his feet.

"There, now we're evenly matched," I told him with a triumphant smile.

His face turned red. "You bitch," he growled, cradling his broken wrist. "I'm going to kill you. You could have been my mate, my everything, but instead you acted like a whore," he spat. "You fucked Lachlan. You let him *mark* what is mine!"

An unholy light came into his eyes and I realized that Brayden Kirkpatrick had lost his grip on reality a long time ago. I couldn't believe that I never noticed.

When he mentioned the mark, I lifted my hand to my now smooth shoulder. His eyes followed the motion, widening in shock. "It's gone. How?" His red face turned purple as he charged me. "What did you do to my mark, you cunt?"

I planted my feet, letting him run toward me in his rage. Just before he reached me, I stepped to the side and jabbed my hand into his throat. His feet flew up and I slammed him onto the ground, holding onto his neck with rigid fingers.

His eyes rolled when his head hit the hard earth and I heard the air leave his lungs. Winded, he twitched and flailed.

"I got rid of your mark, Brayden," I murmured, leaning closer.

"Because you had no right to claim me. So I'm going to tell you one last time—I'm not your goddamn mate and I never will be."

I must have missed the knife sticking out of his boot earlier. I gasped when it slipped too easily between my ribs. I knew immediately it hit something vital by the agony and the strange tingling sensation that encased my body.

"If I die, I'm taking you with me," he sneered. "Either way you'll be mine, whether it's in life or in death."

When he pulled the knife free I felt the rush of blood and cried out, but I didn't loosen my hold on his neck. He tried to stab me again, but I was ready this time. I grabbed his hand. His eyes flared with victory when I released his throat.

Until the blade sank into the soft flesh beneath his chin. I ignored the fiery pain that speared through me as I shoved with all my might, never taking my eyes from his shocked gaze.

"Then I'll have an eternity to torture you," I whispered. "I'm almost looking forward to it."

He gurgled around the blade, his hands weakly tugging at the hilt. Then I watched the light go out of his eyes.

I didn't like killing. I never had.

But in this case, I felt none of my usual pity for the wolf that lay before me. He didn't deserve my pity.

I pressed my hand to the wound on my side, unsurprised by the amount of blood. Still, it gushed far more than I thought it would. Shit, I knew it was bad.

I ripped the bottom of my shirt and packed it against the wound. I reached into my pocket, looking for my phone. Maybe I could call for help.

My hands were sticky from the blood and the touch screen refused to work. I wiped both my hand and the phone on the only clean spot on my jeans and only then would the phone work properly.

I saw that Calder had called. With shaky hands, I tapped the screen with my thumb to automatically call him back.

He answered on the second ring. "Where are you?"

"In the…woods," I answered, suddenly breathless.

"Where?"

I glanced around. "Southeast of town. I don't know exactly where." My voice was soft, weak, and I hated it.

"We're coming for you. Are you hurt?"

I glanced down at the blood seeping around the edges of the soaked piece of my shirt. "Yeah. I, uh, I don't know if I'm going to make it until you get here," I replied.

"Goddammit!" Calder snarled. "I don't wanna fucking hear you say that again. You hold on. Finn is with me. He can heal you."

"He can't heal the dead, Calder," I muttered, my vision dimming. I blinked, wondering if a cloud had covered the sun, but realized it was my eyes. I was losing too much blood too quickly and the world was going in and out of focus.

"Shut up, Chloe. You hang on." I heard him say something to Finn, but my ears were buzzing. "Finn is coming for you. Once he's locked on to your location, he's going to cast a spell to take him there."

"Calder," I whispered. "Tell I-I-Ian that I'm sorry," I stuttered over Lach's first name as a shiver wracked my body.

"Tell him yourself," he replied sharply.

I couldn't argue with him because I fell into oblivion.

CHAPTER THIRTY-FOUR

Lachlan

THE SOUND OF the shotgun going off in the distance made my blood run cold in my veins. I ran faster, not bothering with stealth any longer. I knew in my bones that something was wrong.

The minutes it took me to reach Chloe stretched into hours. Time was elastic, my fear making each step seem to last an eternity.

When I reached the clearing, I knew immediately that Brayden was dead. The knife sticking out of his chin was a clear indication. I skidded to a halt next to Chloe's prone body, my throat closing at the sight of so much blood.

Falling to my knees, I pressed my hand to her neck. The pulse was there, but it was so weak. I covered the wound on her side with my hand, trying in vain to staunch the flow of blood.

I could hear Calder's voice in the distance, but my focus was solely on Chloe. At the sound of a light step behind me, I whirled with a growl. Finn lifted his hands in a gesture of peace and it took me a moment to recognize him.

"Help us," I demanded.

He moved to Chloe's side, his strange eyes already glowing. "Lift your hand."

I did as he directed, watching as he placed his palm over the wound.

"I will do what I can," he said. "But she is hovering near the edge."

"Whatever it takes," I snarled. "I don't care if you have to suck the life out of me to save her. You do it."

He nodded, closing his eyes. "Kerry, I need you," he whispered.

The wind around us picked up and I caught the scent of his mate, but she never appeared.

A light appeared beneath Finn's hand. I watched as Chloe's body twitched. With the depth of the wound, I knew that it hurt, but her body was too weak to do more than jerk slightly at the pain.

Reaching down, I took her hand, leaning over her head. "You listen to me, Chloe MacArthur. You will not die. You will live and you will be my mate. I need you and you need me. You hear me. *You will not die.*"

"Keep talking," Finn murmured. "I can feel her. She's on the brink."

"I love you, Chloe," I whispered. "I won't be able to live without you."

Her shaking body arched as she gasped, but her eyes remained closed. I glanced at Finn, but his eyes were still shut with a look of fierce concentration on his face.

"Dammit, Chloe, you can't give up," I commanded, squeezing her hand. "You have to fight for me. And for yourself."

The uncontrollable shivers that shook her limbs began to slow. This close to her neck, I could hear her heartbeat grow stronger, though it was still sluggish.

Out of the corner of my eye, I saw the light radiating from Finn's palm fade and his head fell forward. The wound on her side was still open, but the blood was no longer flowing from it.

"Don't stop, Finn," I demanded. "She's not completely

healed."

His eyes lifted to mine, no longer glowing with his power. "I can't do anymore, Lachlan. But she will be able to heal herself and she will live."

"Are you sure?" I asked, looking back down at her pale face.

"I am," he replied. "The wound was too deep for me to heal it completely, but she will live."

The tension filling my body flowed out and I stroked the matted hair away from Chloe's forehead.

"Your mate will be fine in a few days, Lachlan," Finn reassured me. "I swear."

It seemed my debt to a vampire had just grown larger. I met his eyes. "Thank you," I murmured. "I owe you more than I could ever repay."

He looked down at Chloe, his mouth curving into a tired smile. "If you take care of your mate, that will be payment enough. Kerry has a soft spot for the both of you."

I didn't argue with him, knowing that I would owe him for the rest of my life. This was the second time he'd healed Chloe. Until the day I died, I would give my aid to the vampire and his witch mate whenever it was needed.

CHAPTER THIRTY-FIVE

Chloe

I SWUNG MY legs over the side of the bed and stood up.

Gram appeared in the doorway before I'd taken more than a single step. "You need to stay in bed," she stated.

"It's been three days, Gram. I'm healed, just a little weak. Exercise and food will be the best things for me."

Her brows lifted. "What did I say?" she asked, crossing her arms over her chest as she leaned against the doorjamb.

I met her stare with a level one of my own. "I'm not going back to bed. Darrell is in a holding cell, waiting to be interrogated, and Brian Kirkpatrick is being held by the Tribunal. I need to be up and taking care of business."

"I said I would wait until you were better before dealing with Darrell. And the Tribunal will wait for your testimony against Brian as well."

I sighed as I slipped on a pair of leggings beneath my t-shirt. "Look, the only way you're getting me back into that bed is if you knock me unconscious. I know my limitations and I won't overdo it, but I need answers. I've waited two years, don't make me wait another day."

"What's one more day after two years?" she tossed back to me. But she echoed my sigh, sounding just like me, and moved away from the door. "Fine, I'm not going to force you, but only because I don't want to have to explain to Lachlan how his m—" she paused. "How you were injured again. I don't think even his respect for me would keep him from trying to tear me a new one if I did."

I gave her a confused look when she stumbled over her words. She was right though. Lachlan had been a protective shadow, always hovering over me, since I'd been injured. When I awoke in Carter's farmhouse the night after Brayden stabbed me, he'd been sitting in a chair next to the bed. That was where he stayed the next night as well.

Last night, he'd climbed into bed next to me after I was already asleep.

We hadn't talked much. I had slept a lot, only waking to eat, shower, and use the bathroom. Now, I was feeling more like my old self. The wound on my side had closed, leaving behind a small pink scar where the blade entered my body. I was still sore, but considering I'd been at death's door three days ago, I would take the slight ache in my abdomen.

"Fine. We'll go to the police department." My grandmother paused by the door as I slipped shoes onto my feet. "The Tribunal sent a representative. We gave him all the photos and videos. Darrell was removed as alpha of the pack and we were given permission to deal with him as we saw fit as long as Carter agreed."

"Why Carter?" I asked.

Gram shrugged. "Because he's the new alpha."

"They're not conducting a Call?" I asked.

She shook her head. "The representative offered, but the pack refused. They requested that Carter lead them. I think this is the first time that an alpha has been put in charge by vote rather than battle." Her eyes darkened. "I worry that other wolves will hear about this and try to challenge him."

I smiled at her. "I don't think Carter will have any problems taking care of any and all challenges that come his way."

Her mouth curved up at the corner. "Yes, you're probably right. That wolf is more than he seems, isn't he?"

"That he is," I said, running a brush through my hair and pulling it into a ponytail. "Let's go."

"Only if you eat something first," she argued.

Knowing that I would get what I wanted more quickly if I followed her directives, I went downstairs and plowed through several rashers of bacon leftover from breakfast that morning and a banana.

"There, I had a snack," I told her as I rinsed the grease from my hands in the sink.

"Did you even chew?" she asked. At my level look, she sighed. "God, now I understand why my mother laughed when I told her I had a granddaughter. You're just like I was at your age."

"Thank you."

"It wasn't a compliment," she muttered beneath her breath.

"Considering I respect you more than any other she-wolf I know, I'd beg to differ," I retorted.

She smiled at me.

"Now, stop stalling and let's go," I stated firmly.

Gram grabbed the car keys and Nicholas appeared at her elbow. "Where are you going?" he asked me.

"To the police department," I replied.

He glanced at Gram, his eyes clearly stating he thought this was a mistake. "Does Lachlan know?"

Gram shook her head.

"Sophia, you know that—"

Gram lifted a hand, silencing him. "That's between Ian and Chloe. I refuse to get involved."

Nicholas' mouth pressed into a thin line but he stopped arguing.

What the fuck was going on here? Why was everyone acting so strangely? I pondered my questions as we walked outside to the driveway.

I climbed into the SUV, gingerly buckling the belt across my lap. "Since when do you call Lachlan *Ian*?" I asked.

Gram shrugged, backing up and turning the car around to head down the drive. "Since he asked me to."

She left it at that. Accustomed to Gram's tendency to be closemouthed, I didn't ask anything else. We drove in silence into town, not speaking again until I'd stepped out of the car and walked toward the front door of the building.

"I want you to stay outside of the cell," she stated, taking my elbow in her hand.

I frowned at her. "Why?"

"You're still recovering, Chloe, whether you admit it or not. Darrell knows what he's facing now that the Tribunal has given us permission to deal with him as we see fit. I wouldn't put it past him to attack you in hopes that we'll kill him to protect you." Her face darkened. "I don't want him to get away so easily."

I nodded. "Fine. I can do that."

I followed Gram inside, waving at Tom, Miss Emma's husband. He was helping Carter get the office back in order. Carter wanted to make him an officer, but Tom refused, stating he didn't have the temperament for it.

I could see Carter in his father's office, talking on the phone. The expensive, heavy furniture it once held was gone. In it's place were utilitarian pieces, mostly made of metal. They were also old. It was clear that Carter intended to take his job seriously and that he wasn't planning to waste pack money.

He nodded to me, his mouth moving as he spoke to whoever was on the other end of the line. I nodded back and followed

Gram into the holding room.

As soon as I saw the bars, memories flashed in my mind. The ropes and Brayden's bite on my shoulder.

Unconsciously, I lifted my hand to my neck. The sensation of smooth skin beneath my fingers broke me from the overwhelming thoughts. Brayden was dead and I no longer carried his mark.

But in destroying his wound, I'd also removed all traces of Lachlan from my flesh as well.

That I regretted.

A movement in the cell caught my attention and I stepped forward. Darrell sat on the cot in the corner, his eyes burning with rage and hatred.

"So you survived after all?" he spat. "How lovely."

I grabbed a metal chair from against the wall and sat facing him, just out of his reach should he be stupid enough to try and stick an arm through the bars to get to me.

"I did," I replied, crossing my legs and resting my hands on my knees.

We stared at each other until Darrell finally looked away.

"Why are you here?" he asked.

"You know why."

He briefly glanced at me out of the corner of his eye before resuming his study of the floor. "Your parents, you mean," he mumbled.

"Yes."

"And if I don't tell you?"

For the first time since we entered the room, my grandmother spoke. "You will. Eventually."

Her final word hung in the air, the threat it held clear. My grandmother disliked the use of torture, but that didn't mean she wasn't capable. She was well versed on a wolf's body and the ability a shifter had to withstand pain. I didn't want to know how she'd come by that knowledge, but I sensed it wasn't from anything she'd read in a book. Information like that was cultivated through practice.

Darrell shuddered then sighed. "The Kirkpatricks approached me and I agreed," he answered.

"I doubt it's that simple," I snapped back. "Start from the beginning."

Darrell's eyes met mine for a moment. "Brayden Kirkpatrick came up here to propose a mating between the two of you. Specifically for political purposes. He wanted your parents' approval and backing." Darrell scoffed. "Why he thought your parents could bring you to heel, I'll never know, but he was convinced that you would agree if they were on his side."

"And what did my parents say?" I asked, already knowing what the answer would have been.

"No." Darrell laughed harshly. "Not only did your dad say no, he smacked that pup a good one for even thinking about forcing you into a mating you didn't want. He said forced matings were outlawed centuries ago and threatened to go to the Tribunal if the Kirkpatricks didn't let the matter drop."

"And why did they come to you?" I asked.

Darrell's eyes lifted to mine, the malevolence in them making my flesh prickle. "They knew I wanted the pack," he replied with a shrug. "It was a mutually beneficial arrangement. When your parents were out of the way, Brayden could make you his mate without worrying about retribution and I would have the pack."

Gram stepped forward, drawing even with the chair at my side. "Did they just assume I wouldn't notice there was an problem?"

Darrell laughed again, the sound rough and devoid of amusement. "Brayden was convinced that he could force Chloe to play along. Otherwise, he intended to do to you what we did to your son and his mate."

My grandmother's growl rolled through the room, deep and intimidating. Even I slouched a little in my seat beneath the dominance she projected toward Darrell.

"You're a disgusting excuse for a wolf, Darrell Whelby," she said, her voice deeper than usual. I knew she was holding on to her control by a thread.

His expression said he knew it, but it also showed that he didn't give a damn.

"How did you find us?" I asked Darrell suddenly.

Confused by my change of subject, he blinked as he turned toward me. "What?"

"How did you find Lachlan and me after we left your cabin?"

He smirked. "I wouldn't have if you hadn't gone grocery shopping in town." He tapped his temple. "People owe me favors all over the state. They pay attention when I ask them to."

I glanced at my grandmother and knew she was thinking the same thing I was. We needed to find out exactly who his contacts were and take care of them.

I rose to my feet, done with this conversation and with Darrell. "Enjoy Hell, Darrell. Be sure to give Brayden my regards."

I left the room, feeling his eyes on me the entire time. Gram followed me, her expression forbidding and cold.

"We will mete out his punishment as soon as you're well," she promised.

I shook my head. "Do it tonight. Or even now. He doesn't deserve to breathe another minute for what he did."

"But you're still weak," she argued.

I shook my head. "I killed the man responsible for the murder of Mom and Dad, Gram. Even if he didn't do it himself, he set the plan in motion. I'll leave Darrell to you and Brian Kirkpatrick to the Tribunal." I cleared my throat. "But I do have one request."

She looked at me, waiting.

"Allow the she-wolves he abused a chance to get their pound of flesh," I stated.

A slow, frightening smile crossed her face. "Why, that sounds like a fantastic idea," she drawled.

I shivered, uncertain what might be in store for Darrell, but whatever it was, I hoped it was excruciating and it lasted for days or even weeks. It was no less than he deserved.

"I'm tired and I'd like to go back to the house and take a nap. I believe my grandmother would insist on it," I said.

Her eyes moved over my shoulder and an unreadable expression crossed her face.

"You're right, I do insist. Unfortunately, I have some things to discuss with Carter. You'll have to get a ride back with someone else."

"I'll take her," a quiet voice offered behind me.

I twisted around, already knowing who would be standing there by his scent. I'd smelled him as soon as we exited the holding room, but he hadn't been in sight.

Lachlan was a few feet away, his eyes glued to me, moving from my ponytail down to the slip-on sneakers I'd shoved on my feet earlier.

"Make sure she eats again too," Gram directed, heading in the direction of Carter's office.

I tried to ignore the awkwardness between us, but it was difficult. We'd agreed to see how things went after this was over, but now that it was done, I was uncertain.

"My truck's out front," he said, gesturing toward the street.

I nodded and walked outside, surprised when he opened my door for me, helping me into the cab though I was perfectly capable of getting in under my own steam.

I watched him with narrowed eyes as he moved around the front and slid into the driver's seat.

"Buckle up," he directed.

I did as he said without argument. I stared unseeingly out the window as he reversed out of the parking spot and headed out of town. It wasn't until we'd been on the road for nearly ten minutes that I realized we weren't heading in the right direction.

"Where are we going, Lachlan?" I asked.

His face was grim when he answered, refusing to look at me. "We need to talk."

CHAPTER THIRTY-SIX

Lachlan

M Y HANDS GRIPPED the steering wheel so tightly that the leather creaked ominously and the hard plastic beneath it compressed in my grip.

Chloe stared out the window without speaking. Her skin was still paler than normal and despite all the food her grandmother and I had been shoving at her the past few days, she'd lost weight. All her energy had been directed toward healing the wound that Brayden Kirkpatrick inflicted.

Last night I hadn't been able to take it any longer. She moved and whimpered in her sleep and I knew she was having nightmares. I'd climbed into bed with her, wrapping her in my arms.

I'd done it for selfish reasons as well. I needed her close to remind myself that she was really here, within reach. The past three days seemed surreal.

I had a mate. Another mate.

Finding one's true mate over the course of a lifetime was amazing. Surviving their death even more difficult. But to have a second mate, it was a blessing beyond comprehension. It was rare. I'd only heard of a handful of wolves that had found a second mate after losing their first.

Now I could count myself among them.

I pulled down the drive that led to Darrell's cabin. At my request, Calder and Mason had come to remove all the cameras, leave our bags, and fill the fridge. I fully intended to keep Chloe here with me until she was healed and acknowledged me as her mate. I wanted time with her, just the two of us. I also had her grandmother's blessing.

When I'd mentioned the idea, she said, "Don't make any plans for a few weeks. That she-wolf is more stubborn than anyone I've ever met in my life." Then she eyed me. "You know how to make pancakes? Because that's one way to soften her up. She loves 'em."

Her eyes widened when my cheeks heated and I realized I was blushing for the first time in fifty years.

"Well, isn't that interesting," she commented. "Don't worry. I won't come rescue her if that's what you're wondering." Then she stared at me, her green eyes narrowing. "However, you *will* treat my granddaughter like a queen or you'll answer to me."

I knew enough of Sophia MacArthur's reputation to understand that she meant what she said. And that she was a damn sight scarier than her granddaughter.

"I love her," I stated. "All I want is for her to be happy."

"Then we'll never have to have this conversation again," Sophia said. "Because that means you'll do whatever it takes to make that happen."

Then she surprised me by giving me a hug and a kiss on the cheek. "Welcome to the family, Ian Lachlan. I couldn't have picked a better mate for my Chloe."

With her approval, I'd gone about making my plans.

Though, now that we were here, I wasn't sure where to start or what to say.

"Let's take a walk," I invited Chloe. "Sophia mentioned you've been antsy today. Then maybe you'll sleep better when you take your nap."

She studied me for a long moment and I wondered what she was thinking. Since she'd woken up after nearly dying, Chloe had been different. Quiet and distant, as if part of her remained on the other side of the veil. It made something in my chest twist painfully.

"Okay," she finally agreed.

I jumped out of the truck and rushed around to the other side before she even unbuckled her seatbelt. The look she gave me when I opened the door and helped her down clearly said that she thought I was nuts.

I took her hand and led her around the cabin toward the trees, walking slowly so she wouldn't push herself too hard to keep up.

We didn't speak, but she did leave her hand in mine, loosely gripping my fingers. I wanted to tighten my hold, to lace our fingers together, but I sensed that she would only withdraw if I tried to hold on too tightly.

When we reached the clearing where we'd practiced sparring and made love only a week ago, I stopped. Somehow, it seemed right.

I turned toward her. "How are you feeling?"

Her eyes flicked up to mine. "Better," she answered honestly. "I'm still tired a lot and hungry all the time, but the pain is almost completely gone. Just a twinge every now and then if I move too quickly or stretch too far."

I squeezed her hand gently. "I'm glad." I hesitated before I asked, "Do you remember anything from when Finn and I found you?"

She shook her head, her eyes gaining a faraway look. "No. I don't remember anything after I passed out."

I sucked in a deep breath, my heart picking up speed in my chest. It seemed so much easier to say what I felt when I thought it would be my last chance.

Then I realized that this still might be. My mark was gone from Chloe's neck, the scar healed. She could reject me and move on. It would be over.

My stomach felt hollow at the thought. I couldn't lose her.

I cupped her cheeks in my hands and laid my lips on hers, a light, nearly reverent kiss. Loose tendrils of her hair tickled my face and neck as the breeze blew through them. I'd grown to crave the peaches and honey scent that emanated from her skin under the warmth of the sun.

Chloe's hands came up to my wrists, holding me but not tightly. It was almost as if she felt the same fear I did—that the harder I tried to hold on, the faster she would slip through my fingers.

I lifted my mouth from hers and looked down at her face. Her eyes were still closed and her cheeks finally had some color in them. Slowly, her lashes lifted until our eyes met.

When she looked at me, all my fear vanished. This was right.

"I love you, Chloe," I murmured, brushing my lips against hers once again.

Her eyes were dazed when I raised my head again, but they sharpened far quicker than I liked.

"What did you say?" she breathed, her hands gripping my wrists tighter.

"I love you, Chloe MacArthur, and you're my mate."

She swayed against me and, for just a moment, I thought it was going to be that simple.

Unfortunately, Chloe MacArthur was as unpredictable as I thought.

She straightened her spine, backed out of my grasp, and stared up at me. Her eyes were level and nearly accusatory. "Why are you saying this?"

"Because it's true," I replied.

She shook her head. "You're confused."

I took a step toward her and she retreated once more, keeping the distance between us the same. "No, I'm not, Chloe. For the first time in nearly two years, I'm seeing things clearly." When I moved forward again, she repeated her withdrawal. "Why are you backing away from me?"

"Because I don't want you to touch me right now," she shot back.

Her words hurt at first until I looked at her hands. Chloe's face might not give much away, but her hands were clenched in tight fists, the knuckles white, and tucked against her hips. She was distressed.

"Why don't you want me to touch you, Chloe?" I asked softly. "Is it because you'll want to touch me back?" I lunged quickly, taking her hand in mine, and flattened her palm against my chest. "It's okay. I want you to touch. I'll always want your hands on me."

Her breathing grew rapid as her eyes stared at her palm against my sternum. "Don't do this, Lachlan."

I could see the cracks in her composure. Something told me that I had to break through now before she had a chance to shore up her defenses.

"When you're touching me, you call me Ian," I murmured.

This brought her eyes to mine. "You hate it when people use your first name."

I inched closer. "I do." Brushing the hair back from her face, I leaned closer. "Except when the person is you."

She stood perfectly still as I took another step forward, close enough that her hand was sandwiched between our chests, her palm still pressed to my heart.

Chloe licked her bottom lip but didn't take her eyes from mine. "You love me?" she asked.

I nodded, lowering my head so my cheek brushed hers. "I do."

"But you didn't want another mate—" she began.

I sensed the tension creeping back into her body. "I changed my mind," I interrupted. "But only if it's you."

Her body shook against mine, as though she were fighting the urge to run or draw closer. I couldn't tell which. "But Brayden's mark—"

Once again, I stopped her. "Is gone. Finn removed all traces. I can't smell him on you any longer. Or me." I ran the tip of my nose down her neck and felt her tremble again. "But I would like to change the last part."

"Lachlan," she began.

I kissed her then, not a gentle touch of my lips to hers, but a merging of mouths full of longing. My tongue slid into her mouth and she responded. Her fingernails dug into my chest and her other hand lifted to my shoulder, clutching hard.

The more I kissed her, the more she gave me. Chloe's body softened against mine, allowing me to gather her closer. I lifted her off her feet, still kissing her as her legs wound around my hips.

Somehow I managed to carry her back to the cabin without walking into a tree or falling into a hole. I barely noticed the steps as I took them two at a time. The screen door banged against the wall as I fought to open the interior door, and then we were inside the cool, shadowed room.

Without breaking the kiss, I moved straight to the bed and laid her down on the mattress.

Only when my body pinned hers did I lift my mouth. The pink was back in her cheeks and her eyes sparkled in the familiar way I'd grown to love.

"Please don't make me live without you, Chloe MacArthur," I pleaded. "I'm begging you."

CHAPTER THIRTY-SEVEN

Chloe

I LOOKED UP at Lachlan's beloved face, so sincere, and raised my hand, tracing his cheekbone with the tips of my fingers.

His eyes were so blue and warm. He was looking at me as if I were the only other person in the world.

"What if you regret it?" I asked him, forcing myself to voice my deepest fears. "It's forever, Lach. You'll never be free of me."

His eyes closed at my words, as though they hurt him. When he lifted his lashes, my breath caught at the raw emotion in his gaze.

"There is nothing to regret, Chloe. Not unless you don't want me."

My throat constricted at his words. Of course I wanted him. I wanted to hold on to him and never let him go.

"I—" I stopped and licked my lips, gathering my thoughts. "I do want you," I whispered. "I have since…" I trailed off.

"Since when?" he pressed.

"Since I realized you were my mate," I replied, so softly that I was surprised he could hear me.

"When did you know?" he asked, smoothing back the strands of hair that had come loose from my ponytail.

I couldn't meet his eyes any longer. It was too difficult to bare myself so completely. "Not long after Belinda died." My words fell between us and I felt him go completely still on top of me. The only movement in his body was the beating of his heart. He wasn't even breathing.

I forced myself to continue. "You were so…broken. I wanted to heal you." My breath hitched. "If I could have brought her back, I would have. I hated to see you in so much pain."

I felt a tear trickle down my cheek and cursed myself inwardly. I'd cried more in the last few weeks than I had my entire life.

"So that's why you stayed," he breathed.

"Yes."

His thumb traced the trail of dampness the tear left behind. "That's also why you left, isn't it?"

"Yes," I answered. "You were finally getting stronger. You didn't need me anymore and it—" I couldn't continue because my throat convulsed. I swallowed hard, forcing back more tears.

"It hurt," he finished.

My throat wouldn't loosen enough for me to speak so I nodded my head.

"Chloe, look at me."

"Lachlan," I began.

"You call me Ian when we're in bed together, Chloe. You have since the beginning."

My eye opened at the thread of steel in his voice and my gaze collided with his. Though he didn't look angry, there was a resolve in his eyes, as though he'd made up his mind about something.

"Ian," I whispered.

"I'm sorry, Chloe," he apologized. "I'm sorry that I put you through that."

My hands squeezed his shoulders reflexively. "Why should you be sorry?"

His lips brushed my forehead. "Because I learned over the last three days that there's no pain like the one you feel when you watch your mate suffer. And you bore that in silence for nearly two years. For that, I am sorry."

My heart thumped against my breastbone, one hard bump. "I would do it again because you needed me," I replied.

"Jesus, Chloe," he said, his voice rough, before he kissed me again. "I can't let you walk away now. Not after this."

I couldn't breathe as his mouth found mine once more.

When he lifted his head, he said, "I'll spend the rest of my life making it up to you."

I shook my head. "There's nothing to make up, Ian. I wanted to do it."

"Then you have to stay with me," he insisted. "Because I still need you. I'll always need you."

I looked up at him, seeing everything I'd ever wanted wrapped up inside him. Love, warmth, family. He was offering it all to me.

"Make me yours," I said, curving my hand around the back of his neck. "Now."

He kissed me again, giving into my urging touch. As our mouths opened, our tongues tangling and tasting, his hands moved to the hem of my t-shirt, lifting it over my head. Beneath it I wore a simple cotton tank that disguised the fact that I wasn't wearing a bra. It followed my t-shirt to the floor.

My own hands were busy, diving under the hem of his tee as well. He reached over his head, his hand grasping the material between his shoulder blades and pulled it off.

My flip-flops had fallen from my feet when he laid me on the bed, but he released my mouth and straightened, tugging my leggings and underwear down my thighs, over my calves, until I lay bare before him.

He rose to stand at the end of the bed, unbuckling his belt. I watched as he kicked off his boots and socks and shoved the jeans off. When he rejoined me on the bed, we were naked, our bodies twined together skin-to-skin. He barely took his eyes from my face as his hand roved over my body, trailing over the pink scar tissue on my side, down over my belly button, and from hipbone to hipbone.

I laid my hand flat on his back, smoothing it over his skin. My fingertips brushed the bumps of his spine and I felt the flex and bunch of his muscles beneath my palm. He was warm and heavy, his body enveloping me.

When his fingers dipped between my legs, I gasped and arched my back. The sharp hunger I felt for him was insistent as though it had been months rather than days since he'd last touched me.

"Ian," I breathed.

He smiled before he kissed me again, his finger circling my clit. As my hips began to move, his mouth moved down my neck, the tip of his tongue light against my skin.

Then his mouth captured my nipple and I gasped again. His lips tugged and sucked at my breasts as his hand continued to move between my legs, his fingers toying with my clit before they slid deep inside me.

"I want you inside me, Ian," I demanded, my nails digging into the flesh of his spine.

"I am inside you," he whispered against my skin.

I shivered at the sensation of his voice vibrating against my breasts. "That's not the part of you I'm talking about."

I felt his smile and retaliated by dragging my fingernails over his back in the way that I knew drove him crazy.

He groaned and removed his fingers from my body. Moving over me, he reached between us and guided his cock to my entrance. I lifted my legs, my thighs hugging his hips, as he slid inside.

He stilled when he was fully seated in my body. "There, I'm

inside you."

I growled at him. "Move, Ian."

He pressed his hips tighter to mine. "Say please."

I shook my head, resisting even though I wanted to give in. My pussy clenched hard as he nudged a place inside me that made my nerve endings spark. It was enough to crack my resolve. "Please, Ian."

He withdrew and thrust again, his movements slow and deliberate. He set a languid rhythm that felt good but wouldn't bring my body to the clamoring release it ached for.

"Ian, faster," I urged.

"No," he replied.

My nails dug into his ass as I pulled his hips toward mine, pushing him to move more quickly. "Yes," I hissed.

"Your injury is still healing," he argued.

"You're the one who's about to be injured if you don't stop teasing me!" I growled.

He chuckled, his hips moving at a faster pace, but it still wasn't enough. When I snarled at him, his chuckle turned into full-fledged laughter. He lifted me, turning us so that his back rested against the wall. With one hand supporting my spine, his other splayed across my lower belly putting his thumb in just the right position to roll against my clit.

I leaned into the hand on my back, giving him room to maneuver as I rose and fell against him. As the orgasm swelled within me, he pulled me up and gripped my ponytail in his hand.

When the first wave crashed into me and I cried out, he sank his teeth into my shoulder exactly where his mark had been before. This time I didn't fight the urge. I turned my face into his neck and latched on.

He groaned against my skin and I knew he was coming. Together we rode out the orgasm, our bodies crashing together as it seemed to continue on and on. When it finally ebbed, something clicked within me, a void in my heart that was no longer empty. I lifted my mouth from his shoulder and ran my tongue over the mark I'd left behind. I felt Lachlan do the same. Then he pressed a gentle kiss to the bite.

"Now you're mine," he murmured. "And I'm yours."

"Always," I replied.

CHAPTER THIRTY-EIGHT

Lachlan

AFTER I MADE Chloe mine, she insisted she needed a bath. Then she dragged me into the tub with her. I'd never been one for soaking in a bath, preferring a shower instead, but she converted me.

Afterwards, I carried her back to the bed and we slept together naked until mid-afternoon.

I awoke to something brushing my face. I swatted at it without opening my eyes and heard Chloe giggle. I cracked one eyelid and saw that she was using the end of her ponytail to tickle my nose.

"Oh, you're awake. That's great," she said cheerfully. "I'm hungry."

She yelped when I pinched her ass and retaliated but I ended the fun before it could get carried away.

"You're still healing," I stated. "No wrestling for at least another week."

"Then you should make me something to eat," she retorted. "Since I am still trying to regain my strength."

"I think you're just milking it now," I replied, but I still got to my feet. Chloe did need to eat more often to fuel her body's efforts at putting her to rights. "What do you want?"

"Pancakes?" she asked innocently, her eyes moving toward the kitchen table.

I groaned, turning my back to her. "No, no pancakes. You'll get ideas. I'll make pasta."

She sighed, but when I turned toward her she was smiling.

As I went about putting together the meal, she watched me, reclining on the pillows on the bed. "I could get used to this," she said.

I shot her a look. "You act like I haven't cooked for you before. As I recall, we took turns making meals while we were here."

"Yeah, but now that we're mated I figured you'd turn into a slob that forgets how a stove works."

I tossed a bit of Parmesan cheese at her, but she snagged it out of the air and put it in her mouth.

"We never talked about where you want to live," I mentioned casually. "Now that Darrell is no longer in charge, would you want to move back here?"

She chewed, staring at me with a thoughtful expression on her face. "No, I don't think so. I love it here and the wolves I grew up with, but it's not home anymore."

"What about North Carolina? You would be closer to your grandmother."

Her eyes met mine. "Wherever you are, that's where my home is. Home is in the heart and soul, not a place on a map." She paused. "Actually, I think I'd like to stay in Dallas at the pack compound. Our pups would enjoy playing with Ricki and Calder's little ones."

When I dropped the spoon I was using to stir the pasta sauce, she laughed.

"Pups?" My voice was high and tight.

"I'm going into heat in a few days. Unless you pick up some condoms in town, there will likely be a pup around Christmas-time."

Shifter pregnancies were shorter than human ones. If we created a pup soon, I might have a son or daughter by Christmas. My chest compressed as I imagined Chloe with a pregnant belly, then holding a tiny bundle to her heart. "What do you want?" I asked.

She got up from the bed and crossed to me, placing a hand on my chest. The knot inside it loosened immediately. "I would love to have a child with you, Ian, but I'm more than willing to wait."

I stared down at her, imagining her eyes staring up at me out of a child's face. "I want children with you. Tomorrow or ten years from now."

"That's a beautiful thing to say, Ian, but it doesn't tell me what you want to do when I go into heat." She cocked an eyebrow at me, waiting.

"No condoms," I murmured.

A smile spread across her face, so full of joy and hope that it took my breath away. "You'll be a fantastic dad," she replied.

"I just hope we don't have triplets like Ricki and Calder."

Her smile faded and her eyes widened. "Oh my God, do multiples run in your family?"

Laughing, I shook my head. "No. All my ancestors had one pup at a time."

"Maybe we should wait a bit before having pups. Ten, maybe fifteen years," she hedged.

I couldn't stop the roar of laughter that escaped me and I looped my arm around her waist. "No way. Now that you brought it up, that's exactly what I want."

Then I kissed her. The pasta was overcooked by the time I was done, but it was worth it.

After dinner, we each carried a beer out onto the porch and enjoyed the warm evening. The fragile connection that bound us after the mating bite was growing stronger with every hour. I could feel her inside me, a constant warmth.

I hesitated to bring up a topic that might upset her, but I was concerned.

"What are you thinking?" she asked me, tilting her head to rest on the back of the chair. "I can feel your worry."

I took a deep breath. I'd forgotten this part of the mating bond—the sharing of moods and thoughts. It was nearly impossible to hide things from a mate, not that I wanted to.

"Why didn't you take part in Darrell's punishment?" I asked. She'd been so determined to make him pay for what he'd done to her parents that her decision to bow out surprised me.

Chloe twisted her head and met my eyes. "A lot of reasons. I've had to kill before, and I'm certain that as pack enforcer I'll be required to do so again. This time, though..." she paused, gathering her thoughts. "Darrell Whelby hurt so many people. Yes, he took my parents from me and Gram's son from her, but the females that he hurt over and over deserve the chance to make him pay." The corner of her mouth curled up in a smile that held no amusement. "And, honestly, I think any punishment they could dream up would be far more creative than mine."

"You said there were a lot of reasons," I said softly. "What are the others?"

"I've been too close to death the past week. Brayden's death. Your death. My death. I don't want to swim in a sea of blood for the rest of my life. Killing shouldn't be the only thing I'm good at," she murmured.

"It's not the only thing you're good at," I replied, sitting up straighter in the chair.

She smiled, small and sad. "I know, Lach, but I don't want to walk too close to that line. It's too easy to cross over and never return. I've seen the wolves that exist hand-in-hand with death. They forget that life holds meaning and beauty." She hesitated. "They forget to live."

I understood then what she meant. "Then I'm glad you stood aside."

"Speaking of living, fancy a run in the woods under the full moon?" she asked.

I glanced up, shocked to see the full moon hanging in the sky. I hadn't noticed the waxing moon for months if not years. "Yeah, I think I would," I replied slowly.

With a wicked grin spreading across her face, she stood and began to shuck her clothes. "If you catch me, maybe I'll give you a prize."

Before I could do more than put my beer aside and stand, she was already naked and leaping off the porch. She shifted mid-stride, letting loose a challenging howl as she dashed across the open field and disappeared into the trees.

I stripped and followed her in the blink of an eye, eager to chase my mate.

When I did finally catch Chloe, I made sure she understood that the only prize I wanted was her.

CHAPTER THIRTY-NINE

Chloe

One month later

THE SUN WAS setting over the MacIntire pack compound, but the place was buzzing with activity. Wolves were milling about in the open field where we gathered for pack runs.

Only the tall grass had been mown down and raked up a few days before. In the center of the clearing, stood a tree. It was huge, it's branches covered in fairy lights and paper lanterns. Chairs were arranged in rows facing the trunk. Though the moon was full, shining down so brightly that we didn't need other lighting, there were lanterns set everywhere, the candles inside casting a gentle glow. More fairy lights were strung along the backs of the chairs.

It was romantic and beautiful. The perfect setting for a mating ceremony. Though wolves didn't marry as humans did, when true soul mates found one another, the pack often celebrated it with a ceremony during the next full moon. All the pack members would watch as the mates made vows to one another, then the entire pack would shift and enjoy a run beneath the moonlight. It was an ancient and wonderful tradition.

Ricki and Lachlan had planned the entire thing to surprise me. I thought we would make our vows in the moonlight, surrounded only by our family and pack mates. Having been raised human,

Ricki wouldn't hear of it. She insisted it should be special.

I glanced around and realized that Ricki's idea of special also included a cake and champagne, so I had no complaints whatsoever.

A shrill whistle pierced the air and the wild activity ceased. Ricki stood in front of the tree where Lachlan and I would make our promises to each other and clapped her hands.

"Everybody sit your asses down!" she yelled. "We need to start."

I laughed as wolves grumbled and found seats. My grandmother sat in the front row between Carter Whelby and Nicholas. Miss Emma and her husband, Tom, were further along toward the end. Other wolves from what was once called the MacArthur pack were there. After Carter became alpha, he changed the name to Prater at the pack member's insistence.

Several members of my grandmother's pack were in attendance as well. Though the MacIntire compound usually remained half-empty, tonight it was full to bursting. All of the empty houses were filled with guests and friends.

I watched from my position on Ricki and Calder's front porch as everyone settled down, their voices hushed as Calder and Lachlan took their positions beneath the tree.

I looked down at the simple cotton dress I wore, glad that I'd allowed Ricki to talk me into it. The halter straps tied behind my neck and left my back bare to just below my shoulder blades. The dress fell to my ankles, clinging to my figure without restricting me. The white material would glow in the moonlight.

I'd drawn the line when Ricki tried to fix my hair. I fully intended to go for a run with my mate after the ceremony was over and any effort to curl or pin it would be wasted in the end.

Ricki bounded up the porch steps and stood next to me. "You ready?"

She glanced down at my empty hands and frowned. I had refused to carry a bouquet of flowers as humans often did, preferring instead to walk to my mate with open hands and an open heart.

Clearly, Calder still needed to explain a few things to Ricki about the differences in shifter mating ceremonies and human weddings. Otherwise the poor unmated she-wolves of the MacIntire pack would face this every time they found a mate. Most of them would be unable to deny their alpha female anything she wished, buckling beneath the weight of her dominant personality.

"I'm ready," I replied.

We walked down the porch steps and out into the clearing. Every eye in the field was focused on me, but I didn't notice. The only thing I could see was Lachlan. Once again, Ricki had failed in her attempts to get the male shifters to dress up and he stood beneath the tree in nothing but a faded pair of jeans and a tank top. Most of the male wolves were dressed in a similar fashion. Their attitude was that the fewer clothes to remove before a shift, the better.

Ricki moved to her chair as I walked down the aisle created between the seats. Someone, meaning Ricki again, had sprinkled flowers along the path. Rose petals and stemless daisies were scattered beneath my feet as I moved toward Lachlan.

His eyes never left mine as I drew closer, gleaming in the candlelight. He took my hands as we faced each other in front of Calder. As the alpha of the MacIntire pack, he would preside over the mating ceremony as a gesture of his approval of the match.

"Let us begin," Calder stated, his voice carrying through the night air. "Before your pack, you will make your eternal promises to each other. Do you both come willingly into this mating?"

"We do," Lach and I said together.

"What is your vow to Chloe MacArthur?" Calder asked Lach.

I stared up into Lachlan's eyes as he spoke the words to the

---

ancient rite. "I, Ian Lachlan, swear that my life belongs to you, Chloe MacArthur, until we are separated by death. You will live in my blood, nourish my bones, and become a part of my soul."

His hands held mine tightly as he vowed his life to me. I smiled up at him, feeling his sincerity through the connection between us, the bond of true mates.

"What is your vow to Ian Lachlan?" Calder asked me.

"I, Chloe MacArthur, swear that my life belongs to you, Ian Lachlan, until we are separated by death. You will live in my blood, nourish my bones, and become a part of my soul."

"Do you accept these vows from your mate?" he asked us both.

"We do." Once again, Lach and I answered in unison.

To the wolves behind us, Calder lifted his voice. "Bear witness to two true mates!"

Howls and claps broke out among the pack, the noise growing deafening.

Once again, Ricki's influence entered the ceremony as the cacophony died down.

"Kiss your mate, Lachlan, so we can cut that damn cake!" he whooped.

I laughed as Ricki's low growl reached my ears, knowing that Calder's words weren't what she instructed him to say. Then Lachlan took me in his arms and pressed his mouth to mine. The kiss grew heated and wild, eliciting more howls and yelling from the pack.

When he released me, my knees were weak. Lachlan rested his forehead against mine as he held me close. "You are in my blood and bones, Chloe MacArthur. Without you, I would be an empty shell."

I wrapped my arms around his neck tightly. "I love you, Ian."

His mouth brushed my ear as he asked, "Do you really want

cake?"

I shook my head.

"Then let's go for a run."

While the rest of the pack was distracted with cake and champagne, Lach and I slipped away. We left our clothes on the back porch of his house, shifted into wolf form, and loped into the trees surrounding the compound. When we burst out of the woods close to the lake on the property, I shifted back to human form and held my hand out to him.

"Make love to me, mate, in the light of the full moon."

Lachlan shifted and took my hand. Together, we sank down in the grass. He kissed me then, our tongues tangling in the lush kiss. There was no urgency in his touch as his hands moved over my skin, his fingertips trailing from my shoulders to my breasts. As his thumbs swept over my nipples, drawing them into tight peaks, I curved one hand around the back of his neck and smoothed the other over his hip before moving it between us to stroke him lightly.

Lachlan nipped my bottom lip before moving his mouth lower. He pressed a kiss to the mark he'd left on my shoulder, a bite he repeated often to keep the imprint of his teeth fresh in my skin. He wanted everyone who saw me to know that we belonged together.

Then he moved lower, stopping to flick my nipple with his tongue. I gasped but he continued on his journey until he reached the small scar on my ribs. He kissed that as well, noting the wound that had nearly taken me from him before we mated.

I threaded my fingers in his hair, enjoying the fact that the strands were growing quickly. Though I loved being able to see his face when his hair was short, I'd always liked his hair long. I knew that he was growing it out for me.

His mouth returned to my breasts and he ran the tip of his tongue along the bottom curve of each, making me shiver at the light contact. When his mouth finally captured my nipple, I sucked in a sharp breath.

My hands roved his body, running over the corded muscles of his biceps and chest. When I reached between us again, curling my fingers around his cock and stroking him firmly, he growled. His hands captured my wrists, pinning them above my head.

Unwilling to submit, I twisted suddenly, rolling us both until he lay beneath me. He grinned when I straddled his hips and released my hands. I lifted up, guiding him inside my body and we both groaned as I sank down until he filled me completely.

His fingers gripped my hips as I began to move, preventing me from picking up my pace.

"Ian," I whispered. His name was a plea. I was desperate to move faster, my body no longer content with the indolent motion of my hips.

Without releasing me, he pulled me down as his body bucked, driving himself deeper inside of me. He repeated the act again and my body tightened in response. Only then did one hand move from my hips to the center of my body. His thumb pressed against my clit, rolling firmly, and I cried out, my head falling back.

Our bodies crashed together over and over until I was begging for release. Lachlan put his other hand between my shoulder blades, urging me to lean down, and his mouth closed around my nipple, sucking hard.

At the contact, my climax rushed over me. My muscles trembled from wave after wave of bliss and I collapsed on his chest. His mouth closed around the mark on my neck and I felt his teeth break the skin once again. I mirrored the gesture, sinking my teeth into his flesh as my orgasm renewed.

His body jerked beneath mine with a growl and I knew he was coming. As we both came down from the pinnacle, Lachlan's arms drew me tighter against him and he remained deep inside me.

We lay there together, our hearts beating in unison, and I was awed by the love that emanated from him. When I recognized him as my mate, I never thought that he might one day return my feelings. Now that we were together, I promised myself that I would never forget how blessed I was that he was able to love me in return.

As the moon rose in the sky, my mate and I made love over and over, celebrating our love with the gift of each other.

It wasn't until a few weeks later, when I found out that I was pregnant, that I realized we conceived our child.

EPILOGUE

Rhys

I KNEW AS soon as I opened my mailbox that the brown package inside was from her. Somehow she always found me.

Sure enough, when I looked at the return address, Kerry Gayle's name stared up at me.

"How in the hell do you find me?" I mused to myself. I could almost picture her secretive smile, knowing that would be the only response I would get to my question if I asked her in person.

I carried the envelope into the house. It was the only piece of mail I received that day, which wasn't uncommon. Since I moved to this little rental home in Austin a couple of months ago, I rarely found anything in my mailbox. Unless it was from her.

The first envelope she sent came to the seedy motel I'd stayed in right after I'd left Dallas and contained an amulet on a long, thick chain. Confused, I'd opened the note enclosed with it, wondering why in the hell she would be sending me jewelry.

Rhys,

This should help you out with those pesky electrical problems. I had a dream about you riding a bike everywhere. Since you'll never be able to pick up chicks that way, I thought you might be able to use this.

Love,
Kerry

The words were ridiculous, since I wouldn't need a strange invention with two wheels to reach a desired destination. I had the power of teleportation. If I wanted to go somewhere, I picked a place and made myself appear.

I'd almost thrown the amulet away, thinking that it was a cruel joke, but the promise of being able to use the phone or a computer, maybe even watch television, had been too much of a temptation. When my hand closed around the pendant dangling from the chain, I felt the pulse of power within the stone.

Instead of chucking it into the trash, I slipped the chain over my neck.

Since I had issues with electrical equipment, I never used the lights, phone, or television in my hotel room. Instead, I lit candles and read books. Unsure what to expect, I lifted the remote control and pressed the power button. Immediately, the television came on. Slowly, I approached it, expecting the usual sparks and flashes that accompanied my proximity to any device that used electricity. Nothing happened.

When I reached out and touched the screen, the television kept working, not even a flicker of disturbance due to my presence.

I stared in disbelief, shocked that the witch had taken the time and effort to make an amulet that would allow me to interact with the outside world. She knew nothing about me except the fact that I had helped her kill my brother. When Cornelius died, I'd left, thinking that I would never see or hear from the witch and her friends again.

It seemed I was wrong.

From the time she sent me the amulet to now, at least once per month, a little gift would arrive. Most of the time it was a DVD or a CD, but occasionally Kerry sent pictures. No matter how much I moved around or where I went, she always seemed to know exactly where I was.

It should have worried me, but somehow it was comforting. I'd been lonely for so long in this world, always hiding what I was and evading my brother. I'd never had a friend, and when I touched the gifts she sent me, somehow I knew that Kerry Gayle considered herself my friend.

The package she sent me today was larger and heavier than the others.

Curious, I tore it open, staring in surprise at the box that fell out. It was a cell phone. I hadn't bothered to buy one since I had no one to call. I lifted the lid and removed the little device. It felt odd in the palm of my hand. There was a note attached to the top with an arrow and the words *Press here to turn the phone on.*

I followed the directions, watching as the screen lit up and the shape of an apple popped up. A few seconds later, I stared in wonder at the tiny screen, full of icons.

Before I could even touch it, the phone began to emit a ringing noise and I saw Kerry's name flash on the screen.

I tapped the green button and lifted it to my ear.

"I see you got my present," she said.

"I did."

She paused and when I didn't say anything else, she chuckled. "You're supposed to say thank you when someone gives you a gift."

I smiled. The witch wasn't scared of me in the least. "Then thank you for my gifts," I replied.

"You're welcome."

"But I do wonder why you insist on sending them," I said.

She didn't reply right away, the silence stretching between us. "I have a feeling that we will see each other again, Rhys. And when you need me, all you have to do is call."

"I doubt I would need a phone to reach you should I really need you," I quipped, my tone dry.

She laughed, the heaviness of the moment dissipating. "No, you wouldn't, but you might want to call someone else sometime soon."

Unsure how to take her cryptic response, I didn't say anything.

"I'm always here if you need me, Rhys," she stated quietly. "Whether you like it or not, I'm your friend. And I like to keep in touch with my friends."

I heard the slight click as she disconnected and took the phone from my ear. Despite her attempts at lightness, I sensed the undercurrent of fear beneath her words.

As I stared down at the tiny device, I wondered what the witch had foreseen that worried her.

Whatever it was, it was obvious that she didn't intend to let me face it alone.

~ The End ~

The Blood & Bone series will continue with Rhys and Savannah's story. Souls Unchained (Blood & Bone, #2) will release July 18, 2017.

Author's Note

When I was writing the *Bitten* series, I originally planned for five books. Just five books.

You know what they say about planning, right?

Anyway, as I finished up **Love Bites**, the fourth book, I realized that I loved Chloe MacArthur. She is such a great character, strong enough to stand on her own, but soft in many unexpected ways. I knew that would nurse Lachlan back to health after Belinda died, even before she realized he was her mate. Not exactly something you would expect from a pack enforcer and resident badass.

I wanted her to find her happily ever after.

Then I wrote **Bite the Bullet** and Rhys appeared. Would he be good or bad? In the end, he helped the women. As I worked on his backstory, I realized that Rhys had a lot of unhappiness in his long life. I hated that. I wanted him to finally be free and to find love as well.

Then I thought about several other characters that I wanted to explore and stories I wanted to tell. But I still wanted to finish the *Bitten* series. To me, the chapter for those five ladies was closed. I wanted them to move on. It was then I decided to write the spin-off series called *Blood & Bone*. I don't have a definite number of books in mind for this series, but I've already planned the first three with a possibility for two more.

But you know what they say about plans...

Sign Up for C.C.'s Monthly Newsletter

www.ccwood.net/newsletter

Blogger Sign Up for C.C.'s Master List:

http://bit.ly/2mieXgm

Contact C.C.

C.C. loves to hear from her readers!

Facebook:

www.facebook.com/authorccwood

CC's Sinners (Reader Group):

http://bit.ly/CCSinners

Twitter:

www.twitter.com/cc_wood

Instagram:

www.instagram.com/authorccwood

Pinterest:

www.pinterest.com/ccwood01

Email:

author@ccwood.net

You can also sign up for blog updates and C.C.'s monthly newsletter on her website!

www.ccwood.net

About C.C.

Born and raised in Texas, C.C. Wood writes saucy paranormal and contemporary romances featuring strong, sassy women and the men that love them. If you ever meet C.C. in person, keep in mind that many of her characters are based on people she knows, so anything you say or do is likely to end up in a book one day.

A self-professed hermit, C.C. loves to stay home, where she reads, writes, cooks, and watches TV. She can usually be found drinking coffee or wine as she spends time with her hubby, daughter, and two beagles.

Titles by C.C. Wood

Contemporary Romance

Novellas:

Girl Next Door Series:
Friends with Benefits
Frenemies
Drive Me Crazy
Girl Next Door-The Complete Series

Kiss Series:
A Kiss for Christmas
Kiss Me

Novels:

Seasons of Sorrow

NSFW Series:
In Love With Lucy
Earning Yancy
Tempting Tanya

Westfall Brothers Series:
Texas with a Twist

Wicked Games Series:
All or Nothing

Paranormal Romance:

Bitten Series:
Bite Me
Once Bitten, Twice Shy
Bewitched, Bothered, and Bitten
One Little Bite
Love Bites
Bite the Bullet

Bitten Origins:
Destined by Blood

Blood & Bone Series (Bitten spin-off)
Blood & Bone

Cozy Paranormal:

The Wraith Files:
Don't Wake the Dead
The Dead Come Calling

Made in the USA
Middletown, DE
25 May 2021

40359530R00159